Isabel's Healing

Ryeland Press
Books By Women For Women

A Ryeland Press Book

By

Maggie McIntyre

DEDICATION

This book is dedicated to all the front line medical and support staff who have worked so hard to look after people through the Corona Virus pandemic. Words can't convey what we owe you. Thank you so much.

Published in 2020 by Ryeland Press

First Edition

Cover Photo: Attribution to Cottonbro from Pexels
Cover Design: Karen D. Badger
Formatting: Karen D. Badger

ISBN   979-8-650898-73-3

Maggie McIntyre

ACKNOWLEDGMENTS

Thanks and appreciation goes to my brilliant cover designer, formatter and editor, Karen Badger of Badger Bliss Books. If this book comes to life, it is mostly all down to you.

Isabel's Healing

Chapter 1

"Bel, you might call her something other than, *The Girl*!"

"Well, what am I supposed to call her? I've not even spoken to her. I can't remember her name, Brianna, Bramble, whatever...? You and my dear brother have fixed this up with hardly a nod in my direction.

"Has the thought ever crossed both your minds that I might actually appreciate having some say in who has to come and look after my every need, and yes, I bloody well mean 'every need' for the next eight weeks?"

Claire Bridgford sighed a very small sigh, but buried her impatience under sympathy towards her much younger sister-in-law. Bel was now balefully glowering at her from the passenger seat of the Grey Citroen Berlingo, a car which Claire and her husband had driven as a second vehicle for more than ten years.

It was large enough to carry Bel, her wheelchair and all of her academic books and files to the cottage they had booked for the next two months. Claire's husband Edward had driven ahead with clothes, medical necessities, and a large box of groceries. It was an expedition which Claire had never thought was wise, and it now seemed more foolish than ever.

Bel, with two broken arms, crushed ribs and a badly broken lower leg and right ankle, was more bandage than person right now. She was completely incapacitated, until they could at least get some of the casts off her limbs. She was also in constant pain. It was no wonder she was in a foul mood.

After a month in the hospital, all Bel wanted was to get away from people, to go up into the Welsh hills and hide away, nursing her bruised and battered body, her mental exhaustion and shattered nerves, and something she rarely shared with Claire, her truly broken heart.

Now she knew she was making things worse for everybody, by her senseless grumbling. She felt ashamed, but couldn't seem to control her anger.

Claire persisted. "Her name is Bryony. I'm sure you do remember, unless the anesthetics have really done your head in. We couldn't consult with you very much while you were in the hospital, could we? You were completely out of it most of the time, but we're sure she'll be suitable.

"Edward has interviewed her on Skype, and she has good references. She's a final year medical student. She's bright. She'll be a good caregiver and assistant. It's only for eight weeks, or less, if you decide to curtail this experiment and come back home with us. So try not to prejudge, eh?"

Isabel, or Bel, Bridgford bit her lip and met Claire halfway on her request. She let her head, with its still thumping headache; give a tiny nod of assent.

Of course she should be nicer to her brother and sister-in-law, who'd returned home just to help her. They curtailed their long-planned summer holiday in Tuscany, then arranged her transfer from London up to Liverpool by ambulance, and had visited her in hospital daily from their home twenty miles away. It had been for nearly a month now.

Her nemesis had been some car crash. The little Fiat Panda she drove 'met' a ten-ton truck head-on, just after the lorry had careened down an access road down onto the M25, the orbital route around London. The truck's driver suffered a major heart attack and died before their vehicles even collided. His truck then destroyed her little car, pushing it, and what was left of Bel, back up the motorway for more than fifty yards.

The ensuing carnage had made the TV news, for it had blocked the M1 for the rest of the afternoon. It took a fire and rescue team three hours to cut her out of what had once been her vehicle. Those were three hours she could well live without remembering.

The flashes of recall she did have were all of red-hot, blistering agony. Isabel had already coped with twenty years' of intermittent pain, after a series of misadventures during her more than active life, but the time following the crash were by far the worst days of her life.

Claire was now driving them placidly along quiet country roads which wound their way out of the lush and fertile plains of South West Cheshire into the border country between England and Wales. South of the famous Snowden mountain range, it seemed a semi-mystical land of rolling forests, and tight, sheltered valleys, she remembered from childhood outings, home to sheep farmers, and self-sufficiency buffs. This was the first time Bel had escaped the confines of a hospital ward in more than a month.

"How much further?" Bel knew she sounded like a child asking, 'Are we there yet?'

"Another forty miles, just under an hour on these windy roads. Are you thirsty? Do you want me to pull over and give you a drink?"

"No, don't worry. I'm fine. Let's push on. I am keen to arrive."

Claire still couldn't really understand why Bel wanted to hole herself up in Wales so much. She was more than welcome to stay with her and her husband in sensible, suburban Chester. They could buy in care on an hourly basis, and while Isabel's mental instability and mood swings were still a cause for concern, Claire wished she had heeded their advice.

What would she do up there in the hills all day? Isabel had a book to write, she knew, but she always had a book of some sort to write, and her still troublesome concussion would surely prevent her achieving very much on this new project.

Isabel waited now for her headache to settle. "Sorry, Claire. You've been wonderful, both of you. It's just..."

"I know. It's been hell, and so frustrating for you.

But I'm so glad we could rent you the house for the summer, and the girl, Bryony, she told Edward she's a fast typist. She will be able to type up your book, as soon as you feel strong enough to dictate the first chapters."

"Yes, but the deadline for the first draft remains September 1st. My whole year was planned around getting it done on time. The UN Climate Change summit...I'm supposed to have something published for distribution by the conference next year. I've wasted a whole month already!"

Claire sighed, and they drove on, using her GPS to locate the little white cottage, perched by itself along a track at the top of a long winding hill. Edward was already there, unpacking the suitcases and boxes from his car, and waving at them as they approached.

"Hi, as you see, it is a nice cottage. The key was under the old milk churn, just as they told us. I think the previous tenants must have moved out very recently, because the Aga still feels warm. I've switched it back on. I know it is summer, but you will need it for cooking and to heat the hot water. Everything comes off it, so I hope you won't feel too warm, Bel.

"The beds need making up, but there is plenty of linen available. I've left everything for your caregiver to sort out and arrange for you as you want it, and there's a guidebook explaining everything about it.

"Now, I had better go and fetch this girl, Machynlleth station now. Let me help you out of the car and into your wheelchair first though."

He reached down and helped Isabel swing her legs round and hop up onto one foot, but she needed his help to balance and sit down in the wheelchair. She was secretly suddenly nervous, now she had achieved her goal of actually arriving at the cottage.

Edward noticed her looking around.

"Well, here, you'll have very few distractions. The woods are vast, and this is on a private road. Only a handful of walkers if any will come up here to disturb you."

It was a beautiful spot, and as isolated as she had hoped,

and the view was magnificent. But as Isabel well knew, one can't live on a view.

Edward left them to drive ten miles south to Machynlleth, to collect the girl from the train which would arrive about 4:30 pm. If the train was on time, they would soon have sight of his grey Peugeot edging its way back up the valley.

Claire pushed the wheelchair inside the cottage, bumping slightly over the door lintel, which jarred Bel's nerves and made her grimace in pain. They went from room to room, and saw the clean linen left out for each bed, at the two far ends of the one-storey cottage.

It was a typical Welsh long house, probably two or three hundred years old, but thankfully modernized. The bathroom at least was updated, and had room for a wheelchair to enter, park and turn.

Claire wheeled Bel back into the living room and then at her request took the chair back outside and parked it under a larch tree in the front garden. They both gazed down the valley and over to distant fields and woods dipping away to the southeast.

It was truly a beautiful Welsh summer's afternoon, with a light refreshing breeze. Isabel suddenly hated it for not matching her personal physical misery and mental frustration. Black clouds and pouring rain would at least indicate some cosmic empathy. Bel started to extend her pessimism into a general moan about the new girl.

"Probably it will be too quiet for her, if she's used to university in central London. She'll have to cook, and do the laundry, drive, and manage the bloody chair in and out of the car. She'll have to help me dress and undress. She'll even have to get me on and off the loo!"

Bel knew she would detest every personal indignity she would have to suffer at the hands of this girl, who had just answered the advert her brother had placed in *the Lady* magazine of all sites.

The Lady! Bel would never have described herself as a Lady. She was an explorer, an anthropologist, a ferocious campaigner for women's rights, and exposé of the FGM scandals still rife in so much of the world.

She had spent half her forty-two years in and out of sub-Saharan Africa, and she had headed up one of the most sharp-edged and radical aid agencies, worked to change legislation in three continents.

Yet here she was, grounded by some-one else's heart attack, a random connectivity which meant her normally strong muscles were becoming completely wasted, her bones crushed and her ligaments in a mess. It had also devastated her immediate plans and made her outrageously furious with the Universe.

"Yes, I know it's been very hard for you. But at least this will be better than in the hospital. You can maybe build up a relationship. At least with one assistant, you won't have to keep reintroducing your particular problems. You can train her. You're good at training."

"Am I? There are many folk who would disagree with you. I've become quite snappish in my old age."

"Bel, stop that! You are not old. You're only forty-two for God's sake. Compared to me you're a spring chicken. You have a life ahead of you still. I know the last three years have been tough."

"Understatement of the year...but with this on top of everything..."

Bel was tempted, just tempted, mind, to feel thoroughly sorry for herself, but she knew that was not the way to promote good healing. She acknowledged she was lucky to be alive, not like the wretched driver of the lorry.

Now though, she had to brace herself against the prospect of this new caregiver, the random girl who had answered the advert and said she needed a job with accommodation, just for eight weeks until the end of August, when the girl was due to return to London for her final year's training in clinical practice before she qualified as a junior doctor.

Eight weeks seemed a lifetime to endure living with someone. By then, Isabel seriously hoped she would either have died or gotten better. At times she wondered if the first option wasn't her preferred outcome.

"I just wonder what this girl is like, on a day to day basis. How good will she be at taking direction? Will she be one of those chatty Cathies who never shut up?"

Bel was self-aware enough to realize her normal rate of progress, whether on grass, city-street, or African bush, was extremely fast, and she went through assistants equally swiftly. Their average tenure was nine months, after which they usually either collapsed, decided they urgently needed to do a full-time Master's Degree, or found someone to make them pregnant. One assistant had even gone so far as to have twins, simply to escape.

"Oh well," thought Bel gloomily. "I just hope she isn't as bossy as me. We won't last a week together if she is."

If things became desperate, she could send the girl packing for the cost of a local taxi and a train ticket. But what would she do then? She couldn't bend her arms, so she couldn't feed herself. She couldn't even blow her own nose, or wipe her own backside.

"Here they are!" called out Claire suddenly. "I can see the silver from the car glinting in the sunshine. I will go and put the kettle on." And she retreated inside to the kitchen.

Bel turned her head a little, and squinted in the sunshine. She should be wearing shades. She could see the Peugeot ascending the hill below, turning corner after corner, and bringing her savior, or maybe her nemesis, up to her door.

Bel tried to scuff her chair forward with her one workable foot, but it wouldn't budge. She realized of course that Claire had set the brake on and with both arms in plaster there was no way she could release it. She almost cried with frustration, and eventually violently kicked out at the sandy gravel under her foot, so a whole shower of pebbles flew up into the air.

Isabel's Healing

Maggie McIntyre

Chapter 2

In London, two hundred miles to the south-east, Bryony Morris had also been having a bad day. Her boyfriend Aiden, golden boy of their year's cohort, and ridiculously talented on all fronts, was supposed to be seeing her off from Euston Station, but he'd been really late picking her up, and now she was in danger of missing her train. They shot through the congestion charge check points in his old van, and screeched to a halt in front of the large London train station.

Bryony reached behind her to grab her rucksack and messenger bag with her precious lap-top.

"You still haven't said "Yes." Now you're going off to the back of beyond for eight weeks! When can I see you?"

Ignoring the traffic wardens bearing down on them, Aiden had jumped out of the car as she prepared to run into the station. He hugged her clumsily as she was already putting her rucksack onto her shoulders.

"Here! Kiss me at least!"

Their lips briefly touched, and she gave him a squeeze as compensation.

"Honestly, Aid, I'm not sure. Maybe in a month or so. It all depends on my patient, and it's a long way. Look, let's Skype or Facetime. I'll keep in touch, I promise!"

"Well, thanks, make sure you do. And I need an answer. Mum's already asking me when we are setting the date. She really likes you."

"I know, and I like her too, I like both your parents, but that's not really the point, is it? Look, I must fly! 'Bye!'"

And she was gone, sprinting off towards the barriers before the trains.

"Ok! Ok! Keep your hair on! I'm leaving." Aiden

shouted irritably at the warden bearing down on him, and revved up his van. As well as having to pay to enter central London, he didn't want to be prosecuted for illegal parking as well. He pulled out quickly and rejoined the traffic heading west towards the Marylebone road.

***

Bryony caught the train by the skin of her teeth and collapsed into a corner seat. All she had were vague directions to a cottage called Ty Bach, or 'Little House', and the promise that someone would meet her at Machynlleth station, a name she could barely pronounce.

'Little House' didn't sound promising, especially since she discovered the phrase was also a euphemism for a toilet in Welsh. Not a good omen. She could barely pronounce the name of her destination station.

"Single with student railcard to Machynlleth?"

"Yes."

The guard scribbled something on her two little cards.

"Change at Birmingham New Street."

"Is there a snack bar on this train?"

"Sorry. Trolley service only. It will probably get down to this end before we get to Birmingham though."

Bryony was doubly frustrated, as she normally planned all her expeditions down to the nth degree, but somehow today everything had turned to mud underneath her. The washing machine in her accommodation block had not been switched on properly, so by the time she noticed it, her laundry cycle was an hour late, and her clothes, hastily stuffed into her rucksack, were all still damp. She'd intended to catch a bus down to the railway station, but Aiden had suddenly called, offering her a lift, and she couldn't refuse. But their argument, or rather his hectoring and her hedging about, the previous evening still rankled. She would really have preferred to slip away to her summer job quietly, even if the issue of their future relationship remained unresolved.

It was quite simple really. For some strange reason, Aiden wanted her to agree to a formal engagement after a year of dating, and Bryony had huge problems with that. She knew it was the guys who normally had commitment issues, but the thought of marrying Aiden, a charming hunk though he was, filled her with a secret dread. She wasn't even quite sure why. He had been surprised, even affronted, and was now almost bullying her to agree. Maybe he was worried she'd meet someone else in Wales. But honestly, how crazy was that idea?

Still, she had made it onto the train, and the right train at that. Look on the bright side. This was a journey to what sounded a good job, an eight week contract to look after a woman who had been in a road accident, and who needed a caregiver until she was back on her feet. She was also apparently trying to write a book and wanted someone to type while she dictated. It all sounded a nice peaceful summer, which would give her the space to sort out her head.

By this stage in the academic year Bryony was exhausted, as all medical students approaching their final year would expect to be. But the promised job would keep her through until September. The pay was excellent with full board and all expenses thrown in, and for someone who had been a child caregiver since the age of eight, domestic duties and mopping up after just one person in a wheelchair presented little challenge.

The train gathered speed out of London, and she looked at her shadowy reflection in the window. She saw someone she recognized, a young, relatively fit, and anonymous medical student who just needed to catch up on her sleep to be on top form.

Bryony arranged her rucksack as a pillow, and leant back on it, closing her eyes. She was more than halfway to becoming a fully-fledged junior doctor, so she could sleep anywhere and anytime, given half a chance. Within three minutes she was fast asleep, and when the tea trolley did come rattling through the carriage, she never knew about it.

Four hours after leaving London she finally arrived at the little mid-Wales station, and pulled her rucksack up onto her shoulders. She was one of only three people to get off the train, and she quickly identified the man who had come to meet her. He had a pleasant, academic sort of face with grey hair, and looked like a retired professor in his sixties, which was of course just what he was.

"Hello! You must be Bryony. I'm Edward Bridgford. Let me help you with your bag." And he led her out of the station straight towards his car.

It took thirty minutes to drive up to the cottage, and Edward used it to assess the character and capabilities of the young girl beside him. She certainly looked fit and strong, slim and easy on the eye. But looks weren't everything. How would she possibly cope with his mercurial and volatile sister?

He asked her about her medical studies.

"I'm almost finished. I hope to be a surgeon, and have been heading that way in my electives."

"You said you'd cared for your grandmother. You must have been young. How long did that last?"

"Oh, right through my teens. But I had to. I owed her a lot. She brought me up after my mother died of cancer when I was eight. But she had a stroke when I was twelve, so could not get about very well after that. I also nursed my great aunt. I do know all about personal care."

In fact Bryony had taken this job, apart from its good pay and full board, as an exercise in trying to gain some more practice in the art of being a perfect hands-on healer. If she was honest, she reckoned she had a better chance of speaking fluent Welsh in eight weeks, than in achieving this though. She had never felt a natural nurse.

Forced out of necessity to care for both her grandmother, and her great aunt had made her domestically very competent and almost immune to embarrassment over the issues to be encountered in personal care. But their constant complaining had made her inwardly impatient with people she considered 'moaners'. And working in a trauma unit as a student reinforced this. When you'd been with people who literally had had their guts falling out after a major accident, it made you inclined to dismiss people who cried over a stiff neck.

By then they were approaching a set of old gates with *TY Bach* signed on them, and they could see Bel kicking at the gravel like a petulant child.

From her hated wheelchair Bel could see her brother turn to the girl beside him and say something, but couldn't work out what it was exactly.

In fact Edward was saying, "My sister, as you see, has still some way to go before her injuries heal. It's been very frustrating for her. I'm afraid you'll need a good deal of patience." He spoke cautiously, which only emphasized his euphemistic assessment.

Bryony Morris nodded in reply but her eyes were fixed on the woman in the wheelchair. Maybe now wasn't the best time to mention it, but patience wasn't her strongest suit. An A in diagnosis, OK, but a self-awarded D in patience, and a complete Fail sometimes in bedside manner.

Oh, well, at least she knew all about compound fractures. She pulled herself out of the car and walked over to meet her new employer and patient. She smiled to hide her nervousness. This, she soon realized, was her first mistake.

"What are you smirking at?" were Bel's first remarks to her. "Never seen an actual accident victim before?"

The words fell from her mouth unbidden. Bel had been so anxious not to appear pathetic and impotent she slipped far too far the other way, and knew she simply sounded rude and hostile, oh, and stupid. Of course the girl must have seen accident victims.

The young woman in front of her actually jumped backwards a step, whether in fear or repulsion she couldn't tell. They simply stared at each other for a second or two, and then Bryony gave a little shrug and pressed forward with the greeting she had intended.

Bel's hostility surprised her, as she had not been prepared to be instantly disliked, but she knew in normal circumstances she came across as intelligent, civilized, and self-confident. She wouldn't be cowed within the first three minutes of their meeting.

So, she ignored the questions, and because Bel was in no position to shake hands, folded her own back in a defensive body position but smiled politely.

"Hi, I am pleased to meet you Miss Bridgford. This is truly a beautiful location and I am very happy to have arrived at last."

"It's Dr."

"What?"

"Dr Bridgford. PhD, not Medical. But you had better call me Bel I suppose."

"Oh, sorry. Bel, then. I'm glad it's not a medical doctorate at least. Can't have two of us clashing on the best way forward all the time."

"I'm sorry, I wasn't aware you are a qualified doctor? Nor were you employed to offer medical opinions. It is basic personal care which I need, and for you to give me my necessary painkillers at the right time of day, and night. But most of your work will be either in the kitchen preparing food and cleaning up, keeping the house straight, or acting as an amanuensis helping me write a book on climate change. How good is your IT, are you on top of all the Office programs at least?"

"Well," Bryony thought, "Not exactly charm personified!"

She ventured to reply in kind.

"Yes, with Word and Excel anyway. Actually, in answer to your earlier questions. I wasn't smirking. That was my friendly face. And, secondly, in fact, I have seen too many accident victims. You can't avoid them in a busy London teaching hospital. I've been seconded to

Accident and Emergency, and worked in Triage for twelve weeks earlier this spring. I hope to specialize in emergency surgery after I qualify next year."

Bel looked up at her sharply, but her temper and nerves both began to settle, just a little. The girl wasn't a mouse at least. After the initial shock, she had shown no fear, rather a realistic attitude to injury, based on her obvious short-term forays into dealing with seriously damaged bodies, and sustained by what Bel suspected might be a decent sense of humor.

Oh, well, it would be an advantage if one of them had a cheerful disposition. Her own *joi de vivre* had been completely splintered weeks before, just as thoroughly as her car's shattered engine.

Ted and Claire, watched this opening exchange with obvious apprehension, and now chipped in to try and improve the atmosphere. They made small talk about the heat of the afternoon, how tired Bryony must be how regular the trains were from London. Ted pulled her small suitcase from the back seat, and Bryony lifted out a rucksack onto her shoulder. She obviously travelled lightly.

Claire, unlike Bel, looked at Bryony and liked what she saw. She was an attractive girl, first of all, and if Bel had to look at one person for weeks on end, then it was good her eyes weren't subjected to anything too disagreeable. She also looked normal, the sort of girl who would fit in anywhere, and also, thankfully, not gay! Isabel didn't need any more complications of that nature during her convalescence.

Bryony was only slightly taller than Bel, and slim enough to look very good in the jeans and high-end T-shirt she wore under a light blue linen jacket. She had tawny blonde hair tied back in the ubiquitous soft ponytail style all girls seemed to go for these days, and her eyes were green.

She also appeared strong enough to haul Isabel in and out of bed and the shower without damaging her own back. Isabel had lost so much weight since the accident, that shouldn't be a problem, but she hoped the girl would be very gentle with Bel's frail body and fragile bones.

"Let's go inside, shall we?" said Claire, "I've made some tea and brought along some scones, and the warmth is fading a little bit now outside. We can discuss all the necessary practicalities better in the kitchen."

She went to release the brake on Bel's chair, but Bryony stepped in.

"Let me," she said firmly. "I might as well get started straight away."

Bel flinched at the thought of anyone moving her chair and carelessly bumping her, but the girl managed to wheel her in, and even up and over the door lintel without hurting her. She decided to start by talking about the cottage, rather than her own physical issues.

"It's a traditional Welsh long house, which means it's all on one level, one important reason we chose it, but it is small, very small for two strangers to co-exist in. There are two bedrooms, at opposite ends of the house. Yours will be in there." She nodded her head towards the end door leading out of the kitchen.

"There is this kitchen, with an electric Aga which heats the hot water and warms the whole house really, then the living room, and beyond that my bedroom and the bathroom."

Bryony looked around. She enjoyed the smell of the summer invading the cottage. It was light now, with windows all facing south, but in the winter, it would probably be dark and damp unless the Aga ran constantly. The ceilings were low, but high enough not to bang your head on them.

"I can smell wood-smoke," she observed.

"Yes, we only arrived this afternoon, but the previous tenants must have lit the wood-burner in the living room," explained Edward.

"Our plan is for Claire to return next Friday, and then once a week to give you a full day off. Bel can't be left on her own at all yet, but we understand you will need time off to recharge your own batteries. The hospital only released her if there is someone here to help her take her medicine in the night and be there constantly in case of an emergency."

Bryony breathed an internal sigh of relief. It was more than she had expected. There would be breathing holes in the ice at least.

"Thanks, that's cool. But I haven't anywhere near enough to go overnight. If you could just manage to come and stay 9am to 9pm, that will be fine. And I'm used to broken sleep."

Bel wanted to take some part in this induction.

"As soon as my arm casts come off I'll be perfectly OK to be on my own for a day. I won't be able to drive, obviously before the end of your contract. There's a market in Machynlleth on a Wednesday. Maybe you can drive me down. I know the way. Otherwise the fridge is well stocked. I presume you can prepare basic meals."

"Basic meals, yes. I'm sure we'll be fine. Could I see your list of medicines please? And when do they expect to take the casts off?"

"My arms, in ten days, I hope. This right leg was badly smashed, so that may be longer. My arms and ribs aren't yet healed enough to cope with crutches. Hence I'm confined to this chair, or the bed."

Bryony looked at her new patient with a little less dislike and a measured amount of regard. "Brilliant bone structure..." was the first unbidden thought which hit her brain.

Maggie McIntyre

Chapter 3

Bryony thought Dr. Bridgford was really very beautiful behind the scowls and grumbles. She had what might be termed Irish good looks, with black hair, just beginning to have flecks of grey, and very clear blue eyes, fringed with extravagantly thick lashes set on a face with high cheekbones.

Her eyes stared out from all under a short haircut, which must have been very well styled not long ago. Now though, after a month or so of neglect, it looked flat and uncared for. Her fringe was rather too long for comfort as well, as it fell over her field of view, and she couldn't even brush it away.

Isabel decided to say something more about the medical issues the girl would have to face.

"The trouble with the pain killers is that they make me rather nauseated, so I have to take anti-sickness medication. Then there's the problem of constipation, so I have to take something to counteract that. I can't tell you how bloody furious it all makes me, how frustrating."

Nights spent sweating in pain had obviously taken their toll. Bel had deep grey shadows under her eyes, and a few wrinkles and frown lines across her forehead and at the corners of her mouth. In earlier years and months, she had probably been in the sun too much without protection, and it showed in her face, and through the faded tan on what Bryony could see of her hands.

"Let's go through to the bedroom, so I can see what they've prescribed for you."

She pushed Bel's chair through the living room and into the bedroom behind. Beside the bed there was a large suitcase, open but still unpacked, full of papers, a lap-top and several books, all too heavy for the woman to hold on her lap, let alone read. A commode chair was placed discreetly behind the bed, which was a double one and covered with a Welsh woven throw.

The room was simply furnished, but not unpleasant. A large collection of pills and medicines covered most of a side table, and Bryony read through the long check list on a clipboard beside them.

"I haven't had the chance to arrange things as I like them yet. Perhaps that can be your first task."

Bryony surveyed what would be her main centre of operations. Obviously Bel would not be able to move, even to scratch her own nose for quite a while, and she would need nursing 24/7. After a month in hospital, under an even tighter regime, no wonder her nerves were frayed and her temper gone from bad to filthy.

Bryony braced herself for a good few days of bearing the brunt of Bel's tongue.

"Six days, and then I get a day off," she thought. "I can do it. I can get through it. The woman really needs me, and I can save all my wages here."

Making a dent in the enormous student debt piling up round her ears had to be a priority. And the physical process of healing did genuinely fascinate her. What makes a person well, what gives them good health; this had always been of great interest.

At least Dr. Bel Bridgford had genuine reasons to be miserable. Her pain must be acute, judging from the very high levels of opiates and especially morphine she'd been prescribed.

Bryony looked at the panoply of drugs, and wondered how quickly she could get the patient to reduce her intake of them. They were all addictive, so there was a fine balance between achieving effective pain control and falling into dependence.

Claire explained more about the house and their plan for Bryony to have use of the Citroen Berlingo for the duration of her posting.

"It's a high vehicle, so we hope Bel might be able to

sit in the passenger seat without too much trouble. We drove over in it today," she said.

"It would be good if you can get her out for an hour or two's drive now and then. She is used to variety, and she will be prone to cabin fever if she's too confined."

"The person in the wheelchair can still speak!" snapped Bel, deciding she was sick and tired of being talked about as if she wasn't even present.

She turned her head so she could look at her sister-in-law. "Thanks for all you've done, Claire, but I think I can take it from here. You've a long drive home, so I advise you both to set out before long."

Her brother and sister-in-law took the not too subtle hint and decided to leave. They gave Bryony their phone numbers and the ones for a local doctor, as well as the department at the Countess of Chester hospital where Bel had been treated. Bryony watched as they both awkwardly kissed Bel on the cheek.

"She's not very used to being kissed by them," she thought.

"I'll be back in a week," said Claire, "But call me tomorrow evening will you, to give me a progress report? And I can be here in less than two hours if necessary."

"Oh, don't fuss the girl," were Bel's final words. "She'll be fine. We both will. We'll see you next Friday."

Bryony watched as the Peugeot containing her last link with normality slipped away down the hill and round the valley. Then she turned to the woman who would be her sole responsibility for the next two months.

She knew they were probably not going to be best mates, or anything like it. More than anyone, Bel reminded her of a ferocious math teacher who had once petrified her in high school, but she had a mission to get the woman well again, and she was determined to succeed.

"What would you like me to do first? Or what do you need doing most urgently? "She asked.

"I need the bathroom," muttered Bel. "I'm trying to make it to the loo during the day, and just use the commode at night."

"Right you are."

She wheeled the chair into the bathroom, grateful there was room to turn it round, and helped the older woman shakily stand on her one good leg. She wore a long kaftan like dress, with one arm in a three-quarter length plaster cast which went above the elbow, and the other strapped in front in a rigid straight full cast. She had the functional use of neither arm, which made her naturally unbalanced, and caused her to wobble dangerously as she stood up.

Bryony held her up as gently as she could, while pulling her underwear down as quickly as possible and then helping her sit on the toilet. To be so dependent on others for so long, must have been very hard for such an obviously proud and self-sufficient woman.

Bryony's medical training had taught her to see other people's bodies as objects, things which functioned, or didn't, not embodiments of personality or sex appeal, or anything personal. But it must be different for Bel, and difficult not to be embarrassed to be half naked and vulnerable in front of a complete stranger.

However, her own complete lack of being fazed, or even seeming to notice Bel's body as anything more than a battered machine, helped them both deal with the essentials. Bryony was relieved to be able to rearrange the woman's clothes afterwards, get her back in the chair and out into the living room without either hurting her or being snapped at too much. At least she'd achieved something. She could unpack the suitcases and arranged the books and papers later.

"What now? Would you like to eat something?"

"No, not at all. I want to make a start on the book first. Now you're here. Are you going to be up to this job, do you think? As you can clearly see, I'm a difficult patient and a demanding employer."

"Bit late for second thoughts, surely? My lift to the station won't be back for another week. No, if you can put up with me, I'm sure we'll be fine. I like projects. And you're giving me a great one."

"Oh, yes, and what is that?"

"Getting you back on your feet, so you can take off and run whatever it is you run again. And helping you write your book."

"How do you know I run anything?"

"Oh, all that natural authority must be used for something. You must be CEO of a large company or something."

"Nothing like that. Look me up on Google if you must. Now I have a very tight deadline to meet. I need to complete 150,000 words with footnotes, by September 1st. That's only eight weeks away, so we need to achieve 20,000 words a week. I'll be aiming for at least 3,500 words a day, six days a week, which should give you ample time to type up, edit and correct over the weekend."

"This seems to be very ambitious. Please don't forget I get Fridays off."

"Oh! No, I suppose we'll have to allow that, so we'll work Sundays through to Thursday, then use Saturday as an editing day."

"What's the book about?"

"The end of the world as we know it."

Bryony pretended not to be shocked, and smiled professionally at her obviously mad patient.

"Ah, right. Then I see your point about urgency. I had better get my laptop ready. Do you have a password for the WiFi?"

Bel indicated the modem on the bookcase close to her chair, and Bryony went to open her lap-top and get connected. She could already see the black clouds over Bel's head beginning to disperse now that she was talking about her work, and her own tiredness and hunger retreated somewhat. They could afford to work for an hour or more before the next round of medication was due, and she could then maybe rustle up some scrambled eggs for supper.

She parked Bel by the kitchen table, and sat at right

angles to her. She opened her lap-top, checked that it was almost fully charged, and connected it up to the internet. Despite the remote location, the signal wasn't bad, which was a relief.

If things were lonely and difficult here, then she could still Skype with her friends, listen to a podcast or favorite audio book and maybe even watch her own preferred movies. It also meant she could call up a doctor or even an ambulance if Isabel suddenly took a turn for the worse, or had an attack.

She knew she had cracked ribs and a compound fracture of her lower leg and ankle, so anything was possible. The responsibility of her position began to impinge on her confidence. There was really no-one else here, to help. She decided to key in some emergency contacts into her phone before anything terrible happened.

"Are you going to take all night setting up?" Bel seemed ridiculously impatient, and lacking in empathy. It was almost as though she wanted Bryony to dislike her.

"Do not let her upset you!" Bryony told herself firmly. "She is just a patient, in pain. Just treat her as you would someone in the hospital. Remember, it's not personal. She doesn't know you."

"I'm ready now. You can dictate to me, and I'll follow with typing it straight onto the lap-top. Then I'll sort out the grammar and spelling later. I'll try to keep up. Right...one, two, three, let's go!"

Bel leaned back as far as she was able, and closed her eyes. Then she started to speak, slowly but in fully formed sentences, and in a very musical low voice completely unlike her earlier snapping and snarling. It was rather easy to follow and transcribe, and Bryony felt her fingers tripping lightly over the keys.

The clear voice and the gentle clicking kept going, and chapter one of what was obviously going to be a profound, even ground-breaking, book began to take shape.

The subject matter of the book, the imminent threat of climate change, sounded very compelling, in fact something anyone could become absorbed by, but of course the opening paragraphs were mainly based on setting the scene and the parameters for Bel's arguments. Her thesis rested on the universally recognized premise that the whole earth was at a point of crisis, a tipping point of global warming which within their lifetime might be irreversible. What Bel had to offer were many case studies where the rising sea levels, droughts, floods and general climatic catastrophes had direct negative impact on the lives of the poorest, in particular women, who grew the bulk of the world's food on the poorest soil.

Bryony kept her head down and concentrated on the words rather than their meaning. As Isabel spoke, she could just about keep up with her. The woman certainly knew how to dictate efficiently to someone who didn't know shorthand.

Bryony liked to think she was as environmentally aware as the next girl, but her degree course and further training had been so focused on the physical construction of the human body, and its medical needs and issues, that she had had hardly any time to consider global issues or politics.

She read articles mainly in the British Medical Journal, and just caught the news headlines first thing or last thing at night as she crawled into bed, and set her alarm for ridiculously early calls. She had no time to be out there protecting the environment. This sudden shift of emphasis, this new use for her IT and manual dexterity on a keyboard was astonishing Bryony, not least because of the feeling of mental fresh air it was blowing through her brain cells.

She was only worried that Dr. Bridgford would overdo it. She looked quite fragile, and at times her eyes stared wildly into the middle distance, as she fought to find the right words. The summer evening faded from gold into a soft purple duskiness all around the isolated cottage and the song of the birds faded. It was even later when Bel finally fell silent, her voice almost dried out with fatigue; Bryony already had well over three thousand words in front of her on the screen.

"There you are, ma'am, you've achieved more than your first day's target. Three thousand four hundred and fifteen words."

"Humph. I will see tomorrow how good a fist you've made at typing in what I've written and not making a complete dog's dinner of it. And don't Ma'am me please. My name's Bel."

Bryony stood up and stretched her aching shoulders. "Yes, that's something I wanted to ask. Isn't your name really Isabel? Would you mind very much if I called you Isabel? Bel sounds like a dog's name. It doesn't feel respectful. And I also had a favorite doll once I called Isabel. It's much prettier."

"Hmm, you have hardly been here ten minutes and already you want to change my name to make it *prettier*? What nonsense! Anyway, no-one has called me Isabel since my parents died. How fixed are you on this bizarre notion?"

"It's not bizarre, I think if I stay with you for the next eight weeks, do all your washing and ironing, cook edible meals and get you out of all that plaster then I believe I'm allowed to think of you as an Isabel."

"Now you're being ridiculous!" Bel glared at Bryony, unsure if the girl was making fun of her. "You sound just like Anne of Green Gables, wanting to be called Cordelia."

"Not me, you. You look like an Isabel."

"Oh, very well, it means very little to me. But in that case I'm more likely to just call you 'Girl'. Bryony sounds like an overgrown rosebush."

"Touché, I know. I don't care for it either. I didn't choose it. Sorry about that. Do call me Girl if it amuses you."

"Stop teasing. It won't work with me. You must know by now I've completely lost my sense of humor."

Bryony decided it was maybe time to change the subject.

"You must be thirsty. Let me fetch you a drink of

water. I'm really rather hungry as well. I expect you're the same. I thought we might eat scrambled eggs tonight, if that's OK? "

"Oh yes, I forgot the time. It has dragged itself along now for so many weary days. This was the first time since I regained consciousness I haven't been watching the hands turn on the clock, willing the hours away. I suppose eggs might be OK, but don't leave them too runny, and no more than two for me, and half a slice of toast! I've quite lost my appetite."

"Like your sense of humor? Don't worry, we'll find them both together somewhere and restore them back to you again."

"Stop being so fanciful. I thought you were supposed to be sensible."

"I am sensible, when I have to be, like now. But I am glad you know about Anne of Green Gables. It was my favorite story when I was young, being an orphan and all."

"An orphan?"

"Yes, but please don't think I mentioned it to make you or anybody feel sorry for me. It's just made me rather resilient, that's all."

Isabel did not know what to make of the girl talking so openly about such personal things. She acted as though regaining one's sense of humor was like some sort of treasure-hunt, but she seemed competent enough around the kitchen.

Within fifteen minutes they were both looking at nicely scrambled eggs and grilled tomatoes with a side of buttered toast. Bel sat there and pointedly said nothing, until Bryony jumped up and apologized with an embarrassed smile.

"Oh, of course, I'm so sorry!"

She picked up a fork and began to feed her patient who glared at her like a hungry baby eagle.

Maggie McIntyre

Chapter 4

Between passing bites to Isabel, Bryony ate her own supper, and was pleased to see both plates were empty very soon. Then she picked up a glass of water, and held it to Isabel's lips while she swallowed.

All this, having to be fed like a quadriplegic, reminded Bel of how frustrated she was, and her scowl returned.

"Is this how it's going to be all the time?" enquired Bryony innocently.

"What?"

"Your expression of suppressed fury? I am sure you have other expressions you could use. How about trying 'weary resignation,' or hey, maybe even 'Surprised relief at eggs being edible'?"

"Don't make fun of me!"

"I'm not, not really. I just think you'll feel better if you smile once in a while. You do smile nicely, I expect, though I have not seen one yet. Isabel, smile for me, just a small one, please?"

"Don't make..."

Bel felt the corners of her mouth turn up just a fraction, despite her best efforts to stay grimly serious. The young woman was impertinent, but maybe she had a point. Frowning so much was making her stiff neck even more uncomfortable, and wasn't helping her headache.

"There. Will that do, girl?"

It was a quarter smile at least.

"Yes, you only need to do it once an hour or so. I can live on very little."

"Don't think you will get me to smile on demand. Now, go and get all my pills, or the pain will take away even that much."

Bryony counted out the different colored capsules, and fed them to her new employer one by one, helping her swallow each with a glass of water.

"Now, I had better unpack for you and make up the beds." She emptied the suitcase and put all the clothes away as neatly as she could, right down to underwear and socks.

All of Isabel's clothes were simple and loose-fitting, but all were good quality and there were several Italian designer labels sneaked in around the items. So Isabel had a secret penchant for nice clothes.

Bryony was pleased to see some human fault-line in Isabel's moral high ground. She obviously didn't live like a nun anyway. The make-up and body wash, as well, were all from Clinique or Clarens, but maybe they were presents. Isabel had no make-up on, and her face revealed her exhaustion after all their book work. It was time to encourage her to turn in for the night.

When she had unpacked, Bryony then made up the large double bed in the main bedroom, and slipped a waterproof mattress cover under the bottom sheet. She had seen it discreetly folded in the box of other medical paraphernalia, so it was obvious Isabel or her caregivers had expected it to be useful. When everything in the big bedroom was shipshape, she carried through a set of single sheets and made up her own bed in the little far room.

Then she assisted her through to the bed room, and found a nightgown in her drawer. It had buttons all up the front, and was the very plain sort sold in hospital shops.

"Will this do?"

She showed the garment to Isabel who nodded in bored resignation. As Bel sat on the commode chair, Bryony gently pulled her kaftan up and off her shoulders completely and then paused to look at Bel's physique before she replaced the clothing quickly with the night gown. She had been looking to assess how underweight she was, but Bel seemed to assume it was more a judgment on her body's current sorry state.

"I know I'm a mess," she stated flatly, as Bryony fastened the buttons up the front of her nightgown, and then folded her clothes and put them over onto a chest under the window.

The older woman obviously couldn't tolerate anything as constricting as a bra, but her nakedness in fact showed very pretty breasts which almost glowed in the late evening light. Just below them, her ribs were strapped round and round her chest, binding which would need changing soon, and her torso was still marked with yellow and purple bruising.

"Yes, your body might have taken quite a battering, but it will only be temporary. And your brain obviously isn't impaired. I'm in awe of how well you can think and dictate like you do. It's a miracle after all the anesthetic you must have endured, and all these pain-killers they've put you on."

"Personal observations from you are superfluous. I know what I can and can't do. But I'm actually ashamed to admit it; - I am quite frightened of the pain. I've never been before. But this has been something else."

"I know. It must have been hell, but I promise, I'll try and manage the pain relief so you are never more than uncomfortable from now on. I have done a module on analgesics. Now let me lift you up and put you into the bed. There. Good."

The cast on Isabel's lower leg was heavy and she needed help to lift it up onto the mattress. Once this was done, Isabel lay back on the pillows, her face exhausted. She shut her eyes.

"A module on analgesics"? She thought it sounded almost like a spoof. She was sure she could write such a course herself, the amount of pills they'd stuffed into her.

But at least the girl was better qualified than the other candidates who had responded to the Lady advertisement. She should not have belittled her medical training. She knew how much hard work was involved in becoming a doctor.

Bryony gently shook her shoulder.

"Isabel, Isabel, don't go to sleep just yet. Listen. I'll leave all the doors open between this room and mine. If you need me in the night, please call out. I'm a very light sleeper."

"Hmm. Alright. I normally only sleep for three hours at a stretch. You may be up with me again before 2 am."

"Don't worry. That's why I'm here. Goodnight Isabel."

"Goodnight, Girl. And..."

"What?"

"Thank you."

Smiles were obviously over for the day, but Isabel's mouth twitched and Bryony rewarded her with a friendly grin in return. Then she picked up the commode pan and went into the bathroom to empty and disinfect it. When she replaced it, she saw that Isabel had already fallen asleep.

First day over! She moved silently into the kitchen and stacked up the supper dishes. They could be washed in the morning, or some time Isabel was awake. She could see this was going to be like looking after a baby. You had to sleep when they did, if you were going to get any rest at all.

The single bed in her bedroom was narrow, the room chilly, but the duvet was light and cozy and there was space in a narrow wardrobe for her few clothes. As she lay down in summer shorts pajamas she turned to the wall. She had come a long way that day, in more ways than one.

"Maybe I can be a healer," was almost her last thought. "Maybe I won't just have to be just a sawbones after all."

The last wood pigeons decided to cease cooing to each other, and the first owls could be heard hooting to each other far across the valley. The owls hooted again as the night deepened. Bryony fell asleep. If Isabel wanted to call her 'Girl,' she decided she didn't mind, not really.

Isabel's Healing

Chapter 5

Bryony woke just before 3 am and for a moment couldn't remember where she was. Then her bare left foot felt the cool plaster of the wall next to her bed, and she turned over on the narrow mattress. Her sense of location returned and she placed herself in the white cottage tucked against the hill in North Wales.

She listened to the soft, dark silence, but she knew something in the night must have woken her, and sure enough, through all the open doors within the cottage she heard a muffled noise of someone weeping, barely audibly. In a second she was up and hurrying through the shadowed kitchen and living room into Isabel's bedroom. She didn't even pause to slip a dressing-gown over her short summer pajamas.

The occupant was sobbing, too quietly to have been heard by anyone who had not already been used to broken nights, and she was obviously in pain. Bryony turned on the bedside lamp and leaned over her.

"Hey, Isabel, I told you to call out when you needed me, remember?"

She could see Isabel blink in the sudden lamp light and reached across to angle it away from her face. Her face was red and her tears must have been falling for some time, as her whole pillow was creased and damp.

"I...I didn't want to wake you. It's just, oh damn, I've wet the bed, and I can't move a muscle. And my good leg went into a cramp. Oh, dammit! That's not why I was weeping. I'm just so tired of it all."

"Hey, early days yet. I'll soon have you sorted. First thing, let me give you some painkillers. It's time for another round, and once you've had them you'll feel much better. Don't worry about the accident. I can easily change your bed."

Bryony pulled back the covers, and saw that Bel had indeed, had a flood in the night.

"All par for the course," she said. "Here take these," and putting her arm around Bel's neck lifted her gently so she could swallow the tablets along with a few sips of water. They went down her throat, just about, and then Isabel fell back and wondered just how her new caregiver was going to cope with the ruined bed and nightgown.

"I should have worn a pad," she muttered. "I was too proud to ask. They had me catheterized in the hospital."

"No, it was my fault. I was stupid not to suggest it. No worries. We'll both know better tomorrow night. Now, if you can sit up a little, I'd like to move you over into the chair while I make the bed. "

Isabel rolled herself up and over, helped by Bryony's strong pull, and then hopped onto her hated wheelchair. The nightgown came off and was thrown into the laundry basket, and Bryony wrapped her up in her soft blue dressing-gown, covering her nakedness and keeping her warm. She managed to set the foot on her cramped leg against the smooth stone flags of the floor and the stabbing pain eased.

The girl had the bed stripped and the bottom sheet changed in minutes. She was pleased to have remembered to put a mattress protector under it, so there was little harm done. When the sheet had followed the nightgown into the basket, she wiped everything down with a light disinfectant and remade the bed. A cool cotton sheet was placed over the mattress cover, and then she invited Bel to lie back down on it.

"I'm going to give you a little bed wash, to freshen you up. Please wait just a moment." In the kitchen she poured hot water into a basin and fetched a face-cloth, soft, fluffy hand towel and sweet scented soap. When she returned Bel was lying motionless, her face passive, but the weeping had ceased, and she shut her eyes and allowed Bryony to wash her face and then her body and upper legs and afterwards pat her dry like a baby with the towel. Bryony also noticed a jar of talcum powder on the chest of drawers and sprinkled a little over her loins, and between her thighs. Her touch was very light, but confident enough to show she knew what she was doing.

The girl's shadowy figure moved back and forth in the lamplight, and found another night shirt and some underwear in a drawer.

At least she wasn't a chatter-box, thank God. So many youngsters seemed full of inane comments. But for some perverse reason, Bel herself wanted to talk. "You seem very experienced. I thought medical students left all this sort of thing to nurses and HCAs. "

"Oh, it wasn't in training that I learned to change beds. I nursed my grandmother through my teens, after she had a stroke."

"Were you her main caregiver? Surely not?"

"Yes, afraid so. It did curtail the social life rather, though I was so busy with my A levels, I couldn't go out much anyway."

Bryony put a large pad into the underpants and slipped them up over her leg plaster cast and up her hips.

"Better safe than sorry, eh?"

"Is your grandmother still living?"

"No, she died just after I finished my A levels. Here, can you help me give you this new nightgown?"

Bel let the rug slip down from her breasts and held out her arms, and between them they wrapped her back in the nightshirt. It was much more attractive than the previous nightgown, white, with black writing which Bryony couldn't read in the shadows.

She put a hand against Bel's buttocks and raised her butt so the nightshirt could roll down and be much more comfortable. Finally she pulled up the duvet and wrapped it softly round Bel shoulders. The whole episode had barely lasted twenty minutes, but Bel felt she had been awake half the night.

"Does that feel better? Do you think you will be able to sleep again?"

There was no answer to the question but Bel looked less distraught. She had to admit her whole situation was now so much better. She felt almost human again.

Bryony very gently pushed her hair back from her face and looked into her eyes.

"Would you like me to stay until you fall asleep?"

"No, don't do that. I mean, I'll be fine. Thank you."

"Good night then."

"Good night."

The girl walked quietly away and Isabel watched her retreat through the kitchen. Her bare legs and long hair caught a moon-beam as they crossed the kitchen and she looked quite ethereal. She had just had to touch Bel in the most intimate ways and yet she appeared completely oblivious to any physical implications.

It was essentially a relief to see how Bryony had no idea that in fact she might be not just a body, but also a woman, a woman who loved women, a lonely, bereaved woman who had suffered heartbreak and who was more vulnerable just now than at any time in her life. It was a great relief the girl was operating on a whole other level.

Professional, and completely platonic, that was the way to make sure they could live in the same house, not together in any sense, but alongside, like ships in the night. In this way they could finish her book, and patch her up enough to face her world again.

The metropolitan world she had left in London was so different from this isolated rural retreat ten miles from anywhere. They really were together in the back of beyond.

The isolated location of the cottage had suited Isabel's mood as soon as she read about it in the brochure Claire had shown her. Isabel had wanted to disappear entirely at one point immediately after the accident. To begin with, she had felt almost annihilated, a nothing person, scarcely human anymore. It had been horrible, but she supposed it was probably partly due to the shock.

But now the mists were clearing, and she was beginning to regain a sense of self, to nurture a hope that one day she might be healed, that she might be whole again. After the crisis in the night, Isabel, almost for the first time in a month, realized she now felt comfortable, dry, warm, and yes, comfortable.

She decided to let each day take care of itself, not to worry too much about what might be facing her down the line, but to try and be thankful for every moment, every second she was free from pain. It was a comfort to see how efficient the girl had been at nursing, she felt safe in her care, and she easily fell back to sleep.

***

Before she returned to her own bed at the other end of the house, Bryony decided to make herself a mug of tea, and then took it outside to sip as she sat on the stone bench near the front door. The summer night was warm and the air filled with all the tiny night sounds, moths fluttered round the porch light and she could hear the lowing of cattle from a farm far below.

She looked up at the brilliant stars in the sweep of the Milky Way above her head and felt strangely peaceful. There was so little light pollution up here in these Welsh hills that the vision, even with the moonlight, was wonderful.

The hot tea soothed her throat and she almost breathed in the stillness. She sat outside in her pajamas for a further twenty minutes, until she heard the clock in the living room gently strike four, and realized that if she wanted to be awake in the morning, she should retire to her own bed. Like Isabel she was asleep as soon as her head touched the rather lumpy pillow.

Isabel's Healing

Chapter 6

The following morning there was much to do, and Bryony had cleared away the supper dishes, put the washing on and even wiped down all the surfaces in the kitchen and living room before Isabel stirred. She had boiled the kettle and made a fresh pot of tea for them both, not just teabags in a mug.

She carried the tea into Bel's bedroom in a china teacup, and watched as her patient blinked awake. She had drawn back the curtains and the sunlight spilled into the room.

"I didn't tell you to wake me," Isabel muttered, not very graciously. She saw that Bryony was wearing jeans and a red and white striped T shirt. Her hair was tied back tightly into a pony-tail. She looked ready for work.

"No, but it's time for your meds. I know you've been suffering badly from insomnia, not surprising after so many weeks in hospital, but we need a new regime to get things back on track. It is after eight."

"Hmm. Oh, well. Is that tea?"

"Natch. Here, I'll help you sit."

Bel managed to rise a few inches in the bed, and Bryony held the cup to her lips and helped her sip.

"This is better than yesterday's."

"Yes, I used the leaf tea in the caddy and brewed it the old fashioned way. "

"I can hear the washing machine."

"I'm doing it early, so the morning sun can dry all the laundry, including some I brought up from London. There is a little washing line outside, and I found the detergent."

"You've obviously been working early. I am sorry for getting you up in the middle of the night."

"Wasn't that part of the job description? I didn't mind at all, and I was asleep again in no time. But I was thinking, maybe today, later on, after lunch perhaps, can I give you a proper wash, in the chair of course. We can't get those plaster casts wet – but I could shampoo your hair, and put some arnica on all your bruises. Would you like that?"

"Well, yes, maybe this evening, before I go down for the night. We need to put in the hours writing this morning. That's my priority."

"Of course. But I also need to know what you like to eat, what might tempt your appetite. Is the food in the fridge and larder your choice, or would you like me to order in something different?"

"No-one would deliver up here, I'm sure."

"We can find out. You'd be surprised sometimes where these supermarkets deliver to. But if not, maybe on Monday I'll drive you down with me to Machynlleth. You can sit in the car while I nip in the Co-op. I saw it on the way up here. "

The short conversation had tired Isabel out, and after another two swallows of tea, she lay back against her pillows and quite enjoyed watching the girl open the bedroom window and then tidy away all the things which were out in the room. She seemed very methodical.

"You like to put things away," she observed.

"Yes, I do. I am rather Aristotelian. I like everything in its place, ordered, tidy. I don't like clutter."

"Good. And have you always been like this?"

"Since my mother died."

"I'm sorry. You mentioned it last night as well. Do you miss her very much?"

"No, don't worry; it was nearly fifteen years ago. I was a young child. Long time ago now. "

Obviously Bryony didn't want to discuss it further, for which Isabel was grateful. She renewed her decision to keep everything impersonal, and talking about one's dead parent could easily lead onto discussing feelings.

Feelings could lead to relationships being spread out all over the place, and relationships were the last thing Isabel wanted to talk about, to anybody. Her smashed body was one thing, but her broken heart was strictly off limits.

"I'm pleased you like order. Mess and muddle distress me as well. In Africa, in the village round houses, there is no room for any muddle."

"Will I hear more about your times in Africa?"

"Yes, through the course of the book."

"Now, as to breakfast. How about orange juice, cereal, toast and marmalade? Whole grain bread of course."

"Yes, but Marmite instead of marmalade. If there is any."

"I'll look. "

"If we start the book by 9 am, then that will give us the morning. I think that will be enough time to finish another chapter, and if we keep to that we can still have the afternoons for me to rest and to do other things."

"I don't think you should aim for more than three thousand words a day, not at first anyway. It would be good to do a little physiotherapy as well. Have they given you any exercises to do?"

"Not yet. They just sent me out of hospital like a screaming banshee, but as soon as I get my arms free, then I certainly need to build up my muscles."

Bryony made breakfast for them both and carried it back on a large tray to Isabel's bedside. She sat on the bed, and gave Isabel sips of orange juice, then fed her cereal from a spoon, and finally cut up the toast into tiny squares and put them between her teeth one by one.

"I was better at this when I was 12 months old," grimaced Bel as she swallowed and bit another square of marmite toast.

"I'm sorry but either I feed you, or you die of starvation. Here, last one. Now could you manage to give me a smile? Go on, I dare you."

"You are a very forward young thing."

"Go on, smile! I said I could live on one an hour and time's up."

Isabel turned her face towards the sunshine pouring into her bedroom window from the southeast, and decided to oblige. She smiled directly at Bryony, an entrancing transformation of her face which almost took Bryony's breath away.

Isabel was quite beautiful when she smiled, and this was genuine. It reached her eyes and made them sparkle. Bryony had to smile back. It was contagious.

"Hey, Dr. Bridgford, that was some smile. That has set me up for the rest of the morning. How do you feel?"

"I feel...how do I feel? I actually might feel something resembling a human being at last. It's also the first morning I haven't woken with a splitting headache. But I'll feel happier once we are back on the book."

"Right, what would you like to wear? I've washed yesterday's kaftan, so choose something else."

Isabel indicated the chest of drawers, and then nodded when Bryony pulled out a linen top with wide sleeves and matching balloon pants. She put on a soft cotton Tee shirt for her under the linen top, and then slipped a sandal onto her one free foot.

She was seated at the table in the kitchen in no time at all, and while Bryony hung out the washing, Isabel once again channeled her thoughts in creating understandable text. She had found the previous evening's dictation surprisingly easy, but she had a very complex scheme for her book and knew it would not be straightforward to do everything without writing copious notes.

When Bryony returned and opened her lap-top, she was ready.

"To quote you, my girl, one, two, three, go...," said Isabel, and she began to dictate again.

Bryony followed her lead and began to type the words straight onto the keyboard. So it was 'my girl' now, not just 'Girl!' The ice was perhaps beginning to thaw. So far, so good.

Chapter two of Isabel's book began to get much more technical, and Bryony was forced to ask Isabel on several occasions to stop and explain so she could catch the spelling of African tribes and communities correctly and explain terms she'd not heard of before.

"I know about re-iteration, but I'm not familiar with "iteration". Is that development jargon?"

"No! Well, perhaps, if it sounds new to you. Let me rephrase it," and Isabel found easier ways to explain what she meant.

She had lived so long in the world of community development and global campaigning on women's rights; she'd forgotten that it had its own vocabularies and ways of expressing itself. But her head was filled with hundreds of stories, each illuminating in its own right, and she wanted to share them in a way which would be respectful to all the communities she had befriended, and who had befriended her, especially when she was young.

Once Bel was in the zone, the words came easily, and she was so relieved she could remember what she wanted to say. She spoke without pause for more than an hour, and then almost collapsed in the wheelchair.

She realized her headache had actually receded before, only by the fact that now the little man with the hammer was banging on her skull once more. She mentioned it to the girl sitting beside her, twirling a lock of her honey-colored hair in her fingers, and Bryony jumped to attention.

"Hey, dehydration!" Bryony filled the water bottle from the tap and gave Isabel a long drink. Then she took a glass herself.

"It's very good water isn't it? I bet it comes from a local source. It tastes wonderful."

Isabel hoped it wasn't that local! She had enough bugs in her system already from drinking unfiltered water all over the world, and there was no way she could cope with a stomach upset now.

"Maybe I should stick to bottled water."

"No, we'll be fine. I have found in the guidebook to the house in the kitchen, it says the water is totally safe to drink and is fully guaranteed from the tap. You need to keep drinking to flush out the toxins, and the more you drink water, the sooner your bruises will disperse."

After the drink, Isabel insisted they resume the work. She had completed her PhD eighteen years before by exposing sexual exploitation of girls in eastern Kenya, working with Kenyan colleagues on the shores of Lake Victoria, and had then done similar research into women's abuse in the Philippines. In the UK, she subsequently headed up a think tank on domestic violence, and had written several books and papers on that subject.

The more she heard Isabel speak, the more regard Bryony had for her experience and forensically sharp brain, but she could see the woman was grey with fatigue.

"Isabel, can I take you to rest on the bed for an hour, while I correct and check through my notes from last night and this morning? Then you can read through them while I prepare lunch, maybe?"

Isabel was all set to disagree strongly, and then she realized how much her body needed rest.

"OK, just for an hour, mind."

Bryony wheeled her to the bathroom, and when they had coped with the business there, took her back into the bedroom and helped her up onto the bed. She covered her lightly with the throw and the dressing-gown from the previous night, and pulled the curtains across slightly.

As she lay down on the bed, Isabel's head still swirled with the details of her research, and she thought it would be a long time before she could relax enough to sleep. For the last four years she had been compiling notes on the effect of global warming on fragile communities, and had her head full of anecdotal evidence to back up the data.

All this was alongside being executive director of a specialist aid agency, and monitoring projects across four continents. She wondered if she would ever be fit enough to return there, or like so much else in her life, had to be discarded as a shattered dream. Anyway, that was another worrying decision she would have to postpone until another day. Focus, focus! That was what she had to do, focus on her book.

Bryony watched her struggling not to lose consciousness, and helped by gently lifting her reading glasses off her nose and folding them beside the bed. By the time she had reached the door Isabel's eyes were shut and her face looked peaceful. She was already asleep.

Isabel's Healing

Chapter 7

Back at the kitchen table, Bryony did as she'd promised and made as many corrections to the text as she was sure about, then closed the page on her lap-top, and plugged it into the power source to restore its battery. Then she went through to the kitchen and started to peel potatoes. There was minced lamb, onions and carrots in the fridge, and she had in mind a nice little shepherd's pie. The next couple of hours passed very peacefully.

The smell of the meal cooking had woven its way out of the kitchen as far as the bedroom before there was quite an imperious call from Isabel.

"Hey! You, girl!"

Bryony finished laying the table and then went through, wiping her hands on the tea towel she held.

"Hi," she said evenly.

"I thought we agreed I'd only sleep for an hour. It's now nearly 1 pm!"

"Yes, but earlier you seemed angry I woke you, when it was past eight. You obviously needed your sleep. You worked very hard earlier."

"Oh, don't patronize me. And don't argue with me. It's ridiculous to sleep right through the mid-morning. Did you finish writing up the first pages at least?"

"I did, and you can read through them all after lunch. Restful sleep is very healing. I wasn't going to wake you when you were so settled, so please don't be cross."

"Humph."

Isabel wasn't used to being challenged by her minions, but she wasn't sure if Bryony quite fit into that category of staff member. Their relationship was so intimate, and yet so impersonal. She knew it felt weird, and would probably continue to feel weird.

Anyway, the smell of something very tasty emanating from the kitchen stimulated her brain, and she felt motivated to leap out of bed and eat lunch. To do this though required complete help from Bryony.

The girl parked the wheelchair next to the bed and helped Isabel raise her body. She saw her wince, and asked, "Ribs still very painful?"

"Yes, but maybe better than last week. They say it will be six weeks minimum from the accident before they heal, and I'll have some pain for months probably."

"That's why sufficient bed-rest and sleep is essential. See, it's not just me being difficult."

Isabel sighed and almost fell against her shoulder as Bryony stood her up, turned her round and then helped her sit back down in the chair.

"I know. You'll just have to be patient with me when I snap and snarl. I'm fighting this on so many fronts, and my brain wants to fly away and get going on all the really urgent things on my agenda. I'm sorry for my bad temper."

This was very magnanimous from Bel, whom she could see wasn't prone to giving easy apologies. Bryony knelt down in front of the chair and adjusted Isabel's clothes, and then she said, "You know, I really don't mind you snapping and snarling at me. It stops me feeling too sorry for you, which might hamper my efficiency as your caregiver!

"But, Isabel, I do want you to know life will get better. Everyday your body will move forward towards healing, if I have any say in the matter, and I don't want you to worry about whether or not I'm going to stay. I've already signed up for this posting. I can see why I'm needed, and I am enjoying the challenge."

Isabel was determined not to show too much of the huge relief she felt inside at those words.

"I could still sack you, you know," she said, but there was no bite to her words.

"Yes, you could, of course. But you won't, because why

would you? I'm not bad at this caring business, and I suspect you may grow to quite like me by the end. Now let's go through and eat lunch. I've made us some shepherd's pie, with plums and custard for afters. Plums will be good for you know..."

"I know, don't say it!" Isabel cut her off irritably, as she let Bryony push her out of the bedroom, back into the sunny kitchen. The workings of her bowels had been far too much a subject of prolonged discussion with the nurses in the hospital and she was heartily sick of it. She hadn't meant to snap at the girl, though and instantly regretted it.

Bryony did seem to have a calm disposition and more patience than most, and the last thing she wanted was for her to decide Bel was just too difficult a patient to cope with for a full two months, and give in her notice. She gave her a little smile, as a silent apology, and was rewarded with one in return. Maybe the girl was telling the truth when she's assured her she was signed up for the duration.

After lunch, pudding and a cup of tea, all fed to her spoonful by spoonful, sip by sip, she sat in her chair at the table and read the chapter and a half she had finished so far. Bryony had transferred the text from her lap-top onto an even lighter I-Pad, and placed it low on her lap so she could reach it, even with her constricted arms.

She had the strength in her fingers to scroll down the pages and check through the two documents. It was obviously very rough still and would need editing, but it made sense, and was at least a creditable start.

"It's good. You are a careful typist. Well done."

Bryony gave a mental high five, and a visible smile. "Spellchecker is a great help, obviously, but I think we will work well together. You speak at just the right speed for me to follow. Thank you, though, for the compliment, if that's what it was."

Isabel regarded her, now busy washing up and putting away crockery and cutlery from lunch. Her long tawny hair swirled down her back in a very slow wave, held together by a cheap hair band, and her body was toned and fit.

"You are in good shape," she commented, "You must work out or go running or something. You will get very confined with me in here all day. I suggest you take at least an hour off each day to go walk in the woods or something."

Bryony faced her. "No, Isabel. Remember what Edward said. I'm not leaving you alone for more than ten minutes, not while you have no use of your arms even to raise an alarm. If we go out, we'll go together. There may be a smooth enough track we can take the chair along to get some fresh air, and I also have a set of air-force exercises I can use as a mini workout in my own room. Next Friday, when Claire comes for the day, then will be soon enough for me to leave you."

"It's all going to be very intense. I'm naturally very crabby these days, and I'm not an easy patient, as you've seen already. I've got used to being alone much of the time."

Bryony heard what she was saying. Maybe the house was rather too small for comfort. Even if they weren't directly in the same room, they would be in earshot the whole time. She decided to make sure she had her ear phones in if she wanted to listen to music.

"If you get tired of seeing my face, then I can read in my room, or listen to podcasts, but I'm not leaving you alone, OK?"

Isabel sighed, and raised her eyebrows in weary acceptance.

"That was my expression of weary acceptance," she explained, mimicking Bryony's quote from the previous day. Then, without any prodding, she smiled.

Bryony basked in its splendor. "Oh, my word," she thought. "When she does that, she really is stunning."

She said, "Thanks. In return I'll fetch your medication for the afternoon," and she went briskly off to bring a glass of water and tablets.

They worked again on the book together for another long session, and reached Isabel's target by three o'clock, by which time her voice was hoarse, and Bryony's fingers were almost going into rigor mortis. They stopped and Bryony helped them both to another long drink of water. The sun was still shining through the cottage windows, throwing sunbeams against the opposite wall, which showed dust dancing in them.

"You know what you said earlier, about me taking exercise. Well, why don't we try a gentle push along the woodland track? I'll take great care with the wheelchair, and if it gets stuck, well we can just turn back. Let's see how far we can go."

Isabel couldn't think of any reason to object, and allowed herself to be pushed outside. Bryony put an extra cushion behind her back to shield Bel against any bumps. She was concerned how very thin the woman had become, but she'd at least eaten a good lunch. Battling constant pain was just consuming so many calories, and she suspected she hadn't eaten much in the hospital, especially if busy staff had had to make time to feed her. Fresh air would certainly do her good.

The cottage had only a very small garden, mainly given over to parking spaces and a turning circle, but it stood next to the deep forest, where through a gate, a track, covered in larch needles and last year's beech nuts and masts, seemed to wind into the green stillness. It was also pretty well flat, running along the contours of the hill.

Bryony maneuvered them through the gate and into the woods. The green canopy above them almost blocked out the sunlight, but where a fallen tree or a gap in the foliage permitted, bright shafts of sunlight illuminated the woodland with gold, and revealed so many different shades of greens, browns and yellows, that it was like moving through a real wonderland.

The track was firm beneath the tires, and they went further and further. They could hear the summer murmur of the woods, a breeze blowing down from the very tall branches at the top, small birds chattering and chirruping together, not the full-blown concert arias of spring, but a convivial gossiping between nestlings and their parents. Isabel looked up, searching for squirrels' nests.

"The guide book says there are red squirrels still in these woods."

"That would be lovely if we could see any."

Their voices broke the silence, and slightly startled them.

"It doesn't bear thinking about," said Bryony as she pushed the chair round a fallen branch.

"No? What doesn't?"

"The implications of global warming, what your book is about. The whole world needs healing. It's really awful we are only now even coming to terms with it."

"I know. I've been working on it for years. Not a cheerful prospect."

"But can something be done? Enough?"

"Yes. If there's the will. And you, by helping me, you are making a small contribution."

"Well, thanks." Bryony wondered if Isabel was being condescending to her, but decided she wasn't.

"Have you gone far enough? Would you like me to turn back now?"

"I suppose so. You've pushed me for almost a mile. It is so beautiful. I feel, I feel, maybe a little better. But let's go back and see if we can put together another five hundred words."

So they turned the chair and Bryony propelled her patient back down the track. She realized they'd been out for an hour, but there was a little bit of color now in Isabel's sunken cheeks and her eyes had lost some of their dark shadows. This was something they should do together every day, she decided, and by the time they reached the house, back out into full sunshine, her muscles did feel they'd already had a full work-out.

"Shall we stay outside for a little while? We could work at the garden table."

Isabel nodded. "Very well. Go inside and fetch the laptop, while I get my brain into gear."

When Bryony returned she was also carrying a tube of

sun-block.

"What's that?"

"My sun-cream. I want you to have some on your face."

"Far too late now."

"Not at all. Here."

She put a dab on the back of her hand and gently applied it to Isabel's cheeks, nose and forehead, then onto her throat as well. Isabel closed her eyes, and then as the soft fingers touched her throat, she opened them to gaze straight into Bryony's, only inches away.

They stared at each other, before each of them simultaneously lowered her gaze in something approaching shyness. The intensity of that one second bemused and completely took Isabel by surprise. She broke the spell by saying, "What I really need are my sunglasses. Can you fetch them please? They are on the windowsill."

Bryony moved quickly, and fetched the glasses, a top-end brand, reflective, and opened them to place them on Isabel's nose. The woman's expression was now completely hidden. Bryony decided she needed similar camouflage for any inappropriate staring, and went to get her own sun-specs. So, similarly protected from each other's gaze, they got down to business. The book grew some more beneath Isabel's brains and Bryony's fingers.

"Thank goodness we have this project on which to focus," thought Isabel. "Otherwise what would I be doing with this girl all day? There's something about her, which is rather beguiling in its own right. She presents herself as straightforward, scientific, methodical, but there is definitely more to her than that. I wonder what goes on inside that head of hers, really..."

"Isabel. Sorry, what were you saying? I lost concentration for a moment."

Bryony's voice broke into her reverie and Isabel gave a little jump in her chair, almost as though she felt guilty for her wandering thoughts. "Right. Well,

'*Considering the situation of the Tuareg people in northern Mali...*' and so they continued through the tea-time hour, and beyond, as the shadows lengthened into early evening.

Chapter 8

The clock chimed seven and Isabel finally stopped speaking. She had achieved more in one day than she had thought possible, even though her brain felt like a piece of chewed string, and all her aches and pains were returning.

"I promised to wash your hair," murmured Bryony, "And when was the last time they changed the binding on your ribs?"

"Last Monday."

"Well then. Let's tank up your medication, and then let me re-do them and make you feel like a new woman."

"Whatever you think best," sighed Isabel. "I can tell you, I have never felt less attractive in my entire life than I do right now. Feeling like a new woman sounds almost unattainable."

"Sshh. We'll have a light supper, and then when the pain-killers are functioning, we'll see just what your ribs are like under the strapping. I can see a slight improvement in your face color just in the last twenty-four hours."

"Don't forget we must phone Claire and Edward to tell them we haven't killed each other yet. If you find the number on my phone, and connect it for me, I can take the call with the phone tucked under my chin."

Bryony could hear half the conversation while she prepared supper. "Yes, I feel a little better, well a lot better, if I'm honest. No, she's been fine. She's very competent. Honestly. What do you take me for? No, everything's good. You can talk to her yourself if you don't believe me!"

"Girl, come here and talk to Claire. She won't believe that you're not already packing to leave."

Bryony wiped her hands and took the phone. Without thinking, she placed her hand on Isabel's shoulder, and held it there softly while she spoke.

"Yes, Isabel does look and feel better. It's very early days, but we're establishing a routine. No, she hasn't...and anyway, I'm not the crying kind. Yes, I will. Thanks. 'Bye."

Isabel moved her head so she could feel Bryony's hand rub against her cheek for a second.

"What did she say? Was she asking if I'd made you cry? Really! Have I? Did I hear you sobbing yourself to sleep last night?"

Bryony grinned. "No, of course not. Don't give yourself credit for such a silly thing! Twenty-four patients, half with leaking stomas in an acute gastro-intestinal wards at three in the morning couldn't reduce me to tears, so I can't imagine you will. Now come on, I've made lovely cheese on toast on the Aga. Let's have supper. "

An hour later, after copious pills, cheese on toast squares, and sliced tinned peaches, Bryony had persuaded Isabel to trust her enough to allow her to wash her hair. She parked the wheelchair in front of, but facing away from, the bathroom washbasin and let the water run through her fingers until it came comfortably hot. She found Isabel's shampoo, and then, protecting her neck with several towels, helped her tip her head back, and poured jug after jug of the warm water over it until her hair was thoroughly wet. Then she massaged the shampoo through her hair and used both hands to rub it in, rather like an Indian head massage. Isabel's eyes were closed, and she literally purred.

"Oh, that feels so good. They only tried to wash my hair twice in hospital, and it was so painful I screamed. "

Then she was silent, obviously enjoying the sensation too much to waste more words. Bryony let out the soapy water, and replaced it again with the soft Welsh spring water to rinse out the suds. More jugs' full of warm water were employed, and finally a slick of conditioner from her own bottle was combed through.

Isabel put her head up and Bryony wrapped it in a towel, drying it gently against her chest. She realized rather too late she was inadvertently embracing the older woman's head between her breasts.

"Oh, sorry. I wasn't thinking. I do apologize."

Isabel didn't seem to have noticed, or at least, not appearing fazed by the intimacy.

"No matter. You make a good hairdresser. You are multi-talented, aren't you?"

"Am I?" Bryony's raised eyebrows showed her surprise at the compliment. "Do you have a hair dryer, so I can finish the job?"

"I think Claire put one in the suitcase."

She found the hairdryer, and with a one minute blow-dry effectively tamed Isabel's locks. Then Bryony picked up her comb and styled it into a shining cap of black hair. There was a natural curl to it, which flicked the ends up rather sweetly, and she was pleased with her efforts. The fringe was still rather long.

"Would you mind if I trimmed that back for you a little? I think it must annoy you, falling over your eyes."

"Haircutting now? Oh, go on then. But be careful."

"Close your eyes please, and try not to sneeze. It will hurt your ribs if you do."

Isabel shut her eyes, and felt Bryony comb down her fringe and then snip it slowly along with a pair of small scissors from her make-up bag. The girl then surprised her by gently blowing the loose hairs away from her face. She opened her eyes to find a pair of green eyes again only centimeters from her own. They were kind and merry. She decided she liked them.

"Now, sit on the bed please, and I'm going to unwind your rib bindings."

Isabel bit her lip, expecting it to hurt like hell, but the girl was so gentle, she hardly realized when the first cut into the tapes was made and the bandages unwound. She found herself sitting on the bed, her entire torso exposed to view, being examined by this young female, not-quite doctor.

Bryony touched her bruised and swollen ribs, very lightly, and then peeped over her shoulders down at her back. It had obviously been a mass of bruises and abrasions, and still looked very sore, even after four weeks.

She took some salve in her right hand, arnica or something like it, and very, very, gently she smoothed it up and down the bruises. Isabel was transported back in her mind to those blissful times when Carrie had done something similar, but with very different motivation. They had never needed to play doctors and nurses. Now Carrie was dead, and she was simply a piece of meat. The contrast made those stupid tears come to her eyes.

"I'm so sorry. Does it hurt?"

She blinked away the water as she looked up at Bryony's anxious face.

"No, it just reminded me of something, of some-one. It doesn't matter. Well now you've seen the worst, what are my chances of survival?"

"Excellent! No question! The bruising will fade more each day now, and the ribs are healing. I'm going to wrap you up again in binding for a few more days, but the main thing to avoid is any coughing or laughing. So we must make sure we avoid any funny business!"

"Funny business?" Isabel actually smiled at the incongruity of such an idea. She lifted her heavy burden of casts as far as she could, so Bryony could wrap the bandages and tape round and round her ribs.

"I mean, anything which really makes you laugh,"

"But you were nagging at me earlier to smile more."

"Smile yes, definitely. But laughing, no. Laughing is forbidden."

"And crying? Is crying allowed?"

"Oh, of course, you can cry as much as you like. It's a natural way for the body to rebalance its stress. There's a perfectly physiological rationale for crying."

"Let me guess. You chose Science A levels at school, rather than English Literature?"

"I had to, because I wanted to be a Doctor, but I'm not a literary ignoramus. I like reading novels."

"Why did you want to be a doctor?"

"Originally? I had big ambitions to find a cure for leukemia, and breast cancer. My Dad died of leukemia before I was even born, and my mother was only twenty-eight when she developed an aggressive form of breast cancer. But since starting, I've become very fascinated with surgery. I might even apply to be a trauma surgeon with an overseas agency, maybe something like 'Medicins Sans Frontiers.' I've even thought of joining the army as a Medic."

Isabel didn't know how best to respond. Her self-pity seemed quite shallow when she thought what the girl had lived through as a child.

All she said was, "I see."

They were seated next to each other on the bed, and Bryony tugged Isabel closer as she tightened the strapping. The girl smelt of cowslips and summer, somehow. It was a pretty scent.

"What are you wearing?"

Bryony looked puzzled. Surely Isabel could see her T shirt.

"Oh, I see. Not sure. Something by Givenchy? It was just a sample."

"It suits you. Find out the name."

Bryony snorted. Was Isabel actually interested in her perfume? She decided to ignore any implications, and pressed on with her nursing.

"OK. Now lie back on this big towel, and I'm going to give you a gentle massage on all your parts which aren't incarcerated in plaster. It's very therapeutic Aloe Vera. It smells nice and it will help the healing. I use it a lot for any sprains and aches and pains I get in the gym."

Isabel submitted to her regime, and let the girl do her work. It was almost like having one's own spa treatment. Bryony began by giving her a foot massage on her right foot, working the gel into her toes until she squirmed and almost laughed with the tickling.

"Mind my ribs. Don't you dare make me laugh!"

"No, of course. Sorry."

The massage moved round to the sole of her feet and the soft pads of the girl's fingers kneaded her arch and her heel. Then she felt pressure put against her Achilles tendon, and a subtle rhythm built into the massage. Isabel revelled in the physicality of the massage, which worked its way slowly up her one uninjured leg as far as her thigh. She slipped into a delicious dream as Bryony almost played her body under her fingers. She knew the highly unattractive underwear with its incontinence pad would annihilate any hint of sexuality, but while the girl missed out her crotch and hips this time, she did very lightly smooth the gel across her belly between her underwear and the strapping on her ribs.

"When you can bear the pressure on your ribs, I'll give you a back massage. We will also make sure to put gel on your buttocks, to prevent pressure sores."

At the mere sound of the word "buttocks", Isabel felt an involuntary spasm within her vagina, which she couldn't conceal. Was she really in such a pathetic state that a girl could almost bring her up to full blown arousal by a gentle rub? She had not felt a glimmer of sexual feeling since Carrie had been murdered, so the very sensation came as complete surprise.

Whether it was totally unwelcome was something she did not have time to consider, as Bryony had already moved north, and now put both hands up round her neck and gently caressed her collarbones and shoulders. My God, that was unbearably sensual as well. Isabel felt her breasts harden and rise up, aching for the girl to include them in the careful and rhythmic kneading, but stopped herself day-dreaming just in time.

What the hell was she thinking? Bryony had a far-away expression on her face, as though her mind was on something quite different. There was no inappropriate intention in her mind, obviously. Isabel hoped desperately she hadn't even noticed how aroused she was. She decided to curtail the session.

"Thanks, that's fine. If I'm not to catch a cold and get a cough, maybe I should be wrapped up again now and put to bed. And we need to avoid an accident like last night."

Bryony nodded, with a smile, and turned the cap on the bottle of Aloe Vera lotion until it closed.

"Sure. I suggest we do this again each evening though. I'm sure it will be very good for you. I took a short course on massage once. It helps the blood flow and nourishes the skin and the tissues just below the surface."

"Medically sound practice then?"

"Absolutely."

She dressed Isabel in another clean nightshirt, and the cozy dressing-gown, took her to the toilet, and put her into bed in a similar way to the night before, lifting her right leg. She pulled over a spare pillow and tucked it under the plastered ankle.

"I think it would be good to keep it as elevated as possible, especially while you sleep. It will relieve the veins taking blood back up to your heart and help the healing."

"Anything you think is for the best. You're the expert."

Bryony couldn't resist reminding her of her words on their first meeting.

"I thought I wasn't employed to offer medical advice."

"Oh, don't listen to me. I'm a bad-tempered fool."

"No you're not. You're...well, just a little grumpy, but I quite understand why."

"There's another reason I'm grumpy."

"Hmm? What's that?"

"My period is due. I can always tell. I'll probably start tomorrow, as if you didn't have enough mess to clear up."

"That will be no trouble at all, and the wonderful thing is, you'll be so much nicer to me afterwards. Lucky me."

She smiled, and Isabel was completely disarmed.

"Would you like to listen to the ten o'clock news?"

"No, not tonight. I'm just so sleepy. But what about you? Don't you want to shower? Do use the bathroom. Don't mind me."

"Thanks, I will then. I'll try not to disturb you."

Bryony went into the bathroom, and Isabel heard the shower running for five minutes or so, then between half closed eyes she glimpsed the virtually naked girl run past her. She saw her heading back towards her own room, a small towel round her waist. It had only taken one day, and they were perhaps learning to live together. That was a relief, two strangers thrown together. Being gay, you had to be careful, which was one reason why she had fretted about Ted and Claire's choice of caregiver.

But in this situation, nothing could happen. She and the girl, why would they ever be in that sort of relationship? The very idea was absurd. The girl looked pretty straight, and oblivious of her patient's sexuality. Isabel guessed she was just about old enough to be Bryony's mother, and in her own bereavement, she strongly doubted she could ever focus on any woman with desire again. She was resigned to spending the rest of her life alone. She didn't think she could cope with any more emotional pain.

Yet, there was no denying it, Bryony's touch, her healing touch, had been surprisingly beguiling. She liked it, and also appreciated the girl's gentle humor and quiet self-confidence.

Isabel fell asleep very suddenly like a bear in a bed of leaves, and for the first night in more than a month did not wake till dawn's misty light crept up the valley and invaded their cottage the following dawn. It was Sunday morning. She needed the loo, and she lay in her warm bed and thought again about Bryony sleeping at the end of the cottage, behind the far wooden door.

She imagined there must be a boy somewhere, a fellow medic maybe, probably a tall, gangly young fellow on his way to being a successful doctor. They'd probably make a handsome enough couple. Isabel forgot all her firm intentions not to get personally interested in the girl, and wondered how she could discreetly find out more of her back story.

Isabel decided to try to call her and Bryony came immediately out of her room.

"I'm so sorry. I never heard you call before. Were you awake in the small hours? Are you in pain?"

"No, I actually slept through. For the very first time since the accident. I just need the bathroom, and then my meds."

"Hooray. Maybe it was the fresh air in the woods, or all the work you achieved. Give me a few minutes and I'll help you to the loo."

She disappeared into the bathroom, and then helped Isabel to hop through and sit on the toilet.

"Here, put your dressing-gown around you, and sit for a bit. You never know..."

Bel sighed. "Why are we such organic bodies? Why can't we just be spirits?"

"If we were, then I wouldn't have a career in medicine ahead of me, and I need that, if only to pay off the student loan debt incurred to achieve it!"

"Hmm. How much will it come to?"

"By the time I'm finished, something quite scary. I had no money behind me, this is the problem. But many are in the same boat. No point grumbling."

She left Isabel discreetly in the bathroom to see if anything productive might happen, and went back to the kitchen to boil the kettle. Pulling it across to the Aga hotplate, she appreciated the steady constant warmth from the large stove, but the day would most likely be another scorcher. They had had two nights together now, an evening, two nights and one full day. So far so good.

What would Bel like for Sunday breakfast? How about bacon and eggs? She looked in the cupboard and found beans as well, and tomatoes. How about proper old fashioned English, or she supposed, Welsh, cooked breakfast? Then it might sustain them right through until the late afternoon. She hoped Isabel would agree to return into the woods with her. The walk had been wonderfully connective somehow, and the quiet turn of the wheels along the track had been almost meditative.

"I'm ready, girl!" called out Isabel, and she went to assist her. Bryony stayed in her pajamas while she dressed and washed her patient, and also while they ate breakfast together at the table. Isabel smiled at her Winnie the Pooh Pajamas. "Funny nurse's outfit," she commented, in between bites of the food which Bryony fed her. Her smile was sneaking out more often this morning than the day before, and Bryony realized this was probably because her level of pain was diminishing. When it came to giving her all her prescription drugs, she dared to suggest Isabel might just take paracetamol instead of the much stronger analgesics, and see how it went.

"I can top you up later, if you are in real discomfort."

"OK, I'll try. Working takes my mind off the pain anyway, so let's see. Now you go and get out of those skimpy things, and let's kick off with my book again. Even though it's Sunday, we can't let up."

"No, Isabel. I mean, yes, Isabel." They were getting into a routine. It felt good.

Chapter 9

The rest of Sunday morning moved along very peacefully. While she went into the bathroom to shower and dress, Bryony left Isabel in her chair by the window so she could look out at the birds coming down to the feeder. The owners of the cottage had left a large bag of bird seed and another of peanuts in the larder, and Bryony had made sure to keep the feeders topped up. Isabel wondered if there was a bird book in the house. This was probably the case, because a casual glance through the visitors' book with Claire when they had first arrived had revealed a large number of comments about the local ornithology.

"Can you find me a bird book anywhere?" she called to the girl and Bryony left what she was doing and came out with a well-worn volume. It had a list on the fly-leaf of birds which an earlier visitor had seen and recorded, and these more or less corresponded with what they could see that morning. There was an interesting mixed bunch of tits and finches, a nuthatch and a greater spotted woodpecker which flashed up to grab the nuts, showing his or her scarlet collar.

Ty Bach had obviously been a holiday property for a long time, the visitors' book also indicated, but none of the inhabitants had rented it for as many weeks as she intended to. It was a lucky find to come across a property which was vacant throughout July and August at such short notice. But it seemed the owners had intended to return from New Zealand for an extended stay, only to have their plans change at the last minute. Isabel only hoped they had not had such a traumatic reason for their change of plans as she did, but she wouldn't be surprised. Her whole world seemed cloaked in gloom, and she still felt she was teetering constantly on the edge of depression.

She knew just how devastating that could be. The love of

her life, Carrie, had been prone to deep dark bouts of depression. Although never formally diagnosed, she had presented all the signs of being bi-polar. Her highs were ridiculously high, when she would do mad, scarily over the top things. But then her lows were completely wretched, leaving Isabel wringing her hands and wondering what on earth to do to break her out of the black moods and complete lethargy they created. It was while she was on a high however, taking stupid risks, that she had died, so young, at the very top of her game as a film maker.

Isabel stared at the birds, all clustered round the seed dispensers intent of feeding as fast as they could, but still finding time to chat and exchange the time of day with each other, despite the urgent ever pressing need for foraging. They obviously had a complex social life amongst themselves, up here in this Welsh forest.

She wondered how they viewed the world, and whether they wondered what lay beyond their valley. Many birds of course migrated thousands of miles, but these little guys, what did they think about climate change and global warming? She knew she was rambling in her head, but she did feel a connection with them.

When Bryony returned, now looking neat and business-like in a crisp white polo shirt and blue chinos, she pushed Isabel's chair round to seat her at the table, and fetched a cushion as before, to protect her spine.

"Let's get started. I've topped up the lap-top battery, so we can sit here at the table without wires trailing everywhere." She looked the picture of positivity.

Oh, well, better crack on.

Isabel had decided how to organize her stories of climate change impact into various categories, tidal catastrophes from low lying lands like Bangladesh and the Pacific islands, flooding from inland sources like snow melt in the Himalayas, and drought from altered weather patterns as in sub-Saharan Africa and Australia.

It made for a horrendous catalogue of potential disasters, with the loss of large numbers of people's lives. In her present imprisoned state, she tried not to relish her Cassandra-like prophecies of doom. World affairs were far more important than her broken bones after all.

"Of course, the Eastern sea-board of the USA will be as badly affected as anywhere in the world. Half the population there only lives a few meters about the current sea-level."

Bryony had been dutifully typing up her dictated notes for more than an hour and a half, when she finally stopped, and said. "Isabel, this is all so damn depressing. No wonder you find it hard to smile."

She was only half joking. "Is there anything we personally can do now, to help the situation?"

"Well, we need to run the car we have, while we're here. If I was buying a new one of course it should be electric, but I won't be driving for months, and anyway, In London it's hardly necessary.

"The electricity locally is from a hydro-electric plant. I also know I should give up eating meat. If the world's red meat consumption dropped by 50% that would make a real difference, because half the grain and soya grown on the planet goes just to feed livestock."

Isabel was a paid-up member of *Greenpeace*, but she was conscious she now sounded like an editorial from Resurgence magazine, and the moral strictures sounded banal even to her. Bryony didn't react cynically to them at all however.

"Well, say no more. For the eight weeks when I'm here, cooking for you, I can stop using meat in our meals. How does that sound?"

The girl's voice held quite a straightforward challenge, which made Isabel think twice before dismissing it out of hand. There were some meals with meat which she did enjoy very much, but there was no point preaching about it on paper if she wasn't prepared to at least give vegetarianism a go, and as Bryony said, she had her very own catering service on hand to deliver the meals. She just hoped they wouldn't be living just on beans on toast though.

"How good are you at vegetarian cooking?"

"Well, I'm not super experienced. But it can't be that hard. There are dozens of online recipe sites. If in doubt we could always have beans on toast."

Oh, well, she probably deserved that!

"I am sure you can do better than that. Very well girl, look up some ideas and then you could drive me down into town tomorrow and stock up. Let's make it one of our themes for the summer."

Bryony noticed how Isabel had started talking about 'our' and 'we,' and was thinking of something other than her own 5ft 5ins worth of suffering humanity.

"Oh, good. I'll make a spreadsheet and we can plan meals together. Now we've stopped, can I make us a cup of coffee? It's Fairtrade". She grinned as she spoke, but Isabel took the bait.

"Now, stop that, don't mock. I'm not such a kill-joy. Don't make me out to be a food fascist, but when one's been with struggling coffee-farmers on the foothills round Mount Kenya..."

"I know. Blah, blah."

Isabel realized that the girl was no longer scared of her if she could show some cheek and tease her.

Bryony went over to fill the kettle, and qualified her remark. "It's good that you are committed to making the world a better place. I wish I did more."

"You are making my piece of the world a much better place. That's enough for now."

Isabel looked away from her as she spoke, so her eyes and facial expression were hidden, but Bryony felt an unusually warm feeling curl up from her stomach.

"Gee, thanks," she said, in a very poor Groucho Marx impression. "Now I think you should have a biscuit along with your coffee. I'm hoping to build you up somewhat before we go back to the hospital to have you cut out of those casts. I found some in a tin. Tell me your favorites, and we'll get some more with the shopping."

"I never normally eat biscuits. I try to avoid sugar."

"Oh, well maybe I'll just have one anyway. I'll have to think of some other method of helping you regain weight."

"Oh, very well, if you insist. Actually I was being hypocritical. I do like those chocolate biscuits with a slab of dark chocolate on one side."

They sat together, and over Elevenses of coffee and stale digestives, Bryony made up a spreadsheet on her lap-top, with the next eight weeks' dates stretching down the left hand side.

She made three columns for breakfast, lunch and supper, and then with a few others. She called these W, E, S, M, and then another W and another S.

"Whatever are all these letters for?"

"They are a sort of time sheet, to record what we do. W is working on the book. We can record the Hours and we can also put down word-count if you like. E is for fresh air and exercise. You'll get the fresh air and I'll get the exercise. Maybe we can go down to sea sometime and walk along the beach some days. S is for the hours of sleep you achieve every night, and M stands for medicines, the amount you take, as I really hope we can cut back on your potentially addictive painkillers. The other W is for your weight. There's no point recording it while the plaster casts are weighing you down, but once you are free of those I hope to see you put on at least ten pounds before I leave."

"Humph, all very organized. I expect to see professionally produced graphs with all this data before you've finished. And what's with the final S?"

"Smiles. How many smiles I can pull out of you in a day."

"Right little Pollyanna, aren't you?"

"If you like. Look, smile again now, and I'll record it."

"Don't be stupid."

"There, I've recorded it now, and put it in the box. You can't un-smile your smile, not now it's official."

Bel's face cracked out of its normal semi-impatient

frown and she smiled again, she couldn't help it. The girl was ridiculous, but she was also somewhat adorable, though she'd never let her know it. She looked again down at the spreadsheet. All those weeks together in front of them. It couldn't be all work, pain and global misery, that wouldn't be fair on Bryony. They should take some car trips to explore the region, and maybe Bryony had friends she might like to have come to visit. After another hour on the book, the day's word count target had been met, and Isabel decided enough was enough. She had coped very well with the lower dosage of pain relief, but now she needed to rest. With very little persuasion she let Bryony wheel her through to the bedroom and hoist her up onto the bed. The girl pulled three pillows behind her, so her neck and shoulders were supported, and two more under her feet. She felt like a little snooze.

"What will you do between now and lunch?"

"Go over the work we did this morning while it's fresh in my mind, and correct the typos. Then you can read through again after lunch and make any more corrections needed."

"Will you take me into the woods again afterwards? I would like that."

"Sure, I'd like it too. It's so quiet. But we've seen no-one up here anyway since Friday, have we? It's only been just us."

"That's enough."

Isabel closed her eyes, and with a tiny touch of her fingers, Bryony watched her fall asleep. She wasn't sure what she'd meant by her last comment. Did she mean Bryony had blathered on for long enough and she wanted her to stop, or was she trying to say that being with Bryony was enough, was sufficient for her? If it was the second, then Bryony felt endorsed. She was doing her job. So far, so good. But she realized it was very early days. As long as they kept moving forward, that was the main thing.

The process of healing was so complex. Sometimes, as in a stab wound, the healing had to come from the inside out. If wounds festered on the inside, then the body would never recover, but the skeleton, the bones, had a remarkable ability to knit together and might one day be even stronger. The ability to make new bones was something which fascinated Bryony more than anything. And then there was the ability of the body to accept an implant, like a new hip or knee joint, and not reject it. All this truly intrigued her.

But healing also involved the mind, and what one might possibly call the spirit. Isabel was not a happy woman. Why would she be? But there was something else going on behind her eyes, something Bryony could not fathom. She wondered if the painkillers were actually making the woman depressed. It was a known phenomenon. She made a mental note to look it up on Dr. Google and maybe add it into the questions she was already formulating in relation to her patient.

Bryony knew she had at least another hour or more before Isabel would wake, as she had the day before, but she did as she'd promised, and set about editing all her notes. Sitting at the kitchen table, she raised the size of the font to make reading easy and not too tiring on the brain, and saved the documents together in a new folder. Then she worked hard for an hour, and was pleased with the edited version of chapter two.

Afterwards, she brewed a fresh pot of coffee and sat down to enjoy it, while out of curiosity she Googled Isabel's name. There were many entries, but her eye was drawn firstly to a Wikipedia article all about her new boss which ran to several hundred words. She read it with intense interest, but when she came to the personal life details at the end, she took a sharp breath in. It said, *"Partner from 2006 to 2017: Carrie Montarini. 1970 to 2017."* Carrie Montarini was obviously on Wikipedia as well.

Bryony clicked on the name. Carrie Montarini had been a well-known Italian film-maker and photo-journalist, who had specialized in women's issues, and campaigned for gay rights across the world. She'd been shot dead two years before, in suspicious circumstances in Eastern Europe while researching a new lead about sex trafficking of girls from Monrovia into the West.

There was a picture of a handsome, merry looking woman with very curly hair, of mixed race. Against her personal details it cross-referenced back to Isabel as her partner. There were many other references to further reading, which Bryony saved for future reading.

Bryony sipped her coffee and thought about this shocking news in relation to Isabel. It wasn't just the crash which had destroyed her life then, it was losing her lover, her partner of eleven years, under such tragic circumstances. How bleak she must feel, how furious with the world. And, of course, it naturally confirmed her as a lesbian. Had Bryony's gaydar picked any of that up? Well, they had only known each other for not much more than twenty-four hours and nurse/patient intimacy had revealed nothing of that sort.

Bryony found this confirmation of what she had suspected rather unsettling, but decided it was none of her business, unless Isabel wished to make it so. But the fact that Isabel was in reality just like a widow, still grieving over the violent death of her life partner. This doubled her resolve to do the best she could for her, to make her well and help her healing. She was beginning really to respect her, and she physically enjoyed the business of caring for her.

Anyone, gay or straight, would see she was a fascinating, attractive woman, so it was such a shame she considered herself only as a hideous mess. Bryony determined to restore Isabel to full health and re-launch her on the world. There must be loads of legible women out there who could mend her broken heart. It would be a truly worthy project.

Isabel woke in a much better mood than she had the previous morning, and was content to sit and read through their last session's work while Bryony finished their lunch preparation, chicken filets and baby spinach, with new potatoes and carrots.

"Do we have any more meat to eat up before we turn veggie?" Isabel asked her to her back as she watched her stirring something on the stove.

"Well, no, only some tinned corned beef. There is cheese though, and plenty of eggs. We will soon run short of vegetables and salads themselves though. Let's get some tomorrow. I'm quite excited by this project. I've written out some menu ideas. You must tell me your favorites."

"I'm very fond of Italian food."

Bryony congratulated herself on not going pink, well; she didn't think she had blushed. It wasn't as though Isabel had specifically not wanted her to know about her dead partner. In fact she remembered her actually saying to look her up on Google if she wanted to know more about her.

But she did feel reticent about letting Isabel know she had been researching her, and also about how to bring up the obviously painful subject of her bereavement only two years ago. It might be beneficial to talk about Carrie, or rather let Isabel talk, but she would hope for the right moment to slip it into their conversations. Maybe this mention of Italian food was a signpost she could follow, but she was just too shy to pursue it. She wasn't a psychiatrist, or a trained counselor, and had so many issues herself about repressed emotions; she knew she probably was the last person to be any good at it.

So for now, she let it go. They sat at the table, and she cut up Isabel's food. Would each day be more or less the same, right until the end of the summer? Well, no, obviously not. They were now on a planned route with lots of challenges. Healing Isabel's bones and restoring her strength, completing her manuscript to a point where it could be sent off to her agent or editor, trialing a vegetarian lifestyle, there was much to achieve. But Bryony knew she had missed from the list all the challenges relating to her own problems, and it wasn't just her academic work which daunted her. She had one very big decision to make, and some issues to confront. She hadn't been honest with herself about all her motivations for burrowing herself away up here in Wales, the biggest of which sat like a large grey elephant staring at her in her bedroom every evening.

Isabel's Healing

Chapter 10

It all started with sex, or the lack of it, or the reason for it, or her complicated feelings about it. Bryony liked the idea of sex; it was just the practical aspect of it which defeated her. She wasn't frigid, she wasn't prudish, and no, she didn't hate her body.

But from the first time she had tried to experiment with proper intercourse, all the sexual arousal seemed to seep away from her body like water out of a leaking basin. Sometimes she wondered if she needed the female equivalent of Viagra. Why couldn't she climax?

The first time had been with a boy from the boy's grammar school up the road, a boy who used to sit behind her on the bus going home, and make constant rude comments about her "Hoity-toity" airs and graces. Bryony and her best mate Lynne used to sometimes deliberately sit in front of him, in order to drive him and his friend wild with lust, or so they joked.

Really it was just the puppy games all fourteen years old play on wet bus rides in late November, when the afternoons are already dark at 4pm, and nothing lies ahead but homework, and in Bryony's case, a querulous grandmother needing her elastic stockings adjusting.

By the age of fifteen, they'd each paired off. Lynne sat with Bruce Chandler, and they "made out" on the back seat. Bryony tolerated Mike Stubbs and let him occasionally feel down her bra and up her skirt. He was one of the studs from the boys' school by now, and his acne had begun to clear up. Different in so many ways from the other girls in her set, Mike's persistent attentions made her feel normal, like she fitted in, like she wasn't just a nerd, even though she was top in her class in all her science subjects, and was already taking math a year early, to make room for additional math next year.

By the time she turned sixteen, Bryony let Mike have sex with her in his parents' bedroom one Sunday afternoon while they were away visiting his grandmother in Bournemouth. She had been waiting for this for two years, and determined that it would be a rite of passage she needed to get through to get her childhood over and done with.

If she'd had a mother she could confide in, she might have seen things differently, but she didn't. Mum was a picture inside an old diary, one she treasured, but now only looked at a few times a year.

Her grandmother was beyond the pale. They could enjoy an episode of *Emmerdale* together, and her Granny was always pleased when she came home with another good school report, but aside from that, there was no common meeting ground.

Bryony channeled out her grandmother's constant health concerns sometimes, by actually wearing earphones attached to her I-Player list, or an interesting pod-cast while she helped her bath and dress, and counted out her pills. Granny never noticed; she just thought Bryony was 'away with the fairies' as she put it. She was too deaf to hear the music or words creeping out of the I-Phone.

So Bryony had to figure out her own moral compass, and she soon realized that, like smoking (yuck), drinking (Who wants to lose control, and throw up in the street?) and drugs, ('No way!') casual sex was yet another vice she was doomed not to enjoy.

Mike was ecstatic. He had done it. He had actually done it, and with one of the prettiest girls in year 10 as well. They had definitely had intercourse, true. Bryony immediately wiped his "stuff" off her thighs without disguising her distaste for the stickiness, and went off to the bathroom to take a quick shower. When she emerged, she tried to look like a girl who had just lost her virginity to a good-looking boy who proved he could perform adequately. In reality she was totally underwhelmed. It didn't matter, because Mike had enough enthusiasm for them both.

"Great, heh? Fantastic. Did you come?"

"What, hey?" (In less than two minutes of humping? You must be kidding!)

"Er, not quite, but I enjoyed it." Even at sixteen, Bryon knew the expression 'damning with faint praise' but she smiled as well, so that was all that mattered to Mike.

Bryony's overriding emotion had been relief that she'd insisted on being on the pill for at least a month before they tried anything remotely risky. She couldn't get over the difference to one's life as a girl if she had not been so prudent. Two minutes of being pushed and fumbled in return for having to bear and raise another human being? What a crazy system for procreation!

Mike had lasted as her boyfriend only for another couple of months; she just couldn't stand the boredom, coupled with his inappropriate sense of triumph each time. But she did try again; she really did, with other boys, who had different coloring, different speeds, and different levels of sophistication. One had actually read all about the clitoris, and decided to show great respect for hers. He even bit it one day. Bryony told herself she liked boys, she did. She liked being with them, drinking diet coke while they drank beer, swinging on their arm, being courted and kissed and tickled. She liked all those things. She just hadn't found the right guy. That was all.

Then she met Aiden, half way through college, and thought that maybe, he'd be the one. They'd been together now for nearly two years, and she had learned to fake orgasms as well as any star of stage and screen. What had started as her default position of not wanting to crush any guy's ego had moved on to be a result of her guilt at not telling him really what she wanted. But what did she want? She hardly knew. She just knew she felt empty, and a more than a little lost.

Now, the very day before she left London, he had

asked Bryony once again to commit to their relationship, in fact, to agree to marry him, and she had not been able to think of a convincing single reason why she should turn him down. There wasn't any reason, well, except of course for one inescapable fact, that she didn't love him at all, not in the way he wanted, not enough to sustain a marriage which might last fifty years, God help her.

What was she going to say, after so long? "Sorry, it's the stubble?"

So maybe she did love him, but she wasn't in love with him, not love in a way she could hardly imagine. She had to believe in this chimera, this dream that was out there somewhere for her in the universe, elusive, just over the horizon, beyond the evening star.

She had buried this feeling for too long, but it persisted to throw up inconvenient shoots of doubt and sadness. They were like thistles in her otherwise productive life's bean patch. She wanted a love which would include physical passion, excitement, the throwing away of all inhibitions and a total communion of souls. She wanted a love to scare her, excite her, stretch her to breaking point, and also sustain her to the end of her days.

Her true tiny mushroom of self-understanding realized it when she did actually once orgasm in her sleep. She literally dreamed one up, in the middle of the night after yet another unproductive and frustrating session in bed with Aiden. It had been amazing and she actually wanted to cry from the grief of knowing what she'd been missing all these years.

The only problem however was the face which had swum in front of her closed eyes had been, (God help her) the hard but powerful features of her Math teacher back in high school, the one who had coached to an A in additional math at the age of sixteen, and the one who frightened her into correct answers. It was beyond inappropriate. So she dealt with it by dismissing it as a 'weird, I mean, really weird dream,' and then burying it.

Aiden Webster was what her grandmother would have called a 'nice boy,' if she had lived long enough to meet him.

He was undeniably good-looking, humorous, going to pass out near the top of their class in medicine, from a normal family with a mother who adored her, and showing her even more affection than her own relations had been able to muster.

Every one of their friends expected them to stay a couple after university, Aiden included. But by now she knew the special spark, the elusive something, just wasn't there, and she regretfully realized, never would be. Besides, marriage was outdated. Her parents had never married, well probably because they hadn't had time to. The fates had taken them away too young.

Bryony hesitated about calling God into the equation. It sounded irrational to blame a deity one way or another for her singular lack of luck when it came to healthy parents. It would be better just to throw what had happened back over the tennis net as a random missed ball. She was not one to allocate blame, and ranting at a mysterious so-called loving God would achieve nothing. Neither would blame the heavens for denying her the ability to have orgasms.

Isabel chose precisely that moment to break into her thoughts with an inconveniently scary suggestion. "Do you have a boyfriend? I imagine there must be someone. If you invite him up to visit us here sometime I would not object. I don't want to cut you off from all your friends."

Bryony gulped so hard a piece of chicken threatened to go down the wrong way. Because Isabel was in no position to thump her on the back, she had to rescue herself from choking, by swallowing copious amounts of water and heaving the obstruction back up herself. It took several minutes for her digestive system to calm down. Isabel looked at her in astonishment, raising her eyebrow.

"So there is someone? I didn't mean for you to drop dead though, at the very mention of him."

"Er, well, no. There is someone, but he understands

he can't visit, and I won't be free to go south to meet up with him. He lives in Sussex. It's too far. But thanks, anyway."

"I knew it," thought Isabel.

There had to be someone for a girl as attractive as Bryony. Isabel had an unexpected wave of regret sweep through her, and was alarmed by how suddenly unsettled, even sad, the information made her insides feel. Where had that ridiculous emotion come from anyway?

It had to be crushed immediately if that was the case. Some perverse masochism made her pursue the conversation further to help with the crushing of "gay awareness" syndrome.

"Well, I think you should invite him anyway. I'd like to meet him. If Claire is here, then you can maybe go off for a night together."

"No thanks!" Bryony heard herself almost squeak in protest. "Thanks. You're very kind, but there's no need."

"Oh, very well, but if you change your mind..."

Isabel tried to stop herself. What was she playing at? Hadn't she just insisted to herself that she wouldn't even ask about the girl's family circumstances?

She opened her mouth to speak again, but was silenced as Bryony popped in a piece of chicken wrapped up in spinach. She chewed obediently and they grinned at each other.

Something was almost funny, but neither could understand quite what it was. They seemed to be running on automatic pilot suddenly. Lunch continued in silence, and then Bryony said.

"There's some yogurt for dessert. Do you fancy some? "

She had obviously recovered from her coughing fit at the mention of the boyfriend.

"OK."

Now Isabel really did feel just like a baby, being fed yogurt from a spoon and having her chin wiped with a napkin afterwards. She cursed that she couldn't move her arms even enough to reach a spoon into her mouth. She wouldn't be able to clean her own teeth either until at least one of the arm casts was removed.

Bryony had made a game of teeth cleaning first and last thing each day, putting a blob of toothpaste on the electric brush and holding it up to her mouth while she tried to work it round her teeth. Then the girl would switch it off; pass a glass full of mouthwash to her lips and command "Spit!"

It became a silly challenge to see how far she could spit. A disgusting, childish activity, but one she actually enjoyed. In the hospital, such niceties had been impossible.

Oh, well, for now she would just have to continue putting up with being a blob in a wheelchair. Maybe it was divine punishment for all the times she had impatiently pushed people out of her way, or written sarcastic comments about other people's inadequacies in references and reports. Now she could not even sign her own name with any similarity to her original hand–writing. Bryony had to act as her hands, arms, her legs, everything. It was such a relief she wasn't irritating either to look at or to listen to. She really was a pleasant and competent assistant.

Isabel decided to leave it at that. If she developed a crush on the girl, after all these months of feeling absolutely no attraction for any woman after losing Carrie, then that would ruin everything. And she would only embarrass herself and scare her away. The very idea was anathema.

***

Sunday afternoon was spent once again wandering with the wheelchair through the woods. They went further this time, and took a right fork in the track, which meant Bryony had to cope with pushing the chair with its passenger up a long slow incline, and then quite a steep way back down, but Isabel hadn't fallen out, thank God. They both returned home exhausted, but almost as pleased with themselves as if they'd discovered America. Isabel was definitely thawing out, and even cracked a few jokes.

In the evening Bryony suggested she might like to watch television for a while. Isabel left her chair to be seated on the old comfortable sofa in the living room. She patted the cushion next to her and Bryony plumped herself down next to her. The TV was showing pretty banal stuff.

"Chewing-gum for the mind," Isabel called it, but they both enjoyed the repeat of an old film.

Isabel rarely watched TV, so the very activity was quite a diversion and she had used up her day's supply of grey matter, so simply wanted to look at somebody else's life and death struggles. They then watched *Murder She Wrote*, a real Golden Oldie, and Jessica Fletcher's detective problems from the early 1990s filled the mindless banter bill quite nicely.

"Have you noticed how that woman wades through murdered corpses each week without a care in the world? She never seems to lose a moment's sleep over it either."

"Steady work solving crimes must be a great comfort."

The girl looked as though her own eyelids were very heavy. Isabel realized if she didn't nudge her she'd miss her promised massage.

"You said you'd give me a massage," she said hopefully.

Bryony opened her eyes and stretched her arm round Isabel to turn on the lamp behind them.

"I did, and I'm a girl of my word. Here, lie back on the sofa, and I'll do you here."

It wasn't exactly an elegant mode of expression, but as Isabel lay back and let Bryony take off her trousers and top, she sank into a state of semi-consciousness. Bryony, as before, started with her toes and worked up her body, rubbing in the fresh green Aloe Vera lotion. She could almost feel her cells regenerating. Bryony then knelt on the floor beside her, and in places where there was no bruising; she exerted a fair bit of pressure.

She had arrived at Isabel's mid-section when she said quietly," If I pad you up with cushions could you turn over for me onto your stomach? I need to do your back and prevent those pressure sores."

Isabel turned and resituated herself. Her pinioned arms and leg were a complete nuisance but Bryony worked round them. Isabel buried her head in a cushion and lived for the moment.

"Mindfulness," she thought. "Be in the moment. Enjoy the sensation just as it is. No regrets, no resentment, no hopes...ahh!"

Bryony had now stripped back her underwear so that her backside was exposed, like a baby's on a play mat after a bath.

She felt the girl's fingers dig into her maximus gluteus muscles and work in copious amounts of gel. It felt divine, and so cooling, but oh, lord, undeniably sexually stimulating. Just when she thought she could bear it no longer, and would have to indicate something to make her stop, Bryony moved smoothly upwards, and readjusted her underwear. She caressed and massaged Isabel's lower back from the top of her butt upwards, then knelt more upright and moved so she could work her neck and shoulder muscles. She dug into the shoulder muscles, with her thumbs next to Isabel's spine.

"There's a lot of tension up here. I'll give it more time tomorrow."

"Are you surprised?" protested Bel, her voice muffled into the cushion. "Heaving about in the woods all afternoon. I'm lucky you didn't send me flying three hundred feet out of the trees and down the valley at one point."

"Sshh. We made it home safely, didn't we? Anyway, I've been reading about you. You're a fearless explorer. You might have enjoyed it if I'd sent you airborne."

"Oh, yes, but I haven't the time now to recover from a second round of multiple fractures, thank you, girl." Then Isabel thought about what Bryony had just said, "Reading about me?"

"Uh, like you suggested. On Google. I'm actually quite in awe as a result."

"Oh, right. Only *quite?* I see." There was a long pause as she digested the implications of the information.

"Well, totally in awe actually."

"That's good. I could do with more than a modicum of awe right now."

"You know..."

"Yes?"

"Any time you want to, you know, talk about...anything, it would be fine. I would understand, or try to. If you just wanted to talk about it, about...her, you know, your partner. I was so very sorry to read how she died."

Bryony didn't stop her hands, but she held her breath. Had she said too much? What would Isabel say? Would she be angry? But Isabel instead did something sweet, and completely unexpected. She turned her face towards Bryony's hand on her neck and kissed it very lightly.

"Thank you," was all she said.

Bryony realized she was speaking from a heart so full it could scarcely let out more words. The pressure from the kiss was like a butterfly's wing, but the imprint of her lips stayed on Bryony's hand. She flexed her fingers and completed the massage with a light stimulation to Isabel's head in the manner of the Indian masseuses. She knew just how wonderful it felt, because someone who had been on a training course in India had once done it to her.

Isabel sighed, and murmured, "Oh, yes, that's, that's very...relaxing," and then she dropped her head and buried her face deeper into the cushion.

Bryony finished her head massage, stood up to stretch her muscles and then sat back down on the sofa, making room for herself by gently lifting Isabel's head onto her lap. She didn't protest, and simply lay across Bryony's knees with her eyes shut. Jessica Fletcher, as always, solved her case, explaining it all in a very friendly, straightforward way to the murderer, the sheriff and any members of the TV audience who might have missed the vital clue she alone had noticed.

Bel and Bryony stayed together on the sofa until the ten o'clock News. It focused mainly on yet more controversial arguments about Brexit, but Isabel slept through it all.

When she woke, just as the late evening news finished, she awkwardly tried but failed to sit up, so she lay back down on Bryony's lap and looked at her quizzically. She looked funny with her hair on end, smelling of Aloe Vera gel. Her mouth twitched, as she felt Bryony's arm casually resting round her body and across her chest and spoke, without thinking just what she meant.

"I'm stuck. You've captured me. What are you doing here, girl?"

Bryony looked down into her eyes, and gave a very slight shrug. She thought she knew what Isabel might mean though, so didn't entirely ignore the question.

"I don't know, getting you well, making you feel better. Are you comfortable? That's the main thing."

"Yes, I am comfortable. More comfortable than I can tell you."

"Then that's all that matters. Now if you allow me my 10 pm smile I'll release you and help you to bed." And Isabel complied.

Isabel's Healing

Chapter 11

By Monday it felt as though they had been together for more than just one weekend. They were slipping into a routine, one that Bel found very tolerable. She was unwilling to admit it, but Bryony was proving to be a perfect nurse, calm, always pleasant, gentle but firm, and deft when she had to administer personal care.

She washed and dried Bel carefully, and on Monday morning she took up a hand mirror from the dresser in the bedroom, and positioned her in front of the dressing table to show her how the bruises were beginning to fade on her back. Isabel had to agree that the arnica treatment had speeded up their healing, and her ribs were definitely becoming less sore.

"Would you prefer if I left off the strapping today, to see how you go. It might help with your breathing."

"Very well."

"Let me put some more arnica ointment on them for you. Hold on."

Bel sat on the bed, naked to the waist. She was used to exposing herself now to the girl, who had turned her slightly away from the dressing table, and more towards the window, so she could more easily examine her back. The sunbeams filtered through the glass and she enjoyed the warmth. Bryony applied the salve over the bruises, and Bel enjoyed the gentle contact.

No-one had touched her like this, so gently, since Carrie died. Carrie had loved her and had been addicted to her body. She could almost imagine this was such a touch, but of course it wasn't. It still made her shiver though. The plaster casts were chafing her under her arms, and Bryony applied extra cream there, holding up her arms while she rubbed it gently from back to front, almost as far as her breasts. Then she reached for an old soft cotton T shirt.

"I found this in your drawer. I think if you wear it, it will protect the sides of your upper body against the rough casts. Let me cut open the sleeves so I can put in on for you."

She reached for a pair of scissors and slit open the sleeves to accommodate the arm casts, and then she pulled it gently over Bel's head. It fell comfortably down over her body and unsupported breasts. A bra would still be too painful across her back and ribs. Without saying anything Bryony gently lifted Bel's breasts up one by one to settle the T-shirt and smooth it out. The touching sent a frisson of arousal through Bel and she almost moaned out loud, before biting her lip and swallowing the little cry of pleasure.

This was getting ridiculous. She seemed to have no self-control at all. Where did this sudden resurrection of her sex drive originate? Thank God Bryony noticed nothing, and carried on as though everything was normal,

"We'll keep to this system, shall we?" she asked. "Salve on the bruises in the morning and a massage at night? When did you say they want you to return to the fracture clinic to remove the casts? "

"Next Monday, a week today, if all's well."

"Fantastic. Only a week to go then. You'll get through it, Isabel. The time will fly by."

"Fly by? Some hope, but let's at least use the time productively. I'm very tired of living like this, being trussed up like a mummy."

"Yes, I can't imagine it is any fun for you, being so grounded. You are such a high flyer."

"No fun for you either, being stuck here with me."

"No, I like looking after you. I am perfectly happy."

"Really? Truthfully?"

They observed each other, Bel searching for the insincerity she suspected must be somewhere in Bryony's mind, but she couldn't detect anything other than a genuine cheerfulness.

"Yes, really. I wouldn't be anywhere else if they paid me £10,000."

"Not even with the boyfriend? What's he called again?"

"Aiden. No, not even with him." And as she spoke Bryony realized how true that was. The thought did little to cheer her troubled conscience. The weakness of the Wi-Fi signal had been her excuse, but she still hadn't Skyped him, just sent a text to say it was a good job and she was very busy but happy.

She really had to end it with Aiden, but explaining why would be so difficult. Up here, perched on this hillside next to the forest with Isabel, she felt just as happy as she would have been with Aiden, perhaps even more so. It was difficult to excuse, but it was true.

"Well I am grateful, anyway. When I am fully fit again maybe I will take you on a balloon ride across the Serengeti as a thank-you."

Bryony laughed at the extravagant idea, and it made her forget her worries.

"Be careful what you promise. I may take you up on it! Now, are you ready for breakfast, and then another book session?"

"Yes, bring on the bran-flakes." and they went through to the kitchen together, Bryony pushing the chair, and Isabel trying hard not to make life difficult for her by tucking her arms out of harm's way as they went through the narrow cottage door-ways.

***

The first half of the morning was spent barreling through the writing task for the day, but by eleven o'clock they had both worn themselves out sufficiently to mutually agree they could do with a break.   Bryony stripped both their beds and tossed the sheets and pillowcases and any clothes they'd worn over the weekend in the washing machine.

"Monday is wash-day. I know it's not long since we moved in, but I like a system. They may dry in a couple of hours, and if not, I am sure there are spares. "

She was making a fresh pot of coffee as well, and dusting around. She really was very domesticated, far more than Isabel would have been. Isabel decided to press Bryony a bit further on her relationship with the absent boyfriend. She wondered if they were love's young dream or anything like it.

"Tell me about your friend Aiden," she commanded boldly. "I haven't noticed you calling him much."

"There's hardly any signal here for my phone network."

"Well, you could surely use *WhatsApp*."

"Hmm." Bryony sounded very non-committal. Maybe she didn't want to spread out her most intimate relationship in front of some grumpy old woman she had just met. Fair enough. But Isabel pressed on forward. She couldn't resist doing it for some reason.

"Well, at least tell me about him. I'm interested in the sort of young man you would go for."

Bryony opened her phone and flicked through to some photos.

"Here. You can see him if you like. He's there."

She passed the phone so that Bel could see the picture of a conventionally good-looking young man with nice eyes. He looked intelligent, and obviously worked out, judging from his biceps.

"A fellow medic I take it?"

"Yes, we met at the start of Year 3. He transferred to London from Oxford and we were in the same cohort. But he took different specialties from me. He wants to be a radiologist."

"And he's OK with you being apart all summer?"

"Well no, not really. Actually it's difficult, Isabel. Just before I left London, he proposed. He's still waiting for an answer."

"And?"

"And I don't know what to tell him. No, that's not being

honest. The truth is I don't know how to tell him. I don't want to get engaged. I don't think I can,"

"Why not?"

Isabel watched as a faint pink blush delightfully crept up Bryony's cheeks.

"I...I just can't commit, OK? I'm far too young."

"Well, I won't disagree with that. How old are you, in fact?"

"Uh, twenty-three."

"There you are, just a baby."

Bryony for some reason took offense at her comment.

"I'm nearly twenty-four! I was born in August."

"Then you will still be dancing attendance on me when your birthday comes. What is the date of this celebrated event?"

"Oh, I'll tell you nearer the time. I'm not looking to make a fuss."

"I wasn't thinking of any fuss. I thought you might just deserve a day off for your birthday and I can get Claire to cover, so you can get away."

"Thanks, but really, there's no need to bother. I have decided what I need to do with my Fridays off anyway."

"Oh, yes?"

"Yes, it's only 30 minutes on the train from Machynlleth to Aberystwyth, and I have a student railcard, so it will cost hardly anything. I've checked and I can use my University of London library card at the University campus there, so every Friday I can go down and study for my special project for my final year elective."

"Which will be?"

"It was going to be the treatment of compound fractures in children, but I've decided to change it now to holistic aftercare for trauma victims."

"Oh, so I'm to be the subject of your dissertation, am I?" Isabel rolled her eyes heavenward.

"No, well, sorry, not exactly the main subject, but

I've just realized over these few days how important it is to see injured parties as real people. I don't think I had fully taken that on board before. Nor, how it's not just physical recovery that's important.

"The shock of the trauma, the effect it has on one's psychological health as well, one's confidence, all sorts of things. It would be an honor if I could include you in the research, interview you, chart your recovery maybe, but it's not essential if you'd rather not. In any case, of course you'd remain anonymous."

"But you and I would know it is me you're writing about, won't we, and most of your friends and associates presumably?"

"Oh, dear, well if you'd rather not...I don't want to compromise our working relationship."

"Girl, I don't mind. Don't be put off by my negativity. If any good can come out of that stupid accident I'd be pleased to help. Just disguise my real profile if you can, otherwise you can say what you like about me. I have already lost all my finer feelings, so you can't hurt them. I'd like to read the final draft though, when you complete it, just for my own interest."

"Thanks, Isabel. Thanks so much."

"Is this where your smiley graph will come into its own then?"

"No, I hadn't thought. That's purely for my own pleasure, and I will go and add a smiley face to it now!"

Isabel tried hard not to react. The girl was very young and very silly. But despite herself she had made her smile. She was concerned about the mixed feelings Bryony voiced about the boy who had proposed. It wasn't fair on him to leave him wondering. She should encourage the young woman to communicate with him more clearly, either invite him up, or talk to him honestly by internet or on the phone.

But while she wanted to appear helpful, she really didn't want to waste her current very shallow reservoir of human kindness on him, nor on all the other people who must be in the girl's life. If she finished with dishy Aiden, no doubt there would be more boys, more men for Bryony. The girl was like a peach waiting to be plucked from a tree.

Isabel was still so withdrawn into her own unresolved grief over the loss of Carrie's love and brilliance in her life; she felt she could hardly bother to think of what other people were doing, in and out of love all the time, falling in love, breaking up.

It all seemed so trivial, so facile, somehow. When you had lost your best love, your only love, it mattered little how others felt.

Bryony broke into her thoughts with a sudden question.

"So how about that trip down to town we talked about? If we're going veggie, we need to stock up."

She had neatly changed the subject, and had even pulled over a notebook to start to write a shopping list in longhand.

"Do you want to go the whole hog, and try vegan? In which case we'll need soya milk and vegetable oil margarine instead of butter?"

"You are mixing your metaphors slightly. I don't think "the whole hog" is a good way to talk about a plant based diet. But no, I think I should include milk and cheese in my diet, for calcium. OK, let's decide to do it. I'll choose the mains and you can decide on side dishes and desserts. For week one, then next week, let's swap. I'm not a complete control freak."

"Very well. Good thinking."

Isabel's fondness for quick decisions, coupled with Bryony's wish for everything to be tabulated and organized, soon led to them creating a scheme of meal planning for the coming week. The resulting spreadsheet looked promising.

"Monday—something Asian, a little spicy, a Thai based curry dish with stir fried vegetables maybe.

Tuesday—good old British staples, a shepherdess pie made with lentils, or vegetarian sausages with mashed potatoes.

Wednesday—a big mixed salad with eggs and falafel fritters.

Thursday—hearty veggie soup with beans.

Friday—pasta, to meet Isabel's liking for Italian food.

Saturday—black bean burgers with all the trimmings, and chips.

Sunday—a nut roast with cabbage and roast potatoes."

The desserts would either be fresh fruit or a non-dairy ice-cream or yogurt. Lunch could be salads or sandwiches, as the weather was still very warm and not conducive to a cooked meal.

"Well!" commented Bryony as she laid all this out on yet another spread sheet. "Now, all I have to do is to cook it."

They carried on discussing their new diet, and planned meals for the rest of the next two weeks. It diverted Isabel, and made her feel she could get through another seven days of immobility without flying into a screaming fit of frustration.

So what would you like for supper this evening?"

"Well, vegetable curry. How about that? I haven't had a good korma since Kerala."

"You know, you do place-name drop rather a lot."

"I do not!"

"Yes you do. I like it though. It's like listening to a live copy of Boys' Own Adventures. Were you ever at home?"

"Humph. Well, I have wandered for much of my life. Carrie gave me the most stability I've ever known, and she travelled with me as well as taking her own frequent trips. I should have been with her when...I still blame myself..."

Isabel was angry with herself to find tears were running unbidden down her cheeks at the very mention of Carrie's name. This was shocking, nearly two years on, to still be so out of control. But she did feel maybe she might want one day to talk about the great love of her life to the girl. She suspected she'd be a good listener. It would possibly let out some of the pain held tightly in her heart, pain she revealed to no-one, not even Edward and Claire. Bryony said nothing, but simply fetched a tissue and delicately wiped the tears from Isabel's cheeks and eye-lashes. Then she nodded.

"Later. I would love to hear about her. Please do tell me about her."

"Yes, I will. As and when. She was...she was truly the most remarkable woman I've ever known."

"Then you must have been an astounding couple. You're quite something yourself, you know."

"Am I?"

"Sure thing. Now would you like an omelet for lunch, before we go out?"

Isabel nodded.

"No cheese though. For some reason, I don't like cheese omelets."

"Right you are. How about some chopped tomatoes then?" And Bryony went to crack some eggs.

***

Their shopping expedition for vegetarian options went very well. Isabel had never gone out into public in her array of three plaster casts and she was aware she looked, if not freaky, at least a little strange. She wanted to sit in the car and wait for Bryony to do the shopping, but the girl insisted she needed to be with her to make decisions, and fetched a trolley which would clip onto the front of a wheelchair. They had a little stand-off while Bryony held open the passenger door and Isabel just sat there looking very angry.

"Come on, Izzy, come on. You won't like it if I buy all the wrong things. I'm sure you have a favorite brand of ice-cream or crackers."

"Izzy?! Izzy?! Don't you ever call me that ridiculous name again! You do have the most appalling cheek."

"Ok, sorry. But when you get furious, you look like an Izzy. Please just get in the chair, and we can stop wasting your valuable time."

"Hmm, 'Izzy!' Whatever next?"

But Isabel capitulated, and held out her arms to be

helped up from the passenger seat.

Thankfully the co-op supermarket in Machynlleth wasn't too busy, and once she was clipped on, wedged in, and generally sorted, she actually enjoyed the trip round the store.

Chapter 12

If Isabel had been told a week before, just how much better she would feel by the following Friday, in just seven days, she would never have believed it. The time with Bryony in the house had not dragged. In fact as they became better acquainted with each other, their communications became ever easier.

Isabel somehow grew so used to Bryony looking after her that she could be stripped naked, washed, dusted with talc, massaged and manipulated without hardly a care as to how she looked, or what the girl's reactions would be. Bryony always behaved professionally, always treated her with respect, but her touch, her actions were necessarily intimate and personal, and she didn't hide her admiration for Isabel's physical attributes as well as her mind, and her achievements.

"You're so slim, but you are looking a bit less skeletal. I'm sure your bones have a bit more flesh on them now."

"Well, after you've gone to the trouble to cook for me, I suppose I feel obliged to eat the meals, more than I would if I was just cooking for myself."

Sexuality, or anything to do with it, was never mentioned between them however, for which they were both secretly grateful, but Isabel slowly began to feel less hideous, and regain something of her old self confidence.

Bryony applied arnica every morning and the many bruises began to fade right away, from purple to yellow, and even disappear in some places. Each evening she laid Isabel down on the sofa and gave her a therapeutic massage, and every night, as she was so relaxed, Isabel slept right through the small hours into the dawn. Her ribs were still very sore, but following the girl's suggestions, she was trying only to use the minimum painkiller dose necessary to stop her body throbbing with pain.

Her spirits were brighter as a result. If she was awake by 6 am, then Bryony would rise with her, help her to the bathroom, and then make tea for her to drink while Bryony held the cup to her mouth. They shared breakfast in a similar manner as they sometimes sat outside in the little south-facing garden. Isabel called it greeting the sun, and wondered if she would ever be able to return to the morning yoga routines she had practiced for years wherever she lived and whatever her circumstances.

They were sitting like this, already dressed and ready for the day ahead on Friday morning as they waited for Claire to arrive. Each evening they had had a brief phone call as promised, and now they had heard from her as she left Chester by 6:15 am. She would be there by 8, so Bryony could leave in time to catch the early train down to Aberystwyth.

"I expect you're looking forward to a day off. You've worked longer shifts than even the most overworked junior hospital doctor."

Bryony felt she wanted to be honest.

"When I took the job, I did rather dread being up here, with just one other person all the time. But after I met you, it's been so different. I haven't felt trapped at all, and you're not a very troublesome patient, are you? I've learned so much from you already. And we've made our word target, which pleases me."

"Yes, 26,000 words in the bag. And from Monday, after I get the use of my arms back, then everything will be much easier for you."

"Don't expect to have much strength in your arms to start with. I'm researching a regime of physio which can build them up slowly. And Isabel, I won't be late tonight. I'll be back by 8 at the latest. I'll call in the co-op to buy something nice as a treat on my way."

"You're a good girl."

Isabel said it quietly, but she meant it. A day of listening to Claire's good-natured prattling about her book-club, the latest news from the Cheshire set, and how their dog's digestive problems were settling down, was not really a prospect which excited her. But for goodness sake, of course the girl needed some time away from her.

***

Claire arrived on time, as she had promised, complete with a bag of knitting and a thermos of cooling coffee she had not had time to drink en route. She was obviously curious to see how the two of them had survived the week.

Bryony looked very like she had the first day, not panic stricken or exhausted, but Isabel looked far better than she had dared hope. There was a pink blush to her cheeks and she had gained a little weight. Her frown lines looked less pronounced, and her eyes were no longer strained and red. Whatever regime the girl had devised for her was obviously working.

Claire was more relieved than she dared say, because on the journey home the previous Friday, Edward had voiced huge misgivings about leaving his sister in the sole care of an anonymous girl, medical student or not. It wasn't Bryony's competence he had questioned, but his sister's erratic bouts of fury, wicked tongue and very short fuse. But here she was, apparently quite content to sit in her wheelchair in the morning sunshine and have the girl apply sun block to her face, neck and even her one bare leg, in its light sandal.

"Vitamin D is so good for Isabel's healing, but this will protect her from too much sun damage," she explained. "You could reapply it after lunch if you both sit out here for most of the day."

"Hey, I'm here, and I can speak, you know," Isabel broke in, and all three were reminded of her protests from the week before.

"I'm sorry. Of course you are and of course you can."

Bryony had the keys to the Citroen in her hands, and her haversack over her shoulder. She and Isabel stared at each other, and she had a terrible temptation suddenly to kiss her employer before she left her.

It suddenly seemed the most natural thing in the world to do, but of course it wasn't, and wouldn't be at all appropriate, even more so in front of a third party. So she just briefly touched her shoulder, and retreated to the car, giving them a cheerful honk on the horn as she left the property. Isabel and Claire watched her progress as the car descended out of the gate and took its time going down the valley.

"Now then," said Claire, "I'm dying for a drink. OK if I reheat the coffee in a pan on the Aga? I want you to tell me how things have been all week, how they've really been. I can't imagine it's been as plain sailing as you made out on the phone. Can you really stand having her here for the next seven weeks?"

***

Bryony negotiated her day as methodically as she had planned it. On the Monday before she had already found a parking space near to the station where she could leave a car for a full day at low cost, and she bought her return ticket using a student railcard which cost very little. She sat on the train as it carried her south to the University City twenty miles down the Welsh coast, and had that same little thrill from childhood at her first glimpse of the sea from the train window.

Isabel would enjoy this, she thought, and resolved that one day she would definitely pack them up a picnic and take her down to the nearest coastal resort. In fact it was only as the train drew into Aberystwyth station that she stopped thinking about Isabel, and all they had to achieve the following week. She caught the bus from the railway station up to the main University campus where she could access the main library with all its access to academic and technical periodicals. She thought eight days of desk-based research, coupled with her case study of Isabel would be just the right balance for her final year dissertation.

Medicine wasn't taught at Aberystwyth University, but her priceless student card would give her all the online resources she would need, and she was allowed to sit in the main University library and focus on her research. She registered as an external reader, and located a quiet section where she could concentrate in peace.

At lunch she left the seat she'd chosen, and went out for a walk to the student cafeteria to grab a sandwich. The campus was quiet, but there were several cohorts of summer school participants, some learning the Welsh language, others studying the fascinating culture of medieval Welsh literature and all the legends and heritage stories. She was sitting on one of the benches eating her cheese roll, having decided not to cheat on Isabel's vegetarian regime, when a group of American students approached her, seemingly wanting to meld her into their party.

"Hi, we just wondered. Do you speak Welsh? We need all the practice we can get."

Bryony's south English accent revealed her origins. "Sorry, I don't. I'm sure I'm worse than you. Are you here on a course?"

Two of the girls hitched themselves up onto her table and a boy sat beside her. They were as friendly as a group of enthusiastic puppies.

"Yeah, for the summer. We are part of an exchange program with the University of South Carolina. We're doing a unit on Celtic Studies. What are you doing?"

"Oh, I'm a medical student, working in the area for the summer, but I can use my University of London library reading card. I'm doing some personal research."

"Gee, sounds cool," one of the girls replied in that bland, non-committal politeness well brought–up Americans had perfected. She obviously did not want to ask any further questions but she looked at Bryony's physique with un-disguised appreciation. "You work out, you look well-toned."

Bryony couldn't decide if it was an American characteristic to address personal remarks to a total stranger, or whether the girl was just exceptionally friendly.

"Thanks," she grinned in response. "I haven't had time to work out at all this week, but my job is quite physical. I'm caring for someone who is recovering from an RTA."

"RTA?"

"Sorry, road traffic accident. She has multiple fractures and can't move her arms at all right now. Her ribs and lower leg are also smashed up and she needs 24/7 care."

"Ugh. I don't think I want to hear any more. How can you face doing that all day? You know...I couldn't face all that yuck."

"There's nothing to worry about. It's only physical. She's still a whole person, one I'm privileged to work for. "

Bryony felt herself rising in defense of Isabel. The girl's comments were all too common for people who had no personal experience of being injured. There was such an emphasis in the social media culture on physical so-called perfection. Isabel might well fully recover, but supposing she didn't, supposing she'd lost an eye in the accident, or had her face smashed in? The way people would view her might change forever. There was a strange almost atavistic aversion in the human species to disfigurement or even 'difference.' It was something else Bryony added to her list of things worthy of research in connection with her proposed topic for her dissertation.

"I'm sorry; she didn't mean to be rude." The first girl's friend had lingered behind while her mates had peeled themselves away to return to class. She was blonde and tanned and overweight in a rather cuddly sort of way. She virtually snuggled up to Bryony.

"That was kind of insensitive of her, I'm sure, but

she's just never lived in the real world. My name's Melanie, by the way, but folks call me Mel. What's yours?"

"Oh, Bryony. But I'm afraid I must get back now to the library."

"Do you come here every week?"

"This is my first time, but I expect to be here for the next seven Fridays if all goes well."

"So I'll see you, same time next week. Cool. Bye!"

Melanie or Mel shimmied away, her backside definitely sashaying in a siren like message to Bryony. What on earth had just happened? Had the girl just made a date with her, a complete stranger, on the back of two sentences? Well, maybe one of her aims in Wales was to get laid, and she hadn't even noticed Bryony was straight. It was all very bizarre, but Bryony couldn't get her wriggling rear-view out of her mind. She returned to the library, "Mel, Bel, oh hell, too much to think about. Back to the computer and the periodical library files."

***

Twenty-five miles north, Claire and Isabel had also taken a light lunch. Claire had tried her best, but she was much more awkward and embarrassed than Bryony had been about all the little physical inconveniences of Isabel not being able to use her hands. Taking her to the bathroom was as far as she could see herself going. She had made tomato sandwiches though, and cut them into little slippery segments, which she was pushing towards Bel's mouth at irregular intervals.

"So what is she doing down in Aberystwyth all day?" she asked about the absent caregiver.

"She's doing desk-based research...on recovery from trauma. The idea is that it will help her give me even better care, and promote healing. It will make an interesting topic of study for her."

"You're going to let her use you as a case study? Is that wise. Bel? You've always been so reticent about discussing private matters."

Claire was making an oblique reference to what she herself had always been reticent about talking to Bel about, her 'unfortunate' lesbian tendencies and lifestyle.

Of course she wasn't prejudiced, she had told her so years before, but maybe it wasn't something to necessarily bring up in casual conversation with strangers or their Cheshire friends.

The fact that Isabel had lived with a woman for eleven years, and that they had been planning a totally open and wonderfully celebratory wedding before Carrie had died, was an inconvenient truth she never thought to dwell on. It was one area of her sister-in-law's life she just didn't empathize with. She felt sorry for Bel in her bereavement, but she showed no comprehension just how deep the pain had gone, or how longstanding it had been. It surely hadn't been as all-encompassing or profound a grief compared, for example to losing a husband. She was sure she would never have soldiered on like Bel had, if she'd lost Edward. Gay people just didn't understand.

Isabel chewed her tomato sandwich and felt it stick in her throat. At that moment she could read right through Claire's pleasant homophobia and out the other side, and wondered just why she had counted her a close friend all these years. Maybe she needed to replace her as her right hand woman from now on with an out and out lesbian. She would call Jane and invite her up to stay for the following weekend. Then Bryony might have a whole day and a night away, and they wouldn't have to bother Claire again.

Claire wandered happily off into the garden with her knitting after Bel claimed she really needed to rest for an hour or so. Sitting in the chair would be fine, but maybe Claire could dial a number for her on the phone and set it to speaker phone?

She listened to the dial-tone, and then her old friend picked up.

"Bel! Your name came up and reminded me you aren't dead yet! Where are you? More to the point, how are you?"

Jane had a very strong voice. The girls where she taught PE more often called it a fog-horn. She could be heard from one end of the hockey field to the other, even in an adverse wind.

"I've been better. But I'm on the mend. I have an excellent caregiver. Listen Jane, are you still teaching? You couldn't get away for a weekend and come up here could you? I'd value your help, and company."

Jane pushed the phone onto her other ear and took her feet off the staff room table.

"Term ends next Tuesday. It's chaos of course, but I have no plans for the following weekend. Of course I could come. But tell me where on earth you are. I know about the smash. Rotten luck. Do you need some support?"

"Yes, I really do. I don't want to work my caregiver into the ground, and I've imposed too much on my family already."

"Hmm, am I on speaker phone?"

"Yes."

"'Nuff said then. So tell me where you are."

Isabel told her the address, and even remembered the postcode, so Jane could put it into her satnav system in the car.

Jane was head of PE in a large Bristol Comprehensive High School. It wasn't so far along the M4 and then up to west Wales and it would be a very pleasant drive. She'd come Thursday night and leave Sunday. All settled.

Isabel felt pleased with herself for sorting it out. It meant that Bryony would be free to go away for Friday and Saturday nights, and sort things out with the boyfriend. She'd be very pleased, she was sure.

Jane and Bel had known each other more than thirty years, since they had started grammar school together. They had instantly recognized each other as gay, before they had even learned all the words for it, and had been inseparable as best friends.

Jane was extremely active in the LG community all her

adult life and was absolutely fearless and outspoken about sexuality. Only Bel's constant travelling and her partnership with the crazy woman Carrie had caused them to drift apart in the last decade, but they could always pick up where they had left off. They were easy together. Jane remained Bel's oldest and best friend. There was very little she could not discuss with Jane, and knew she'd get a sensible answer.

Isabel's Healing

Chapter 13

By the end of the afternoon, Bryony had almost begun to have double vision, so long had she been concentrating on the library monitors. But she had achieved a good first list of relevant articles which she wished to pursue and felt the dissertation was taking shape. She gathered up her notebook and papers and pushed them all into her haversack. She walked all the way down to the railway station as she felt she needed the exercise, and caught the train back to Machynlleth just after 6 pm. The long summer evening still stretched ahead of her.

After picking the car up, she called briefly at the shops to buy Isabel a packet of the dark chocolate biscuits she liked, and a large bottle of full fat milk, then started north. She knew the route well by now, and realized how much she was looking forward to seeing Isabel again. It was quite silly; just how much she had missed her. She only hoped Claire and she had enjoyed the day together, and that Isabel wouldn't be in pain when she returned. As she drove the Berlingo through the gate, she could see Isabel in her wheelchair out in the front garden, pretty much where she had left her. She seemed irritable for some reason.

"There you are!"

"Yes, here I am, back safe and sound."

Isabel sniffed. She really wanted to say, "I've missed you," but the words sounded pretty stupid inside her head, let alone how they would emerge from her mouth. "Productive day?"

"Very. How have you been?"

"I'll tell you later. Please push me back inside. Claire will need to get home."

She didn't say, "Thank you for catching an early train." Nor did she say she'd been anxiously watching the road approaching the cottage for at least half an hour. But she had. The very act of wasting so much time had irritated her, but what else could she do?

Claire and her topics of conversations had quietly faded by early afternoon, and they had simply turned on the television since then and watched programs about a monkey sanctuary. Claire had cooked egg-plant Parmigiana for tea. She was a good cook, Bel had to admit, and there was plenty left for Bryony. Apart from that the day had been strangely empty.

Claire was too polite to say it, but she now looked very much ready to get away and drive home to Edward and Gardener's World on the TV. It was supposed to include a section on soft fruit, which she especially wanted to watch. She had already loaded her knitting and a fresh thermos of coffee into the car.

"I'll be off then, and I look forward to seeing you both on Monday, after the fracture clinic. You must come by for lunch and to give me a progress report. You'll feel so much better when you have the use of your arms back."

By what Claire had not said outright, but inferred, Bryony guessed that Isabel had been rather fractious and grumpy. The older woman looked at her with some degree of sympathy as she walked out to the car with her.

"Now dear, are you sure you'll be all right? You've survived the first week, and from Monday it will be so much better. I think Bel has organized something anyway with an old friend, so you can get away for the whole weekend next Friday. You've done wonders already. She looks so much better."

After Claire left, Bryony went back inside, not feeling very happy. She knew it was totally irrational, but she didn't want to get away for a whole weekend. She had missed Isabel more than enough, parting from her for just one working day, and she also didn't want to break up her new routine of studying down in Aberystwyth.

As she sat at the table and ate the supper Claire had cooked, she broached the subject. "Um, is it true that you'll have a visitor coming next weekend?"

Isabel nodded. "Yes, so you can have more than one day off. My old friend Jane Walkley will come and care for me. She'll arrive Thursday evening and leave Sunday."

"But..."

"It means you can arrange to go to visit your boyfriend."

"It's too far. I can't afford the train fare."

"Oh, I'll cover that. Don't worry. I think you should go."

Bryony had an insane desire to burst into tears, but her face remained calm. Isabel had been thoughtful and done this for her. Aiden had already texted her three times to try to arrange a face to face chat, but did she really want to go all the way down to London, just to give him very bad news? The answer was a big fat 'No'.

"I...I thought I might Skype him first. It would be free. If your friend comes I can still have some more free time, but up here. I need to go to Aberystwyth to the library, and I could take a long hike on my own on Saturday. Please don't send me away."

"My dear girl, what do you mean? I'm not sending you off like a bag of dirty laundry. I seriously thought you would value the time alone, or with Aiden. Is he really not so important, not your significant other?"

Bryony just stared at her and didn't know how to respond. Then she just silently shook her head. Isabel tried to read her, but failed.

"Oh, well, not to worry. I'm looking forward to seeing Jane, but you can still stay here if you want to. Jane will need your bedroom, but you can sleep on the sofa if you don't mind."

"No, of course not."

The girl seemed oddly pleased she wouldn't get as much time to herself as Isabel had offered. Maybe she just wanted to focus on her project.

"Oh, well, come and tell me all about your day, in more detail. Unless you want to watch the gardening program. I am rather tired of having the television running all day, but Claire seems to like it and I couldn't switch it off or change the channels."

Bryony pressed the off button and gave them some blessed peace. "Now, I'm here to focus on you, and your well-being. How has your day been?"

***

Bryony cleaned up the supper dishes and put what was left of the supper dish into the fridge. Then she fetched her massage oil and Aloe Vera, and Isabel knew that her favorite part of the day was about to begin. Bryony arranged her on the sofa with a towel over her as usual, and began the massage with her left foot. Isabel lay back semi-naked under the towel and breathed out all her frustration and irritation with Claire. The woman had tried so hard to be kind, but she just wasn't on Isabel's wave length.

This young girl on the other hand, she was so empathetic. There was no need for idle chatter. In fact they said nothing to each other for the rest of the hour, but Bryony talked to her with her fingers, through the wonderful fresh smell of the Aloe Vera. She fed Isabel her magic healing mixture of soft and hard massage, and it felt completely peaceful and comfortable. She remembered the girl's questions from a few nights before.

"Do you feel comfortable?"

"Yes, completely."

But that wasn't entirely true, was it? As Isabel healed, she began to feel her libido come out of hibernation, and if she was brutally honest with herself, she did feel sexual desire inside her towards this graceful girl who gave her such good therapy.

She even felt glad she couldn't move her arms because it stopped her behaving appallingly and making a jump on her, kissing her on the mouth, and oh, dammit, wanting to do so much more.

Fantasies rose up in her brain quite unbidden. Bryony's kneading and caressing only stoked the fires, but she couldn't bear the thought of her stopping. The strapping round her ribs had been taken away. Bryony rolled up the towel and flicked the edge of her underwear.

"Shall I get rid of these, so I can do your butt?"

Isabel nodded, swallowed and allowed herself to be rolled over onto her front. God, if she was a guy, she'd have had an enormous hard-on by now.

Thank heaven for small mercies then, but her underwear was still embarrassingly damp. Bryony just removed the panties and she could sense her observing her naked behind.

Isabel had endured enough pain in the last five weeks to last a lifeline, but for one crazy moment she actually hoped Bryony might give her an almighty smack on the buttocks. It might shock her out of this ludicrous crush, or heaven forbid, it might actually arouse her even more.

But of course Bryony did nothing of the sort. She simply reapplied the gel to her hands and very softly massaged her way over and round Isabel's neat little ass, and then very softly up her back. As before she shifted positions to the end of the sofa, replaced the towel over Isabel's body, and then rested the woman's head on her knees as she massaged the tense muscles at the top of her back and along her shoulders.

Only at this point did she begin to talk, and told Isabel about the American students she had met and how one had even flirted with her. Isabel wondered why she was telling her this little story.

"What did you think when she came on to you?"

"I was just surprised. It happens quite often actually. People seem to assume I'm gay for some reason. And she was rather cuddly, big blue eyes and blonde, and that cute Southern accent."

Isabel couldn't resist going through the door which Bryony had opened for her.

"And why do you suppose they think you are?"

"Am I what?"

"Gay, of course."

Bryony stopped moving her hands, but placed them on Isabel's shoulders, in the same position which had earned her a kiss once. She took a deep breath to steady her nerves.

"I've really no idea."

Bryony looked down at the virtually naked woman lying across her lap, and gently smoothed her dark wavy hair with its adorable flicks.

She gulped. "Would it make a difference to you, to us, if I said I'm maybe not quite sure?"

"Of course not. But it might explain a few things to you, if you haven't thought it out before now."

"How do you mean?"

"Think about it, Bryony. Think about your boyfriend and why you are so reluctant to marry him. Think about what turns you on, and what doesn't. Of course. It's a free country. You can do what you like. But in time I suspect you might be happier than you are now if you came to terms with your sexuality, whatever it is."

"I feel terrible. I wanted to be so professional. I wanted just to focus on your physical healing. I never meant to abuse your trust, exploit your situation."

"Whatever are you talking about?"

"This. Even talking to you about being possibly gay. It's just, just that I've never had anyone to talk to me like this before, to advise me. You're so clever, and experienced, I feel I can ask you things."

Isabel decided she needed not to have her head in Bryony's lap and her butt nearly exposed to the air if she was going to continue to have any sort of sensible conversation with her.

"Can you help me turn round and sit up, Bryony? I want to see you when I talk to you." Isabel sounded a little brisk, but not angry. Between them they were able to turn her over again so she was lying face up. Her head still rested against Bryony's knees.

"Now help me up, dear. If you want to use me as a therapist, then you should really be the one on the couch."

With a little assistance, Isabel pulled herself up, purely by using her stomach muscles, and Bryony wrapped her bath towel round her to protect whatever modesty she might have left. Isabel wanted to smile at the incongruity of it all, but as Bryony's eyes were so troubled and she suspected she was close to tears, she didn't want to treat her admission lightly. She sensed this was a pivotal moment for the girl, maybe she had never spoken to anyone about these suspicions over her own sexuality in her life before. If this was the case, she certainly was a late developer.

"Now look here. I am not in any way qualified to give you advice. But whether or not you are gay or straight is not the important thing here. Well, of course, it will be one of the most important things to you, but for my purposes, I am simply happy you are such a competent, skilled therapist, and a gifted caregiver.

"No, don't shake your head. You are. I felt like shit before last week, at my lowest ever ebb and you have brought me back out of the pit of despair. Simple things, like you taking care of me, limiting the pain killers, but making sure I have sufficient to get me through the night. Your care in washing and drying me, in feeding me delicious food, and this, nurturing my bruises and making me feel even a little bit desirable. All this has been intensely healing. I'm not going to criticize you for it in any way. And by the way, I confess I missed you today."

"I...I missed you too."

"Hmm, I did rather hope you might. Was that really wicked of me? It kept my spirits up while Claire went on and on about her flower arranging club and her reading group ad infinitum."

"Do you think I'm gay?"

"Not for me to say, but it would actually be nice if you were. No, don't take it the wrong way. It's just so much easier, so much more relaxing, if one can be oneself with other gay women who acknowledge the fact.

"Lesbians share a culture, a consciousness, even though we often don't flaunt it. I do feel completely relaxed with you. Maybe that's because you're possibly gay, or maybe it's just because you're a lovely, caring girl. Do you understand?"

"If I am gay, what do I do about it?"

"Hey, it's not some sort of weird disease which turns you purple or anything. Think about it for a while, until you get used to the idea. You know denial isn't just a great big river in Egypt as they say. Maybe you should just think about crossing that river over to the other side. Or not, of course. But in my experience, sexuality is in one's DNA. There's no escaping it, nor any long term benefit in denying who one truly is. Have you ever fancied a girl?"

"Not exactly..."

"What do you mean by that?"

"Er, I tend to fall for..."

Bryony desperately wanted to say the most stupid thing she could, which was 'older women, like you.' She stopped herself just in time, and changed it to 'Impossibly unattainable goddess types.'

Isabel scoffed, "Well that won't get you very far! Just open your heart to the possibility that there might be someone out there who's just right for you. And if she's there, she won't be a goddess. She'll be flesh and blood."

"Is that what happened to you?"

"Oh, my love life is like a long tale a-winding."

"Will you tell me about it some time?"

"If life with me gets tedious a few weeks down the line, I

might amuse you with a story or two, not about Carrie, but about a few others of my adventures."

"What about your friend Jane? Was she one of your adventures?"

"No, Jane is a friend, nothing more. She's a big stonking butch, not my type."

Now that they were talking openly about sexuality, if not sex, Bryony felt some of her earlier lack of embarrassment about nudity had vanished. She felt she should help Isabel get some clothes on, and said so. Isabel agreed but wanted to get ready for bed.

"Time for dressing-gown and slippers, don't you think. All this self- disclosure has made me far too tired."

"Right –oh."

Bryony fetched Isabel a nightgown and her blue dressing-gown, and wrapped her up ready for sleep. She did look adorable in her nightclothes, but those thoughts were going nowhere. She helped her into her chair and wheeled her through to her bedroom. They laughed together over the spitting toothpaste game, and Bryony was grateful Isabel was unfazed by their conversation and simply carried on as before. The older woman was somehow much more open and much less defensive than she had been when they had first met.

Bryony knew she could now talk to Isabel about all her conflicting ideas on sexuality. She could ask for her advice. Maybe Isabel could advise her what to do about the fact that she just couldn't get to orgasm with normal heterosexual activity. When Isabel had retired for the night, she once again wandered outside to watch the stars, and think about the river in Egypt. Why on earth had it taken her so long to realize it was even there, and how was she going to cross it?

What she did know was that a major piece of the puzzle about who she was, and what she felt had suddenly slipped into place. The implications for her and Aiden were shattering, but in that case she knew what she should do, and almost, how to do it. The other, far more challenging, thing though was a horrible feeling that she might be developing a personal crush on Isabel herself. That wasn't just like crossing the Nile; it was like plunging right through the Red Sea.

"I am the caregiver, she is my patient. Not a good practice run for a lifetime in medicine if I can't keep my hands off her," she told herself very firmly.

If inappropriate thoughts about Isabel's beautiful face and breasts were completely off limits, perhaps she could channel them elsewhere, maybe even to that pretty girl from South Carolina with her big bottom and round china-blue eyes? Bryony went to bed in her little back room with much on her mind. It was shaping up to be a very strange summer.

***

By some unspoken mutual decision, the Friday night 'coming out' conversation was not referred to again for the rest of the weekend. Isabel was impatient to be back on her book after a day of enforced leisure, and Bryony was only too happy to plunge into it again with her. She needed her brain to focus on other things rather than how cute Isabel looked in her blue dressing-gown.

"Cute?" I'm turning into that American girl," she sighed.

They had embarked on chapter five, which focused on the Bangladesh fishing communities living down the east coast of the Indian Ocean. As before, Bryony was astonished at the breadth of Isabel's knowledge, and her first-hand experience of working alongside the development activists in the villages. These villages were now threatened with inundation from the sea and severe flooding from the Monsoon rains. If the snowmelt from the Himalayas continued to accelerate the whole geographical shape of the Indian sub-continent might change forever, and the country which had supported tens of thousands of years of civilizations might face greater challenges than had ever been envisaged.

Saturday, and Sunday passed in this way, leaving them

both mentally and physically exhausted. Thinking, dictating and writing weren't easy pastimes. Isabel was so sick and tired of the weight of her arms' rigid plaster casts; she couldn't even think how she'd feel if on Monday she was told by the doctors at Chester hospital they would have to remain in place for another week. Her right leg, too, had begun to feel incredibly itchy and weary, and she longed for Bryony to poke a knitting needle down the cast to scratch her leg. It took all of Bryony's skill to stop her falling into a massive grump. By Sunday night, she felt she had run out of strategies to keep Isabel cheerful.

"Would you like to play Scrabble? I see there's a box on the shelf."

"No. You'd win. You'd have to see all my letters, and arrange them for me. You might as well play against yourself."

"All right. Is there anything you would like to do? We've got an hour before bed-time."

Isabel pulled a face, which on a small child would have been called a pout.

"You know what I like. I think it's rather unkind of you not to do it for me tonight."

"Oh, well I thought it was your idea actually to give the massage sessions a break for a while, or am I wrong about that?"

"OK, but I didn't sleep as well last night without one. Maybe I was wrong..."

"I'll get the gel."

Isabel quickly decided that the old sofa in this isolated cottage, miles from anywhere, was her favorite place in the entire world. Bryony sat her down on it, and then lifted her legs up. As the day had been so warm she had dressed Isabel in a pair of loose fitting shorts, over her underpants, and topped with a loose cotton T shirt. Now there was this gay thing between them, (she didn't quite know how better to describe it,) she wondered if she should keep Isabel as fully clothed as possible while she smoothed the Aloe Vera gel into her body, but when she began to open the tube, Isabel made a little grunt of disapproval.

"What?"

"Aren't you going to get rid of my shorts?"

Her eyes flickered down to her clothes, runkled up round her hips and waist.

"Would you prefer it?"

"Of course. We're not in a convent here."

Bryony laughed and began to do as she asked. She undid the shorts and in a moment of wickedness pulled off Isabel's pants as well. She knew what Isabel's body looked like very well by now, but this was a new world. She realized the woman was completely at her mercy, and actually seemed to be enjoying it. Was she flirting with her? If Isabel wanted to be stripped, then well, she was the employer after all. They stared at each other, and then Bryony lifted Isabel's upper body with one strong arm and pulled at her T-shirt with the other. It came over her head, smothering her face, and then Bryony slowly drew it away up her arms. As before, Isabel still wore no bra. Apart from the plaster casts, she was mother naked. Not even a towel covered her. Bryony had never before seen anything which aroused her so much. She had a very frightening feeling that she might be about to cross a personal/professional divide which would change their relationship irrevocably, so it was essential Isabel maintained the upper hand, made their decisions. She quickly reached for a large towel and covered Isabel up.

"What would you like me to do?" she whispered.

"What you do so well...take me away from all of this, from the pain, from all the brokenness and despair."

"I can't promise that, but what I can do is give you a lovely massage," she decided to say, changing the subject away from such frightening feelings. "But then that will be the end of this tube of gel."

Isabel heard her voice drop of its own accord a few tones as she replied, "So, then you will need to buy me some more."

Bryony smiled a smile which lit up her face.

"Of course. Now let's start with your left foot. I'm sorry if you're ticklish, but you know I work to a system."

"Little Miss Methodical."

She picked up Isabel's leg and moved down it until she grasped her toes. A tickle came out of nowhere.

"Ow, stop, Have some pity on my poor ribs." And Isabel felt herself giggling, actually giggling, like a youngster, for the first time in years. The massage comfortably filled the final hour of the evening. Bryony fed Isabel's skin with nutrients and nourished her body with her gentle hands, and by the end she had to shake her gently to wake her up from what was obviously such a peaceful sleep it seemed cruel.

"Come, I have your night clothes. It's time for bed."

Isabel nodded. She lifted her arms to have the nightwear arranged over her, and when they'd finished in the bathroom, obediently fell into bed. She was too sleepy to bother with teeth cleaning games. Just as Bryony thought she had fallen asleep she heard Isabel whisper,

"Bryony Girl, I'm sorry I was grumpy earlier. Don't take it personally."

"I won't of course. But you do know, I take everything you do and say, everything we do together, personally. You are the person I care for, I care...about. "

"That's nice. Night..."

"Good night Isabel. Call out if you need me."

But there was silence from the bed.

Isabel's Healing

Chapter 14

"I can't face breakfast today. I'm too nervous."

Isabel turned her head away from the spoon like a baby refusing a helping of mashed spinach.

"It's only cereal. It might settle your stomach," said Bryony, waving the morsel of bran-flakes around like a fairy's wand.

"No. You eat it."

"Well, OK. Shame to waste it," and Bryony polished off the bowl of cereal in a few spoonfuls. "Now, let's get ready and we can be on the road by nine."

They both knew this was going to be a big day, the most significant one in their relationship so far. Once Isabel regained the full use of her hands and arms, her dependence on Bryony would be much, much less. Bryony knew she was aching to be free, impatient to be able to wash, comb her own hair, and serve herself food and drink.

It would all be wonderful, but Bryony also honestly knew she would miss all the tiny intimate things she had learned to do for Isabel over the last ten days. She felt ashamed, but she wondered if the older woman would now revert to being Ms 'totally competent and independent' and in doing so, shed Bryony's attentions like an unwanted bandage she no longer needed.

This morning, however, she still needed Bryony to replace her own hands. The girl washed her face and tenderly dried it, then dressed her in a smart looking loose smock which they could pull over her casts, and a loose pair of linen trousers. Sun block was applied, and then Bryony asked, "How about make-up? Maybe just a touch of foundation and blusher, to show them you're fighting back?"

"Oh, go on then," Isabel was twitching about in her chair, but allowed Bryony to fetch her small make-up bag and pull out the basic kit she sometimes remembered to apply in her normal life. Bryony smoothed some cream round her face, and then dabbed on the foundation.

"Shut your eyes, and I'll give you some smoky grey shadow."

Isabel did as she asked and Bryony gently held her chin, while she smoothed on the color. The shadows beneath Isabel's lovely eyes had certainly lightened, but her face was still rather gaunt, thinner than it should be ideally.

"I don't want to be a bully, but I hope missing breakfast is just a one-off. We need to keep up the weight gain back to something approaching normal for your frame."

"Are you working to turn me into a dumpling?"

"Of course not, Isabel. I'm sure you've never been heavy in your life have you?"

"No, but it's true. I've never been quite this skinny since I caught paratyphoid once in Syria. That was twenty years ago though."

Bryony finished her make-up session, and held up a mirror so Isabel could survey the results.

"Thanks. Not bad. I look less like something the cat brought in at least. But what about you? Aren't you going to put make-up on to face the big city?"

"Oh, no, I hadn't intended to bother. Who's going to look at me?"

"I always enjoy looking at you," said Isabel quietly, then impatiently waved her head towards the door. "OK, let's be going. Are you sure you can find your way back to the main roads?"

"It will be easy, I'm sure. I have satnav on my phone and we can wedge it so that you can see it and give me directions if I need them."

Bryony helped Isabel in her chair get into the car, and arranged her seatbelt. The wheelchair went into the back of the Berlingo and they set off. She had allowed two hours for the journey and they had more than that before the clinic appointment, so what could go wrong?

In fact, very little did. Isabel did get a little fractious as they approached Chester, convinced Bryony was going the wrong way round the ring road, but it was just her nerves talking. They made it into the hospital car-park in ample time.

Three hours later they emerged from the fracture clinic, both so happy they could not hide the smiles. Isabel was released from all her constricted plaster work and could move her arms and hands almost as well as before the accident. X-rays had shown that the surgeons had certainly done a good job, and while she had been advised to wear a sling on her most badly injured left arm, for a few days, her right arm now swung freely.

She kept flexing her muscles, and enjoyed the small acts which everyone normally takes for granted, reaching for the car door and pulling it open for example. She was still in the wheelchair, but the x-ray on her leg had also shown good bone recovery, and drew a promise from the doctors that if she returned in a week, they expected they could release that limb as well.

"It's not good to wear a plaster cast for too long," said Bryony, endorsing what Isabel knew. "So by the end of the month, you should be back on your feet with the help of crutches."

She had carried out a pair from the clinic, for Isabel to start using, once she could bear the pressure on her arms. They were now heading off to have a late lunch with Ted and Claire.

Isabel sat in the passenger seat and fastened her own seat belt. She almost grinned with the satisfaction of being able to use her right hand like a normal person. She then put her hand up and pushed her hair back from her eyes, laughing at Bryony's raised eyebrows.

"Feels good, eh?"

"Absolutely. You've no idea. Such a relief."

Bryony pulled out of the car-park.

"Can you give me some directions to their house from here, please? I don't have much clue."

"Sure. Turn right out of the gate and then on for half a mile. Then I'll tell you when to turn left."

She watched the girl drive the old Citroen, as calm and competent as ever.

"When did you learn to drive? I don't suppose you have a car in London, do you?"

"No, I've never had a car of my own, but I learned as soon as I was seventeen, so I could drive my grandmother about. My grandfather's old car sat in the garage unused, so I started out on that, but just after Granny died it failed its MOT, and the garage said it wasn't worth fixing."

"You drive well. I feel safe with you."

"Thank you, Isabel."

Bryony didn't know what else to say. She really felt like embarrassing them both by saying something along the lines of "I hope you always feel safe with me," but that would be ridiculous. And when Isabel was fully fit, of course she wouldn't just want to feel safe. She was a woman of action, a go-getter, a boss of goodness knows how many people. Bryony wondered just how big the agency was which she ran. She reminded herself to Google it and sees what its website revealed.

They drove on for fifteen minutes and then Isabel directed Bryony to stop and turn into a drive half hidden by large cypress trees. When they had parked, she helped Isabel get out of the car, still hopping on her one good leg, and sit in the wheelchair as she gave her directions to go round to the side of a big, sandstone house with wisteria tumbling down its front wall. They could see lunch was laid out on a large table on the patio, with a couple of parasols shading the food and the expected diners. Claire came out and greeted them,

"Darling Bel, how wonderful to see your arms free at last. We waited lunch for you both. Come and tell us all about the clinic. Did they make you wait a really long time, or were they keeping to schedule?

Bryony pushed Isabel up to the table, and helped her leave the wheelchair and take one of the dining chairs at the table. Then she parked the wheelchair off to the side, and took her place in the chair next to Isabel Claire had indicated.

"Help me take this sling off," said Isabel. "I'm sure I won't need to wear it all the time and I want to at least be able to cut up my own quiche."

Bryony lifted it over her head, and removed it into her bag. She watched Isabel flex her fingers and then help herself to salad like any other member of the human race. There was nothing now for her to do apart from enjoy her own meal, and so she sat quietly and let the others talk.

She had survived the task of looking after Isabel for the first most difficult weeks of her convalescence, and they had done fine. But she still felt protective of her patient. Isabel was animated, more animated almost than she had ever seen her. Her face looked younger, less strained, and she talked to her family without any of the bitterness or bad temper she had shown on the first day they had moved into the cottage. Ted and Claire responded, with obvious relief on their faces, and the whole lunch party went well.

Bryony realized that Isabel's personality had almost been trapped under a rock over the last two weeks. Now she was funny, witty and full of stories. She could also do a pretty sharp impression of the people in the fracture clinic, not in any bitchy way, but just very amusing. Bryony sat beside her, and was just grateful to be included in the company. She felt, well she wasn't sure what she felt, but she suspected she was about to get even more of a giant crush on her employer than she had felt before. She felt so happy they were going back to the cottage, just the two of them, that she was still needed, that she and Isabel were working on the book project together, but she wondered if Isabel would take back control of her own writing, whether she would want her own fingers to fly over the keyboard on the lap-top.

No, of course not. Isabel had made it plain. She needed her right through the months of July and August, as a nurse, housemaid and secretary. If she didn't disgrace herself by making any embarrassing passes, then the job was secure. They stayed in Chester until 3'oclock, when Ted suggested they left to avoid the later traffic queues out to the ring-road.

"Thank you for making the lunch vegetarian. It was thoughtful, Claire," said Isabel, as Bryony fetched the wheelchair.

"Well, no bother at all. Mondays are meat-free anyway. It's a habit we've developed recently." Then she lowered her voice, "Things still OK?" Claire nodded her head towards Bryony's retreating form.

"What? Oh yes, still fine. In fact we're very compatible. I think she understands me, as far as I let her."

"Well that's a relief."

"Oh, and Claire, Sorry. I meant to say earlier. Don't worry about coming up to baby-sit me in the coming weeks. Jane is coming for next weekend, and then I'll be fine on my own for a few hours on a Friday while Bryony goes off to college."

"Thanks, and I notice you are actually calling her by her name nowadays."

"Am I? I suppose I am. It's a pretty name, don't you think?"

The journey home was very quiet, mainly because Isabel fell fast asleep within ten minutes of leaving the house. She still had some pain-killers in her system, and the morning's activities had obviously worn her out. Bryony didn't mind in the slightest. She was so happy just to have Isabel beside her, the two of them together in a car. She realized she was in real danger of fantasizing a life together where they did drive round the countryside and take trips, like a couple.

"Oh, for heaven's sake, girl," she took a mental take on what Isabel might have said if she'd been conscious. "Don't be idiotic. Just drive."

And so she did.

Isabel slept the whole way home, which meant that by the time they drew into the cottage garden; she stretched and shook her head in disbelief.

"Wow, are we here already? I thought I only nodded off for ten minutes."

"You were dead to the world."

"Sorry, you must have been rather bored."

"No, nice to have a bit of peace once in a while."

"Are you cheeking me, girl?"

"As if."

Bryony smiled one of her 'butter wouldn't melt' smiles. Isabel tried to frown and failed, and they grinned at each other.

"Well, not seriously. I've been using the time to do a lot of thinking, and you know, if your friend is definitely coming, and you will be strong enough by the end of the week to use your crutches, then I think I should maybe use the time to go south and meet up with Aiden, finish it properly. I owe it to him to do that at least. I've been a wuss about it, that's all."

"Yes, I understand. I think it's the right decision as well. Whether or not you're going to explore being gay, it's obvious he doesn't rock your boat. Go with my blessing, but Bryony,"

"What?"

"You will come back to me, won't you?"

"Of course."

They were sitting so close in the car the situation might have been made for a gentle kiss, and then something else. Isabel did that gazing into her eyes trick, which turned Bryony's insides to water, but she pulled away from the magnetic connection and literally jumped out of the driver's seat.

"I've got a scheme for strengthening your arms so by the end of the week you can use your crutches, and you won't need the chair much at all, but for now I think you should still get in it to move around."

Isabel responded equally briskly. "Whatever you

say. You're the medic. Now I've slept I feel full of energy though. If I dictate, could you manage an evening on the book? But what might this scheme involve then?"

"Cans of beans. We can start tomorrow."

"Oh, high tech. I can tell."

"Useful things to do with legumes."

Bryony helped her out of the car and into the chair.

"Sure."

They spent the next two hours writing at the kitchen table, and between them finished another chapter of the book. The word count was now approaching 60,000. The stories were so interesting and at times, heart breaking, that Bryony almost became submerged in Isabel's world. She kept obediently typing, and let Isabel dry up naturally in her narrative, before suggesting they might need some supper before it became too late.

"Shall I fix us something light?"

She went over to the Aga and pulled over a saucepan.

"How about I make some soup and crunch up some toast to make croutons."

"That will be fine. I'm not really hungry, but I agree. It's time to call it a day."

"We should get back onto our meal plan. I have it all calorie counted out so you put on at least a pound a week, and you still seem as slim as ever."

"As long as you have to lift my weight, it seems better to be a little lighter than normal, and if I want to get mobile, surely being slim is no bad thing."

They ate supper together, and Bryony watched her baby eagle serve herself and without needing any help at all, once the food was on the table. She understood that this evening marked the beginning of the next phase of their partnership.

Once she had helped her hop into the bedroom, Bryony could see that Isabel could now undress herself, attend to all the bathroom business without any more personal care and even position the pillows to lift up her bad leg. For some stupid reason this filled her with a sudden deep melancholy.

It was late, and the sun had long set. Isabel lay back on

top of her bed and called her over.

"Sit."

"Hmm?"

"Sit on the bed, next to me."

Bryony sat down.

"Now tell me what's nagging you? Why are you so down in the mouth? Don't think I haven't noticed."

Bryony dropped her eyes and mumbled something.

"Speak up girl, what's the matter? This is the happiest day I have had in three months, more, in a year! But you seem as miserable as I've seen you. Spill the beans."

"I know it's ridiculous. Obviously I'm overjoyed for you. It's just what I wanted, for you to be healed, and today was a major breakthrough. But now you can do things, you don't need me nearly so much, and you won't ever again.

"In your real life, which you'll be going back to so soon, you'll have no use for me at all, and I...I do like to be useful. I'm sorry, I'm being so unprofessional. I don't know why I'm saying this. I'm talking rubbish."

"Bryony..."

"Hmm?"

"You're not talking rubbish, not at all. Here, lie down on the bed next to me, just for a while."

Bryony bit her bottom lip, and almost shivered with pent up physical need. If Isabel wanted her to lie next to her, then oh, where on earth would that lead? The woman was enticing her into something neither of them might be able to control.

She trembled, but as Isabel scooted her hips a couple of feet sideways to make room for her on the bed, she could not resist the invitation and lay down beside her, her head falling back on one of the clean cotton pillows. She gazed up at the ceiling, rather than meet Isabel's eyes, and then was forced to close her eyes altogether as she felt Isabel's touch on her arm and heard her whisper.

"Of course I understand. But don't think I don't need

you anymore. Of course I need you. You are looking after me, and by God I need looking after. We will adjust, obviously. But you are the sweetest assistant I have ever had, you cook beautifully, you drive safely, and you type like a pro."

"But..."

"But what?"

Isabel was forcing her to admit it. She felt squeezed like a little tube of toothpaste. The woman was indomitable. Why was she torturing her like this? Bryony, so normally under control, so organized, so unable to experience real passion, felt she was turning into a puddle.

"It's not that. It's the intimacy I'm going to miss. It's not being able to hold you. I'm sorry, I can't..."

Bryony went as if to jump up and run away, but Isabel's grip on her arm was surprisingly firm, and pulled her back. She then lifted her hand and gently turned her face back so they could look at each other. She smiled one of her devastating smiles and said softly, "So you like holding me?"

"Yes, you know I do."

"Well, if you want to be able to hold me, then what's the problem? I love it when you hold me. Don't you see? Don't you realize I am really, really in need of being held right now? Broken bones heal so much easier than a broken heart. You are my healer, and you have a magic touch. I am not going to give that up very easily."

"You mean? You're not disgusted by me? Isabel, I have to say you do completely turn me on. I think I could be really gay for you. Please let me say it. Please, would you mind?"

"And what would it mean for you? What would being 'really gay' entail?" Isabel's voice was so low and sexy, Bryony could suddenly scarcely breathe.

"I'm not sure, but it might...would you mind if I kissed you?"

"No I wouldn't mind, as you say, but...maybe it would depend..."

"On what?" Bryony felt a little nervous.

"On where you kissed me. I'm very ticklish on the soles

of my feet." Isabel kept smiling, one of her lovely golden smiles, and she put up her face towards Bryony. She had an impish grin, and suddenly Bryony could see totally sexy eyes.

Bryony turned to face her and gently smoothed her hair away from her forehead. Then she bent forwards and lightly felt for Isabel's mouth. It was soft and warm and opened for her without hesitation, and the kiss then deepened and went on for so long she wondered if she would die before she could bear to let go.

Chapter 15

Isabel's teeth parted and she let Bryony's tongue invade her. She felt a kiss full of hunger and need, but also full of promise, enticement, and pure lust. When their mouths did come apart, Bryony could see that Isabel's eyes had dilated into deep, almost navy blue pools. Her still damaged chest was heaving, and there was a sheen of sweat across her forehead which hadn't been there before.

"Oh..."

"Oh. Your first kiss with a woman? How did that feel?"

"I'm not sure..."

"Oh, not sure eh, well we had better try again. Maybe I can do better this time, make things clearer."

"Isabel..."

It was half a plea, half a statement of total acceptance.

Isabel pulled her back down and kissed her full on the mouth once more, and then she followed it with delicious little kisses over her face and round her jaw line. Bryony realized she was enjoying this too much to even say anything or put up any resistance.

Isabel was giving her just what she needed. They were kissing like lovers. Damn it, they were lovers, and an uncompromising acceptance of this fact gave her a lightness of spirit which invaded her mind.

"What a privilege, to kiss Isabel Bridgford."

She put up her hands to capture Isabel's face, and rolled into another deep drinking kiss from those beautiful lips. Still fully dressed, even down to her trainers, she lay on the covers above Isabel's body and absorbed the intimacy of their relationship. When the kiss finished, she lay with her head as close as possible to Isabel's.

"I can't put any weight on you. But could I lie in bed and

just hold you, maybe just for tonight?"

"I haven't slept with anyone since Carrie."

"Sorry, should I go then? Have I taken it too far already?"

"Don't be daft. Of course I'd like you to sleep with me. Here I am in this great double bed all on my own. Anyway, I thought you wanted some lessons on being gay, or was I wrong? How about you go and take your clothes off, and come back prepped for night duty? I'm not going anywhere."

Isabel's eyes were dilated, almost like a feral cat's in the moonlight. Bryony slid out of bed, her whole body aroused and burning with desire. She deliberately wriggled her hips as she walked away, back to her own room, where the cooler air helped her stay focused.

This was it. She was about to lose her gay virginity. It felt like the first time for sex ever. Was she ready? Damn right she was. Isabel was up for it, she trusted her on that one. She needed sex. They both needed sex. Bryony knew this could be the breaking of the ice dam inside her body, that she could cross the Nile once and for all. She slipped out of her jeans and tee shirt, socks and trainers, and then bravely removed her bra and panties. She felt primitive, wild. She wanted to be good for Isabel, desirable, ravishable. She wanted to be taken. It was something she had never felt before.

Isabel's voice sounded from the bedroom.

"Come on, girl. I want to see you in here, now. Get a move on."

She was raising the stakes. Isabel knew just the level of dominance that Bryony would best respond to. She was a natural at this.

Bryony called back.

"Coming. Don't be angry. I'm just...just locking up."

She went first to the front and only door of the cottage and turned the key in the lock, turned out the lights in the kitchen and living room, and then presented herself at the bedroom door. She stood there, naked. It took a lot of courage, but she suddenly felt completely wanton.

Isabel was still in the bed, but she had thrown back the sheet, and had half lifted her nightgown.

"Come and help me get this thing off. You know I really can't stand these horrible nightgowns. They're like army issue."

"Then I don't see why you should have to wear them. I can think of ways to keep you warm."

Bryony lifted Isabel up and pulled off her nightgown completely. The woman was breathing deeply, staring up at her body, and she remembered Isabel had never seen her naked before. Her nipples hardened in automatic response to Isabel's intent gaze.

"Would you like your evening massage now?"

"No, not just now. I just want to look at you. Lift your arms up and tie back your hair."

Bryony obeyed, lifting her hair up and looking around for something with which to tie it. She remembered she had some bands in the bathroom and went to get one, turning it round twice until it was tightly effective as a hair band. Isabel watched her as she fastened her hair up and out of the way.

"Why?" she half asked.

"I just wanted to see your breasts rise up like that. I knew you would have a wonderful body. Turn around, slowly. Yes, like that. Now come closer to me now and kneel above me on the bed."

Bryony sensed just how wet she was between the legs. She had never felt like it before, and the stickiness almost embarrassed her, but Isabel appeared unfazed. She just looked happy, very happy, like a cat presented with a large saucer of cream.

Bryony knelt on the bed and then lowered her upper body so that her breasts fell forward and teased Isabel's face. She could feel herself flooding. This was getting seriously awkward.

Isabel put up her hands and took Bryony's breasts,

cupping each one and then nudging them over so she could grab the right one between her teeth. She bit it, none too gently.

Bryony squealed, whether with arousal or fear she wasn't sure. She began to pant and pushed herself down against Isabel's wicked mouth, grabbing her hair.

Isabel changed breasts and started to nibble and tickle her left nipple. The sensation travelled like a ribbon of fire down into Bryony's core.

"So, you wanted a lesson in what gay women do in bed together," whispered Isabel, her breath arm against Bryony's skin. "Is that true?"

"Yes, Isabel. I think I need to learn as much as you can teach me," she breathed back, and then squealed as Isabel's hand, quicker than she anticipated, suddenly shot forward and felt up between her legs.

"Ah," she breathed in happy understanding. "You're closer to coming than I am. I can see this apprenticeship need not be too long. Lie down next to me and spread these legs, wide. I want you as open to me as you can. I'm now going to give you a fine lesbian lesson in anatomy, my little medical student."

Bryony was released and tipped over so she lay next to Isabel, naked on the bed.

"Cans of beans indeed! I can think of much better therapy for wasted arm muscles. Just lie back and think of England, darling."

Isabel's experienced technique made Bryony understand she was literally in the hands of a master, or rather mistress, of lesbian love-making. Her hand entered her, one finger at a time, teasing open her labia and relishing the wet response. She lay her head on Bryony's shoulder and pinioned her down with her one good leg, then kissed her just behind the ear before tickling it with her tongue so Bryony writhed in excitement against it.

Down below the pulse of Isabel's stroke became faster and deeper. Soon three fingers were inside her and

Bryony couldn't contain her response. Her first orgasm against Isabel's hand came within seconds, and a bright shower of color invaded her brain as the orgasm shot through her whole body like a firework shooting skywards. It was such a wonderful feeling she could hardly contain her screaming, and then remembered she didn't have to worry. This wasn't a dorm bedsit with wafer thin walls, she could make as much noise as she liked, if Isabel didn't object.

There was nothing but distant cows and sheep outside for more than a mile. Isabel was laughing though, a real joyous laugh. She was obviously having a hell of a good time with her hand still inside Bryony, her tongue and teeth nuzzling her ear.

She whispered, "I'm a bit hampered here, with my leg, but you get the picture. How was that, girl? I take it you didn't exactly hate the whole business?"

Bryony could hardly speak, but she pushed the words out as she tried to steady her breathing. "Isabel, I have never, ever come close to an orgasm like that before now. I realize now what it is, what I've been missing. You are wonderful. It was wonderful. I will die happy."

"No time for dying, but I'm glad you weren't disappointed. That was just a practice run, a warm up. Would you like to learn what else two sexy women can do together?"

Bryony's head nodded of its own accord, and Isabel took her hand and placed it right up against her own triangle of pubic hair. She'd opened her own legs and Bryony could feel how wet she was. She gently invaded Isabel's body, and walked her fingers in through the labia and up inside her mistress's secret passage.

Everything inside was warm and soft and silky smooth. Isabel began to moan, so Bryony withdrew just a little and located the firm nub of her clitoris which she began to caress gently, then with a firmer pulse. This came naturally. It was a million times more natural than trying to have sex with a boy, so much more subtle, so much gentler and more effective. She did to Isabel what she had so enjoyed Isabel doing to her, rather shyly at first and then with more confidence.

Isabel moaned again, and then pushed Bryony back deep inside her. She came in a great tearful whoosh of sexual release. Bryony was as happy as a sand boy. She had made Isabel come, she had reciprocated with a simple loving touch, and the woman had climaxed almost automatically. It was so natural. Why had she ever thought it was something so hard?

She lay at peace for a full two minutes before she saw that Isabel had no intention of letting things rest there. The woman was on top of her again, with her teeth, her tongue, and her newly liberated fingers. Bryony was initiated into lesbian sex with what one might call a thorough induction.

Isabel pulled her up the bed until she was virtually sitting on her face, then began to lick and kiss her from the inner thighs up to her clitoris, with long, sweet kisses, which turned her on once more with such intensity she thought she might die on the bed. In all she had four explosive orgasms, and by the end was weeping openly. Then Isabel turned her fiercely over on to her stomach and smacked her sharply on the backside.

"Ow! What's that for?"

"No reason, really." Isabel laughed wickedly. "I just felt like doing it, and it should focus your mind back in the right direction. I can't be doing with sniveling."

Isabel was triumphantly happy. She had been given this gift, the sexual enthusiasm of this beautiful girl. She would have a sex partner now for the rest of the summer. It was like her own ice-cream supply after walking through the desert for a year.

Bryony felt the sting of the slap and decided it was time to take sweet revenge. She gathered Isabel into her arms, and it was almost 2 am before she was done with touching up and tormenting her. They fell asleep in the end within minutes of each other, a tangle of bodies and sheets, and slept right through, until the sun came shooting through the bedroom curtains well after 9 am.

Chapter 16

Isabel looked sideways and managed to pick up her phone. *9:20?* It couldn't be serious! She doubted she had ever been asleep at this time in the morning in her entire life, even when severely jet-lagged and recovering from a three month work stint in Nepal.

But the sunshine outside the window seemed to endorse what the numbers on the screen claimed. Tucked warmly beside her, an arm still laid across her stomach, there was a sweep of honey colored hair and a warm body.

So it hadn't been a dream or a delirium. Bryony had come into her bed and they had made love for hours. Really, the girl was as gay as a jaybird, and her sexuality had ignited Isabel's inner fire, so she had come almost as soon as Bryony had touched her. She just hoped that when Bryony woke, she wouldn't regret the whole night's work and run screaming away into the woods.

Bryony simultaneously was trying to process similar fears as she lay still with her eyes firmly shut. She could feel Isabel stirring beneath her hand, and tried to remember who exactly had initiated all that wonderful sex. Would Isabel be furious with her in the light of day? Would she even perhaps ask her to leave? She didn't want to wake and face the music. She wanted to stay wrapped up around Isabel like this for ever.

In the end, they each took their courage in both hands and opened their eyes simultaneously, gazing into the other's, and smiled.

"Hi," tried Bryony softly. "How are you? Shall I go and make you a cup of tea?"

"Tea," laughed Isabel, "the old British ice-breaker above all others."

"Do we have any ice to break?" Bryony immediately felt insecure, but Isabel put her arms round her and hugged her tightly.

"Not that I can see. How are you, my darling? I'm ashamed to say I feel wonderful. Sex with you seems to have acted as a superb opiate. Who needs pills? I just hope I don't get addicted."

"We did rather go at it, didn't we? I hope I did OK, for the first time."

"You have nothing to worry about at all, Bryony. And I'm afraid to have to break it to you, but there is no ambiguity here. You are without a doubt one of the gayest young women I have ever met. You are naturally gifted at showing your feelings, and you came like a firecracker as soon as I laid a finger on you."

"I did, didn't I?"

"You did, and I did as well, I who had almost decided to take a vow of celibacy before I met you."

"I'm so happy you didn't. Thank you."

"For what?"

"Oh, for being such a good teacher, for showing me how wonderful gay sex is. Can I have some more lessons soon please?"

"My darling, it will be a pleasure, as many as you like. You already have played havoc with my original good intentions to keep our relationship completely impersonal and platonic."

"But we can carry on as before, can't we? I haven't ruined anything I hope."

"No, you haven't ruined anything. I just feel the healing project has just gained a whole new dimension to it. Although you'd better not put last night's activities into your thesis! Let's just accept who we are and what we have, and to answer your original question, yes, tea sounds wonderful. I am just going to try to hop and swing myself into the bathroom, while you put the kettle on."

Isabel gently pushed Bryony out of the bed, and

watched her with undisguised pleasure as she stood naked and reached for a towel to wrap round herself. Bryony turned and helped her in turn to stand, and did a similar long appraisal of her lover's naked body. It was all she could do not to tip them both back into bed for another three hours. But she reached for Isabel's dressing gown and slipped it round her, wrapping it firmly over her breasts and tying the cord tightly.

"Put your weight on my shoulder and I'll take you to the bathroom."

"Thank you."

"My pleasure. I mean my real and complete pleasure."

"Go and boil the kettle. I am thirsty for tea."

"Yes ma'am."

The rest of the day, indeed the rest of the week until Thursday evening, passed in a glorious haze of sunshine, bookwork and sex. They were so content, and Bryony especially was a very happy bunny as she could see the results of her therapies for Isabel really bearing fruit. Her lover had lost all her bruises, and her face had filled out. She no longer looked gaunt and strained and she slept every night in Bryony's arms after each 'lesson' in love-making.

On Wednesday evening, after a long book session, Bryony washed Isabel's hair for her, and also ran a deep bath into which she helped her sink while leaving her plastered leg resting over the side. She poured in some of her lover's expensive shower gel and whooshed it around so there were copious bubbles. Isabel lay back under the water and closed her eyes in bliss.

"Ah, that is really wonderful. I'm not selfish. Why don't you get in with me?"

"I don't think..."

"Do it, now! Come on, you can lie down in front of me."

"Yes, Isabel."

Bryony stripped off slowly, knowing how much she aroused Isabel by slowly turning her back so, as she bent over to remove her jeans, her butt rose up and enticed her.

She slipped off her underwear, and then holding the

edges of the bath slid down into the hot water in front of Isabel, who grabbed her round the waist and pulled her back against her. Then she began to play with her breasts and gripped her crotch possessively under the water. It felt luxuriously decadent.

"Steady, tiger. Is it possible to come under water?"

"If I want you to come, you will come."

"Oh will I? What about you, in that case, oh beloved mistress? What about you?"

Bryony rubbed her backside against Isabel's front, and then put her hands underneath her to tickle her way under Isabel's defenses. Within minutes they were both thrashing about and bath foam was flying everywhere. Isabel won the contest, making Bryony scream as she came in an uncontrolled fit of bucking against Isabel's wicked fingers. In the melee the bath plug was pulled out and to her dismay, Isabel's lovely relaxing bath was disappearing beneath her. She was lucky to keep her bad leg still aloft out of the water.

"Oh, bother, that was unexpected," she said with a deadpan expression. "We had better get out, I suppose."

Bryony felt she was the one supposed to take prime responsibility for their domestic arrangements, so she heaved her body out of the bath, and then helped Isabel. She wrapped her up in a large bath sheet and dried her tenderly.

"Come and lie on the bed, and I will massage all your cares away."

Isabel could now quite easily tolerate lying on her front, so Bryony arranged her like that, and then slowly and lovingly poured a small bottle of massage oil in a pool in the centre of her back and began to smooth it outwards.

"Let's go to town tomorrow and buy another big tube of the Aloe Vera, but in the meantime, I think you'll like this. I bought it in the hospital shop while you were having your casts cut off."

She had a magic touch which Isabel was rapidly

finding addictive and brought her lover up to full arousal without even entering her. But finally, she turned Isabel over and knelt at the end of the bed so she could part her legs and enter her with her tongue.

The taste of Isabel was like a sweet sexy drink of ambrosia. She had never imagined it could be such a delicious sensation, and as Isabel went into full orgasm, Bryony knew she was coming herself, simply by performing the sex act on her mistress. Could anything be more wonderful? She wanted it never to end.

***

Things were about to change. Isabel had practiced, under protest because she thought it was all rather silly, swinging and lifting her arms with a pair of baked bean cans. It had helped in exercising her biceps and triceps, and she could now tolerate using the crutches for a few minutes at a time.

It meant she was almost free at last from the hated wheelchair, so when they went to town to replenish the stocks on Thursday morning, she could swing herself around the Co-op supermarket on her crutches while Bryony pushed the trolley. They also parked down the high street earlier and went into a few smaller shops, a green-grocer and artisan bakery which had wonderful fresh bread. They were buying food with Jane's visit in mind.

"What does she like? Will she mind veggie food?"

"She'll be fine. She has what one might call a robust appetite. Just add in a few bottles of real ale. She'll enjoy a drink or two."

They paid at the checkout, and by then Isabel was feeling a little tired, pleased to sit in the car again, and rest her leg. She handed her bank card to Bryony and said, "Get me £250 out of the cash point will you?" and gave her the pin number.

When Bryony returned with a handful of notes, she was astonished when Isabel simply took her card back and pushed her hand holding the cash away.

"That's for you, for your wild weekend of debauchery in

the South."

"I..."

"Let's go up to the railways station and buy your ticket now. Then you have to go. I don't want you chickening out at the last minute."

"Maybe you know me too well. I really don't want to confront him face to face."

"I think you need to, if only to show respect, and get some closure. I imagine you are rather surer about your sexuality by now than you were before."

"Yes, but I don't want to leave you."

"Oh pooh, we mustn't get too codependent. It will be good for both of us. It will give us some perspective. Besides, you need to have your day in college anyway before you catch the evening train to London. Come on, Bryony, do it."

"Oh, very well."

They drove up to the station at the far end of town, and Bryony bought tickets with her student card. It would be a long journey in either direction, but she was happy to have a return ticket firmly in her grasp at least. Was it true that she and Isabel were becoming too codependent? What did that even mean? She knew she was in love, in love for the first time in her life, and it scared and excited her in equal measure.

After lunch Isabel forged ahead with her book, while Bryony kept her eyes front and followed her dictation as fast as she could. She had never typed so many pages in one go in her life, but her fingers had developed the skills to touch type on the small keyboard, and her mistakes were becoming far fewer.

Isabel had left Bangladesh and was now talking about the situation up much nearer the Himalayas in Nepal, where she had obviously worked with an organization supporting child laborers. The harshness of life in the remote villages was only matched by the deplorable conditions facing children as they were bussed down to Kathmandu or over the border into India.

Many acted as domestic servants, having been promised schooling and 'foster homes', and these were even luckier if you could call it that, than the thousands who ended up trafficked down to work in brothels across South Asia. The harder it became to eke a living from the eroded lands and flooded farmland, the more common the problem was.

"How do you keep going, when there is so much discouraging news, and terrible true stories from every continent?" she asked Isabel, when she was at last allowed to take a break.

"There is a paradox. I have found that my greatest encouragement and positivity has come from the poorest women I've worked alongside. I could tell you many stories about this. And the population of most of the world is so young, a whole new generation has grown up, just in the years I've been working.

"Despite everything, they were succeeding. Acute poverty has fallen, educational standards are much higher, and child deaths are falling. That is, until now, when the climatic changes are the greatest threat to development as we know it. Resources will become much scarcer. Maybe the next war will be fought over access to clean water, not oil."

"Can we stop now? We're on target, and I need to make up my bed for your friend."

Isabel nodded, and let her go from the table. Bryony stripped off the sheets from her bed, and remade it for Jane. Then she went out into the garden and picked a bunch of the flowers growing round the cottage, lupins, valerian and large daisies which she arranged in a jug and carried back into her room.

"There, it looks nice. I hope she sleeps well. Would you like to go into the woods for an hour or so, before she comes?"

"In the chair still?"

"'Fraid so, but it will be cool in there and we do love it, don't we, under that green canopy?"

"Yes, very well, but don't let's forget, after Monday I hope to be back on both feet, skipping about."

"Don't be disappointed if that doesn't happen immediately. Even when the cast is off, I expect they will ask you to keep your leg bandaged for another few weeks, and slowly build its muscles tone back. It might take months, even up to Christmas before it is fully healed. It was a nasty compound fracture."

"Don't remind me. I was frightened I was going to lose my leg in the beginning. Now I have hope the bones will knit together and be stronger than before."

"Well we have another six weeks to make it happen."

Six weeks, that was all? It seemed to Bryony that she and Isabel had been linked together for far longer than two weeks, but in another way the time had flashed by. They left the cottage as they had the previous times, with Bryony pushing the chair and Isabel sitting impatiently in it, but once they had passed through the gate, the magical stillness of the wood worked its charm on them both and they wandered along the trace in blissful silence.

Isabel liked to be quiet, well at least some of the time. She had learned to enjoy her own company as well, and had thought hiding herself away, virtually alone, would be the right ambiance for the healing she needed. But things had not turned out quite as expected. She thought things through as the chair wheeled quietly forwards. Bryony was a gift she had not sought, a blessing she felt she didn't deserve. She was so easy to live alongside, and so delicious to sleep alongside as well. She knew the girl was in a transition stage in her life, that there was no way she could expect her to be here permanently, but it had all been a delightful surprise, and she would enjoy it for the summer.

Chapter 17

They turned back after thirty minutes, and then retraced their journey, seeing the sunlight grow stronger and stronger as the trees thinned and the south-facing exit gate became clearer. When they reached the cottage, they saw Jane's Rav4 Toyota parked up alongside the Citroen Berlingo, and a tall, very fit looking woman perusing the view down the valley with a pair of binoculars.

"I'm watching the buzzards circling on a thermal over there," she said, pointing down the hill to the opposite woodland. Then she turned and smiled at them both. "Hi, Izzy. You actually don't look as ghastly as I expected. So you're still in the wheelchair?"

"Not much of the time. We just went exploring for a mile or so through the wood. It's great to see you. This is Bryony by the way."

"How do you do?" Bryony smiled but kept her expression neutral, as she did when she first met someone, and held out her hand in greeting.

"Oh, she has manners, I see! And you haven't scared her away yet, if she's the same girl you mentioned last week?"

"Yes, I'm the same. I'll just fetch Isabel's crutches and then you can catch up, while I make you some tea."

She disappeared into the house and came back with the crutches. Isabel could then easily hop away from the chair which they folded and parked in the garage, and Bryony left the two friends talking outside, while she went to make tea and produce some little strawberry scones she had baked earlier. Jane stretched out on the garden chair. Her legs were bare beneath shorts and a polo-shirt and her feet were in open –toed sandals. She was tall, slim and athletic and her hair was cut very short so it stood up above her forehead almost like a toothbrush. Bryony busied herself in the kitchen, and was just finishing setting out tea on a large tray, when she heard Isabel call her.

"Don't lurk inside. Come and join the grown-ups."

"I'm coming. The kettle needed to boil."

She walked out with the tea tray and produced the cucumber sandwiches she had been preparing, alongside freshly baked scones and a little pot of strawberry jam. She poured the tea from a real teapot.

"Hey, this all looks good. I'm starving!" said Jane, causing Isabel to catch Bryony's eye with a deadpan stare, but a tiny twitch of her lip.

"Isabel told me you would be, after a long journey. I hope you had a pleasant drive from Bristol."

Jane took the offered plate and helped herself to three sandwiches at once.

"Yes, it was fine. I listened to the test-match on the way over. The time shot by.

"So Izzy, tell me all about everything. I want to hear all about it, and how you found this delightful child to cater to your every need."

Bryony looked across at Isabel to see how she would react, and was concerned for her when she saw the blush which undoubtedly was rising up her cheek. Jane seemed oblivious to the double meaning of her comment, but it was too close to the truth not to veer very near a dangerous precipice. She knew she needed to leave it to Isabel to disclose anything of their relationship she chose to, or not.

"The first thing to say is that Bryony isn't a child, or anything like it. She has been a consummate professional and I wouldn't be as well as I am now if it wasn't for her."

"Wow, girl. What have you been using to sweeten up old Izzy here? You must have been rubbing something powerful into her joints!"

This made Bryony jump, and say, "Oh, shoot, I know what I forgot to buy in Machynlleth this morning,

Aloe Vera gel. What a shame. I'll get some at the weekend, don't worry."

Isabel pretended to scold her.

"Make sure you do!" she muttered, holding her gaze for far too long.

***

Bryony had moved her possessions out of the single bedroom into a neat pile behind the sofa in the living room where she presumed she'd be sleeping for the night. While Jane and Isabel talked after dinner, she hitched up her phone to WhatsApp and connected with Aiden, sitting just outside the front door where there was still a good internet signal. She clicked on the camera button and saw his bearded face appear.

"At last! I was beginning to think you were in a Buddhist retreat," he sounded relieved, but friendly and warm, with no hint of suspicion.

"Hi Aiden, no, I've just been super busy. This is very much a seven day a week job and I'm also studying down in Aberystwyth. But I wondered whether you were free on Saturday. I have the weekend free. Could you meet me in London?"

"I can manage Saturday, but Sunday I promised a mate I'd crew for him on his yacht down on the Solent. What a pity. If you'd told me earlier I could have taken the whole weekend away with you."

Bryony was so relieved they would not have to face a night together that she had to work hard to hide a smile. "Pity, but I only just heard. I've bought a ticket, so I'll make other arrangements for sleeping. Let's meet somewhere, like the South Bank, close to Waterloo station, that place we like for lunch."

"OK, Saturday at 12?"

"Yes."

"How are you honey? You look good, but your voice sounds strained. I've missed you, loads."

She just couldn't return the expected words, "Me too." Instead she said, "You look very sun-tanned, like a real sailor."

"It's been really hot down here? What's it like up there in Wales?"

"Warm, green, quite magical really."

"You don't normally talk about things being magical."

"Well, they are here. This is a really special place."

"How is that old lady you're looking after? Giving you much grief?"

"No, everything is fine. And she's not that old."

"Oh well, whatever. It sounded rather a boring job to me, but at least she's paying you well. I thought we can take a cheap break together somewhere in September, before term starts again. I'd like to take you sailing in Greece."

A sudden, silly chill crossed Bryony's brain. Aiden had meant nothing by it probably, but she didn't want to be taken anywhere by him. She was an adult woman, not someone to be taken along. He sounded so positive, and she knew she was being unfair. How was he to know that she would never be taking a cheap break with him or any other man again?

"Let's talk on Saturday. I'll wait for you at 12."

"I'll call you if the train's late. 'Bye then!"

"Bye."

When she went back inside, she could sense Isabel had been eavesdropping on the conversation.

"Everything all right?"

"Yes. We're meeting for lunch on Saturday in London. Aiden's going sailing on Sunday."

"So where will you stay Friday and Saturday night?"

"I haven't quite worked this out. I have some friends I can call who might let me sleep on their floor."

Isabel looked serious for a moment, and then said, "Hey, No. Stay at my flat. It will be a great favor to me for you to give it an airing, and just check everything is all right. I haven't been back there since mid-May."

Bryony looked startled and bit her lip, "Oh, would you mind? Where is it exactly?"

"North London, top end of Highbury Fields. You can get there easily on the tube from Kings Cross."

Jane looked surprised. "You must have special powers, Bryony. Izzy doesn't normally let strangers anywhere near her flat. She's very jealous about her privacy."

"Bryony is far from being a stranger. She'll be doing me a great service by staying in my place for a couple of nights, and I'll be reassured if she's safely accommodated and gets two good nights' sleep."

Bryony looked from one woman to another. She wondered which of them, Jane or herself, understood Isabel better. Logically it must be Isabel's oldest school friend, but she felt like she and Isabel just had something intangible, a deeper understanding already.

But she could not to presume three weeks acquaintanceship and a few nights' hot sex gave her many rights in anything. The thought made her feel insecure, and she knew she would love to get a better understanding of who Isabel was by staying in her flat for a couple of days.

"Thanks, so much, Isabel. That would be very kind, and a relief. I would have stayed in my college bed-sit, but the university housing people let out all the student accommodation for summer school courses."

She tried to keep her face calm and her voice neutral.

"I'm just going into the kitchen to wash up the dinner dishes. Would either of you like coffee, or cocoa perhaps?"

"Fetch Jane those beers we bought this morning. I think that will more likely satisfy her thirst. I'll have half a glass to keep her company."

Bryony fetched the beers, and two glasses, but shook her head when Jane offered to pour her an ale as well.

"Thanks, but I don't drink."

She went into the kitchen and closed the door to give them some privacy.

She overheard Jane, (for the woman had such a naturally

loud voice it was hard not to), say, "She's quite a little puritan, isn't she? What are you doing, letting her inside your flat? It's full of gay books and Carrie's pictures everywhere."

Isabel murmured something in reply, but too low for Bryony to hear. One thing was certain however. Jane certainly would not be expecting her to share Isabel's bed. A night on the sofa alone awaited.

As it happened, the night on the bare mountain, or even the sitting-room sofa never really happened. They had all retired about eleven, and Bryony had made up a bed on the sofa for herself, using some spare blankets and pillows from inside the wardrobe.

Jane used the bathroom first, and marched off to bed dressed like a rugby player dressed for a match, a Val McDermott novel under her arm. Within fifteen minutes, gentle snoring could be heard coming from the end room.

Isabel let Bryony settle her in bed, in demure enough pajamas, but she held Bryony's wrist and stopped her when she moved as if to go to her own temporary sleeping quarters.

"Aren't you going to sleep with me?"

"We can't. This place is too small. What on earth would she think?"

"Oh, pooh, Jane is already asleep. We can hear her snoring from here."

"So in that case she'll be able to hear us as well. Supposing she needs to come through the room to use the bathroom in the night."

"I'm sure she won't. Why do you think I bought her those real ales? They were strong. She won't wake."

"You are rather a wicked woman. Oh, and by the way, what was that with the *Izzy*?"

"It's a terrible name from my childhood. Why do you think I changed to Bel? But Jane's incorrigible. She's known me since I was eleven and does it to annoy me."

"So she's allowed, but I'm not?"

"You're not allowed to do anything without my consent. And tonight I want you in bed, here, with me. Understand?"

"Yes, Isabel. But be gentle with me. It's been a long day."

Isabel almost smirked with delight. Bryony stripped, pretending it was all a great imposition, and then walked naked into the bathroom to clean her teeth.

When she came back she saw Isabel had pulled out the tie from her dressing gown and was wrapping it round her hand.

"Get into bed, and put your arms up. I don't want you thinking you can go wandering off again in the night."

She tied up Bryony's wrists rather too efficiently with the cord, and then lifted her arms so that she was caught flat on her back. The dressing gown tie was then secured round the metal bed head with a neat knot, worthy of the girl guides Isabel had never joined. She was not one for obeying any rules except her own.

Bryony had no choice but to lie there, exposed and let Isabel work out her physical frustrations and fantasies. This was a sex game which Isabel obviously enjoyed, and was well practiced at. She both hoped and feared it might involve some pain, for some weird reason she was actually fantasizing about that, another first in her sexual apprenticeship.

In fact, all Isabel's assault began with her pulling Bryony's hair back off her face, and drawing gentle patterns across her cheeks and forehead with one finger tip. Then she casually put another finger inside Bryony's mouth and ran it along her inner cheek. Bryony's chest heaved and she couldn't stop herself sucking hard and almost pulling Isabel's hand into her mouth, covering it with kisses.

"Sshh, just lie quietly, like a mouse. I'm going to make you feel so, so good. Trust me. But you must lie still and not make a sound. Can you do that?"

Bryony shook her head. "You know I'm a screamer," she whispered.

"Well this is where I teach you not to be. If you cry out, I won't let you come. But if you are a good quiet little lover, then I will give you a really, really good time tonight."

"I don't think you or anyone will stop me coming under your hand or your mouth, the way you kiss."

"And that's from a girl who thought she couldn't experience orgasms only a few days ago? Whatever is the world coming to? Now, don't distract me. I'm busy here."

Isabel's mouth followed her hand and she caught Bryony's lip in a little nip, before devouring her mouth with kisses. She then kissed her inner arms held pinioned on either side of her head, and began to nuzzle and lick the sensitive areas inside her elbows. Bryony writhed on the bed beneath her. Tossing her head from side to side in an attempt to escape, she only seemed to enflame Isabel more. Isabel's torture session grew more and more enthusiastic, but every time Bryony gave out an involuntary moan she ceased her activities, at one point even turning over away from her with a weary sigh as if to say, "You're hardly worth bothering with."

Bryony wriggled with frustration and tried to entice her mistress back. It was hard to keep her voice down, and she was genuinely frightened of waking their visitor and having her march into the bedroom to investigate the rumpus.

"Isabel, darling, please. Finish what you started. I'll try to be quiet. And if you release me I'll come down on you so sweetly you'll feel like you're in heaven, as well as me." Her whisper was breathed against Isabel's neck, and it tickled her into mock forgiveness.

"Oh, very well, if you put it like that." She turned back, pressing her body tightly against Bryony's and with one hand reached up to release the cords. Bryony's arms slid free and she used them to cup Isabel's buttocks and hold her tightly against her in the dark.

"Jane said I was a little puritan, didn't she?"

"Yes, I will always love her, but she is definitely an

idiot."

"Am I special to you, just a bit maybe?"

"Bryony, you are my whole universe right now."

"Love me?"

"No, of course not. Now, where was I? Oh, yes..."

It was another hour before they slept, and well into the next morning before they woke, but Isabel's thoughtful catering arrangements with the bottles of real ale had done their trick and both of them were up and fully dressed before Jane emerged from her bedroom. Bryony was packing her rucksack for the weekend.

"I must run if I'm to catch the train to the University. Then I'll leave for London in the afternoon. It's a long trip and I have to change in Birmingham."

"Give me your notebook and pen. I'll write down my address and give you my key." Isabel scribbled down the information, and Bryony realized she had never seen her write before. She had very distinctive handwriting which shot all over the place.

"There'll be a ton of mail probably. Could you chuck out the circulars and bring the rest back for me."

"Sure."

"I'm really sorry, but the inside of the fridge might be truly disgusting by now."

"Don't worry. I'll sort it."

Bryony took the door key Isabel gave her and tucked it away in her rucksack, and then she picked up the car keys and hurried towards the door.

"Hey!"

"Huh?"

"Not even a goodbye?"

"Of course, and I'll call you tonight. I've written down your number from last week."

"Come here. Keep safe. I'll miss you."

"Me too."

They stared at each other, very conscious of Jane hovering in the background.

"Oh, come here!" and Isabel pulled Bryony against her

and kissed her on the mouth. "Get off with you then. " Her voice dropped to a whisper, "Don't worry, I'll explain to Jane." Bryony felt herself grow hot and pink.

"Bye, Isabel."

"Bye, my love."

And they were parted.

Isabel's Healing

Chapter 18

The train ride to Aberystwyth was somehow not as exciting as it had been the week before, and Bryony viewed the coming weekend with more than a little dread. She hated causing pain to anyone as nice as Aiden, and none of this was his fault, well apart from being so dense as to not see how unfulfilled she had been over the last two years.

But she switched on her powerful ability to focus, and spent a profitable day in the library. The American students seemed to have dispersed. Perhaps they were out on a field trip or something, as the cafeteria where she took her lunch was very quiet, but just as she was about to return to her favorite library desk, the blue-eyed girl from the previous week came round the corner into the cafe and stopped in front of her.

"Hi, how ya doing, Bryony?"

"Fine. It seems longer than a week since we met. How are you?"

"What'll you have?"

"Oh, tea please." She could spare another ten minutes. The girl ordered for her from the counter and sat down with her as she resumed her seat. The American had a large diet coke, and spent a long time regaling her with the study trips and seminars her group had been doing for the week.

"I'm so sorry; I've actually forgotten your name."

"It's Mel. Melanie. I remembered yours was Bryony."

"Yes, sorry I forgot yours."

"That's cool. You know, you have amazing green

eyes."

Bryony almost choked on her cup of tea. The girl's smile was contagious though, and she seemed guileless enough to be genuine.

"Thank you, though sometimes they're almost hazel. But do you always come on so quickly to someone you have scarcely said hello to?"

"Only when I like someone. And I really like you. I've been thinking of you all week, hoping you would be here. Are you gay?"

This really was beyond the pale! Bryony was about to shout, "No!" but she hesitated and just said coldly, "That really is none of your business."

"I knew you were. I have excellent gaydar. None of the other girls in my group are, which is super boring, and I haven't even found any gay bars here yet, which is very disappointing."

"I'm sorry; I must get back to my studies. I only have a few hours before I have to take the train to London."

"Oh, don't run away. I know I came on really strong, but I understand. I expect you're in a committed relationship. But if it doesn't work out, here's my number. Call me. I'll be here till September, bored, on my own, up for any mindless sex, you know!" She passed over a scrap of paper and actually waggled her bottom on the café chair, widening those large blue eyes. Bryony couldn't believe she was for real, and the scene actually made her laugh.

"You're crazy. You have no idea who I am, or what I'm like."

"Maybe not, but you smell wonderful. What are you wearing?"

It was the same question Isabel had asked? Was she giving out some strange pheromone or something?

"It's by Givenchy, just a sample. I don't even know its name. Anyway this is too silly for words. Goodbye Mel. I hope you find someone else to have a good time with while you're here, but it won't be me."

"You really spoken for?"

"Yes, I'm spoken for. Sorry."

"But you are gay, I am right, aren't I?"

Bryony sighed as she stood up to leave.

"Yes," she said, "I am gay."

Which was how Bryony Morris came out to a total stranger in a cafeteria in Aberystwyth. She almost ran back to her desk in the library, very oddly relieved that it wasn't simply Isabel who knew the truth, and presumably her friend Jane by now as well.

What a strange metamorphosis was taking place within her. No-one had ever assumed she was gay before. She must look for the label on the little perfume bottle, and see what on earth it was called.

***

At the cottage Jane had been giving Isabel a furious dressing down as soon as Bryony had left the property.

"What the hell do you think you're playing at?"

"I have absolutely no idea what you mean."

"Of course you do. You're up to your old tricks again, aren't you? Seducing any poor female who falls in front of your wheels!"

"In my present situation, that's not a very nice metaphor. You're supposed to be here to be kind to me. What about breakfast?"

Jane banged a packet of cornflakes down on the table.

"Look, you can't play games with me. I know it's been a while since Carrie died, and I do know how cut up you were about losing her, but really, your young nurse? Whom you've only known a few weeks? What's that all about? My God, you aren't already sleeping with her, are you?"

Isabel looked down at the table, suddenly finding the pattern of the tablecloth oddly fascinating.

"You are! Bel, really?"

Isabel fought for the right words. "I...we...we sort of

fell into it. It just seemed natural. She wanted to know if she was gay, and..."

"And what? Oh, no, you decided to seduce her so she could find out? You really are the giddy limit, Bel. Even when you're in plaster, women are still in danger from you."

"Stop it. You know I'm not some sort of female Casanova. All I know is that I felt almost dead myself after Carrie's death, and even worse after the accident, and now I feel alive, that my shoots are green again. That I might actually have something to look forward to."

"But she's so young, and in your employ, and are you are telling me she has never had a gay relationship before?"

"She's twenty-three! And yes, no, I think I'm the first. She learned quickly though. She's a natural. She's fun and she likes playing games."

"Don't be flippant. This is serious! And from what I can gather, she has now gone to London to break everything off with her boy-friend, her *boy*-friend remember, just on the basis of being fucked a few times by you?"

"Don't be horrible. I think she's been dissatisfied with him for months. "

"Bel, dearest, don't you see it's you who's being horrible? She probably thinks she's in love, that this is the real thing, when for you it's just like a sex pill, another therapy to make you feel good. Have you any intention of carrying on after the end of August?"

Isabel didn't want to admit just how much Bryony had crept under her skin and was now nestled somewhere deep inside her heart.

"It's not just down to me. She probably won't want it to go on either. Now she knows what's out there, what she can do, how she can choose, the world's her oyster. I've just been giving her a few lessons in lesbian love."

"More like, you'll break her heart, and it'll be me who will have to pick up the pieces, like I had to with those girls before, Sharon, and Rosemary, and what was her name, oh yes, Yvonne, or was it Yvette?"

"That was back in our twenties. You forget I was faithful

to Carrie for almost twelve years, and we'd be together now if she hadn't died."

Isabel's blue eyes filled with tears, and Jane, big sympathetic fool that she was, stopped shouting at her and went across to hug her.

"I know. I'm sorry if I'm upsetting you. But look at it another way. I don't think you are over Carrie, and you may not be, not for another five years, or even ever. Is it really fair on this new girl to string her along, when for you it's only sex, and in reality you're not the sort of woman she should be with. You're far too complicated, too egotistical.

"Anyway, Bryony looks a nice girl, a straightforward girl, but also isn't she a bit too stable and boring for you, a bit too scientific? Don't you normally go for the emotionally crazy trapeze artist types?"

"Stability is something I'm finding I could do with more of these days. Besides, Bryony makes very good scrambled eggs, not too runny or too dry. Just right."

"Bel, you're dangerous. You ought to carry a health warning."

Jane glowered at her friend, and planned to get hold of Bryony and give her some much needed wise counsel before things became even worse.

Bel was a charmer when she chose, but she could also be a witch, and she held a lethal attraction for nice, inexperienced younger women who were dazzled by her intellectual cleverness, her beauty and her virtuosity in bed. But in Jane's eyes, she was, especially now, fundamentally unsuitable for anyone wanting a faithful lover and life partner.

She thought Carrie had only kept Isabel faithful by being even more crazy and brilliant than she was. She knew their long term partnership had been marked by regular spectacular rows and extravagant reconciliations, and was only held together probably by the fact that they had both travelled so much for their respective careers. Out of more than a decade, they had probably only been in the same place at the same time for about four years in total, and that time had usually been split into much shorter bursts of a few months.

Isabel decided she'd been told off enough. It stung when Jane accused her of being egotistical.

"Jane, that's OK. You've made your point. Let's drop it please. This is my summer sabbatical, and I need Bryony with me. She is a gift from the gods who until now, you must admit, have been savagely mean to me.

"I promise to do my best not to break her heart, nor let her break mine, but I'm sure neither will happen. We're just working together on my book. That's our main raison d'etre. But, whatever it looks like, it works. I'm happy. There I've said it. I am learning to take what each day offers as it comes, and today I am happy, OK?"

Jane grudgingly agreed, and dropped the subject. She organized breakfast for them both, and then suggested she took Isabel away for a car-trip.

"Let's go up to Caernarvon. There's a great big castle there, and I can push you round or over the ramparts, depending on how you behave."

"Oh, very well. I can't work without Bryony here anyway."

So they went out for the day, and Isabel was very relieved Jane didn't mention Bryony again. Jane drove them down to the coast and then north round the great mass of the Snowdonia Mountains, standing like great bastions against the Atlantic, and then across the Menai Straits they could see the ancient and mysterious island of Anglesey, the last stronghold of the Welsh heroes who had fought off the English.

Caernarvon was packed with tourists, and the narrow streets were awkward with a wheelchair. Isabel had felt sure she could have managed with crutches, but without Bryony there to help she felt a little nervous. Jane was so strong and quick-moving she'd have never kept up. After viewing the castle, they retreated somewhere outside the city for lunch, and then drove home the long way round, across the mountain passes.

Isabel had bought a small guide book, with several other suggestions for places to visit, and realized she was spending most of her time imagining how it would be if she and Bryony could get out and explore North Wales together. She could not help thinking how stimulating and interesting that would be, compared to the pleasant, but uneventful day she had had with Jane.

She chided herself for dwelling on Bryony far too much, hoping her day had gone well, imagining her on the train, maybe reading, maybe sorting out her notes from the day's research. She knew she wouldn't make it to her flat until about 10 pm, but she hoped very much to get a phone call or at least a text message to say she was there safely. By the end of the evening she was feeling definitely fidgety, and decided to make the call herself.

***

Bryony had had similar thoughts about Isabel, especially when she folded away her notes and walked down to the railway station to catch a train. It took her more than four hours to travel to London, including a change in the great underground metropolis station of Birmingham New Street. While she was there, Bryony grabbed a bottle of water, and a Mars bar and found a window seat on the outgoing London express, where she could rest her head on her rucksack and get some sleep. The previous night had been altogether lovely, but not very restful, and she was now exhausted.

As the train to London finally sped away, she closed her eyes, and met Isabel in her dreams. The vision of her lover showed her strong and fit. She had thrown away her crutches, and she drew Bryony in with her Cheshire cat smile. It was an altogether happy dream which must have come from deep inside her subconscious mind.

When the train finally drew into Paddington, the heat of the summer night in the city hit her like a warm wind, and she prepared to tackle the evening crush on the Underground to navigate her way up to Highbury, to Isabel's flat.

It was 10 pm, and still very warm when she located the address and slid the key into the lock. She pushed open the door past an enormous pile of junk mail and local newspapers. Whatever she had imagined the flat to be like it had not been like this. It took over the ground floor of a narrow Victorian house, with high ceilings and sash windows, and the first thing she noticed in the hall was an artistic clutter of international figurines, musical instruments like drums and African stringed instruments, and large batik wall hangings.

The tiled hall led into an open plan kitchen, full of bright crockery and utensils for the sort of stove-top cooking Isabel obviously favored. A state of the art coffee machine shared the counter top with a slow cooker, and an extravagant array of dried spices and herbs. Beyond the kitchen, through a set of modern French windows, Bryony could see a well planted urban garden with large feature plants and a sitting area next to a small pond. She switched on the lights as she went, each area fascinating her more and more. What a lovely, homely, creative place. It was rather stuffed with knick-knacks and ornaments though, which weren't her style, and she wouldn't have imagined being Isabel's either.

Then she jumped in the air as she heard her phone ring. It was Isabel.

"Hi, you've just caught me as I've walked through your front door. I was about to phone you. Your flat is wonderful. I expected it to be in a block, austere, somehow, functional. It's not like that at all."

"Oh, so that's how you consider me then, austere and functional?" Isabel's voice, warm and eager, contradicted the words which she used.

"No, of course not, but give me a chance. I've been on the road for five hours. I'm just very happy to be here."

"Is it in a terrible mess? No-one has touched it since the accident. There is probably a mass of rotting food in the fridge. I do hope I haven't given you an impossible cleaning-up job to do."

"No, don't worry. I can just chuck everything out if I need to. Is your dustbin obvious outside?"

"Yes. Look, do what you can, but don't worry. You'll find clean bed linen in the chest at the end of the bed. It's a small flat. There's only one bedroom, a living room, kitchen and one bathroom. You can use my bed."

"It's wonderful. I love it. And you have a garden!"

"Yes, that's why we bought it, Carrie and me. If you turn on the switches by the French windows, the water fountain will start to play, and the lights will come on outside. That was her thing. She liked to create theatre wherever she went."

They chatted for a while, very happy to be in touch. Bryony really wanted to know what had happened after she had left, but understood, with Jane still present, Isabel was not likely to spill any beans.

"You will call me again tomorrow, after your meeting with Aiden, won't you?" Isabel sounded almost nervous about that.

"Yes, of course. Now I must sort out a few things here. And Isabel,"

"What?"

"I love your flat, and I miss you."

There was a slight pause, and then Bryony heard the reply she had been hoping for.

"Me too. Goodnight darling."

"'Night."

It brought a smile to her face. Then she took her courage in both hands and opened the fridge door to face what lurked inside.

Isabel's Healing

Chapter 19

Bryony spent most of Saturday morning cleaning and airing Isabel's flat. Thank goodness all the rotting food had been safely locked inside the fridge, not in an open trash can, otherwise the summer heat would have filled the place with a thousand flies. As it was, the mess which had once been fruit and veg, steak, eggs and butter had to be tipped into two bags before tying them up and dispensing them outside into the large bins by the gate.

She did this before she even ventured into Isabel's bedroom. The bed linen smelt fresh and clean, and she decided just to sleep in Isabel's sheets and take them away to wash after she finished her stay. Bryony could smell a faint scent of Isabel's favorite perfume on the pillows, the same as she wore in Wales, and it comforted her as she sought sleep. It took some time, as the two hours she'd slept on the train had dampened her need for oblivion, but eventually the pictures flying through her brain slowed and then turned to mist and she slept from midnight until seven.

In the early morning she flung open all the windows, dusted, polished and wiped down all the surfaces until the whole place sparkled. This gave Bryony a sense that she was repaying Isabel's offer of two nights' accommodation in what after all was one of the most expensive cities in the world, and also gave her a chance to learn something about the tastes and interests of her enigmatic mistress.

A large photographic portrait of Carrie dominated the living room, hanging above the Victorian fireplace. She was definitely a striking woman, and the photographer had caught an arresting tilt to her head as if she was asking a question. She was wearing a blue tunic, reminding Bryony of a Moroccan or Tunisian costume, but her skin was olive and she had very curly hair. Maybe she had some Ethiopian or Sudanese heritage mixed with Italian. Her eyes sparkled and she looked as though nothing would daunt her. Bryony could easily see how she'd make the ideal partner for Isabel.

Bryony gazed at the portrait for a long time, trying to communicate with the lost love of her love, asking her advice, maybe asking her for permission. Her spirit seemed omnipresent within the flat, and Bryony guessed that many of the artifacts and books had been hers.

On the bedroom walls hung classical drawings of naked female forms, and there was a bookcase full of explicit lesbian novels, in both English, French and Italian. There were also a range of books on psychology, and feminist theory. Bryony tried not to pry too much, and avoided opening any chests or the large fitted wardrobe which ran down the inside wall.

The living room was also piled high with books and sets of international political journals and magazines. Comfortable old sofas formed a trio of seating in front of the fire, and the mantelpiece was decorated with little clay figures from South American, African votive figures, and Indian brass work models of Hindu gods.

One low bookshelf contained at least a dozen books with Isabel's name on the spine, and Bryony vowed to spend part of the evening reading those, when she came back from her lunchtime meeting. Her cleaning operations kept her from dwelling on that too much, but she could feel her stomach beginning to clench with nerves as the time grew nearer.

At eleven she knew she should leave. Isabel's flat was restored to pristine and sweet smelling tranquility, so it would be a haven for her later. She made a short list of a few things she could buy for supper, changed into a cotton polo shirt and long shorts, and closed and locked the windows, drawing the curtains against the hot sun beating down outside.

As she locked up and left, she could see all the families and youngsters already playing ball and walking across Highbury Fields. They were enjoying the summer, and maybe, once her meeting with Aiden was over, she might do the same. At the moment though, she felt as though she was going to her doom.

It was really too hot a day for the Tube, so she hopped on the No 4 bus as it swung round the corner towards Islington, and rode it all the way south through the eastern part of central London until it crossed Waterloo bridge. The sights of London still stimulated and excited her, even after five years' studying in the city, and as she sat in the top of the bus, she enjoyed looking at all the tourists thronging the streets, and clustering round the most famous landmarks.

When she finally left the bus just by the South Bank cluster of concrete concert halls and art galleries, it was already nearly noon, and she hurried down the pavement alongside the Thames to where she and Aiden had agreed to meet. She could see him already there, sitting in the open-air wine bar and looking at the menu. He was already tanned, and his beard had grown since the end of term. He looked a hunk.

"Most girls would envy me," she thought, "but that's irrelevant. We have tried this relationship for two years now, and it's run its course. It doesn't have to be about Isabel. I can simply tell him I think there's no point carrying on, that I can't commit to a future without any passion."

"Hi, honey," Aiden said, smiling as soon as he saw her approach the table. He jumped up and hugged her fiercely, kissing her on the mouth possessively for all the world to see, and she had no choice but to let him, before gently pushing him back and taking a seat at the other side of the table.

"Sorry I'm a little late. I caught the bus, and you know how they are."

"No big deal. It's great to see you. How have you

been? Where did you sleep last night?" Bryony explained in as few words as possible, and steered the conversation back to him and what he had been doing for the past three weeks. They looked at the menu together and ordered their usual, a large Pizza Marguerite between them and a beer for him and a diet coke for her.

"How is life in the wood yard?"

"Not bad. I'm building up the muscles. It's pretty boring, but it pays the bills. How about you and your nursing gig? Is it all bedpans and bandages?"

"No, not now, my employer still has one leg in plaster, but we hope it will come off on Monday, and then she'll be working back to full mobility. Anyway, the work is interesting, and I get every Friday off to study."

"Great, more than I do. But I suppose you're on call all weekend. How did you get free to come down?"

"A friend is staying, so she said I could come down for the weekend to see you."

"Very magnanimous of her."

Bryony wanted to leave Isabel right out of the conversation she needed to have with Aiden, but she also would have loved to have talked to him about her undoubted crush, and tell him how wonderful Isabel was. These things were obviously mutually exclusive and one didn't blab to one's current boyfriend about the merits of one's new 'other' love interest.

There was no point in beating about the bush, so Bryony pushed her hair back and tightened her pony tail before saying, "Yes it was. But I needed to come down and have a talk to you in person. I've been giving a lot of thought to what you asked me in June, about commitment and everything. The thing is, Aiden, I don't think I can. In fact, I think we've maybe taken this relationship between us as far as it can go."

"What!? Where did this come from? Are you saying, you're actually dumping me?"

Aiden's face colored, whether with pure shock or embarrassment, she could not tell.

"We don't need to call it that. I'm very fond of you, but I

just don't see us together in the future, and you proposing, well, it brought it all to a head."

"But we've been good together. I love you; you know I love you, since we first met."

"And I love you, but not like that. I don't think I'm capable of being the partner you deserve. There are loads of girls out there who are, I'm sure."

"Oh, and you think that will make it all OK? That you can simply push me off into the highway and I'll pick up someone else, like a fucking taxi-cab."

Bryony could see the anger was growing in him. He hardly ever swore. Then his eyes narrowed, and a thought obviously passed through his mind.

"Is there someone else? Is this why you have suddenly lost interest? Who is it?"

Bryony cursed inwardly and tried very hard not to show on her face the sudden heat which ran up inside her body. The very mention of Isabel made her feel as though she might start to combust. Aiden saw her blush and guessed correctly that it wasn't simply that she was bored with him.

The waiter came with their pizza and placed it between them. Aiden attacked it with his knife and fork and angrily cut it in half. Rent asunder, like their relationship it seemed.

When Bryony said nothing, he continued, now with some more fuel to his fury. "Who is he? Who the hell has turned you against me in just four weeks? Or has this been going on much longer? Tell me, Bry, I deserve to know."

"There's no-one like that. There's no other guy. I just think I am maybe not suited to settling down and getting married. I want to travel. I might even join the army."

They began to eat the pizza, equally miserably, but they were both hungry. Aiden took a swig of his beer, and pulled a face.

"You don't want to join the army. They're just a

load of dykes, the women in the forces."

"That's not true! And how dare you talk like that. But what would it matter if they were?"

Bryony suddenly felt she should be a spokesperson for the entire LGBT community. Aiden looked up at her and whistled through his teeth.

"Where did that come from?"

"What?"

"Sticking up for the sisterhood. Are you insinuating what I think you are?"

"Don't be ridiculous, and stop talking like that. This is about you and me, and about how our relationship has satisfied you a hell of a lot more than it has me for the last two years." Bryony was losing her cool and the truth was beginning to slip out.

"Are you telling me our sex life hasn't done it for you? That's not how you've made out. I remember a lot of very hot sex. You came nearly every time."

Bryony looked round nervously, but their table was away from the others, and he couldn't be overheard. She decided to be honest, and blunt.

"No I didn't."

"What the hell?"

"I pretended. I've always pretended. It's second nature now because it keeps you happy, and it's not your fault. I know that now. It's no-one's fault, but that's the way it is. No heterosexual sex has ever given me an orgasm, alright?"

Aiden digested this bombshell, along with his next mouthful of pizza. Then he said, "So sex with men is useless, but I gather you've found enlightenment on the matter with a woman somewhere?"

Bryony looked hard at her plate, and said nothing. She didn't dare meet his eye.

"Are you telling me you think you're a frigging dyke?"

"Don't talk like that."

"I'll talk any way I want. God, Bry, you know how to bowl a googly. First of all you say you love me, but you don't love me, that you turn down my proposal and you want to break up. Then you let it slip that you've always hated sex with me and have faked every one of those orgasms I thought we were enjoying together. And now you as good as announce the fact that you're gay. Am I right, or is this not a summary of what you've just thrown in my face?"

"Hmm, well, yes, I suppose it's a good summary. Pretty accurate actually."

"So who is Miss Wonderful? Who has initiated you into the joys of penis-less intercourse?"

"Aiden, stop it."

"No, I won't. You go off to Wales a normal person and come back a complete stranger three weeks later. Is it someone you met at college up there?"

"No."

Bryony wished she could just run away, but she was trapped at the table, half way through her meal, and she did want to end this excruciating session as amicably as possible.

"Who is it?"

"I can't say, I just want you to know it wasn't anything you did or didn't do. None of this is really your fault. I know now I've always been gay. I just was too repressed and ignorant to see it before."

"If it isn't someone in the university, then it must be that woman you've been working for, the car accident victim. Oh, Jeese, what a fuck up! Didn't you say she's had multiple fractures and is stuck in a wheelchair, for God's sake?"

Bryony did not trust herself to reply at once. She swallowed her drink and tried to compose her answer carefully before she spoke.

"It's true, the person I have been caring for, is the person who has made me come to terms with my sexuality, but she didn't make any of this happen, neither did I. It's complicated, and I have no idea what will happen. I can only talk about how I feel."

"Stop talking to me like I'm your fucking therapist,

Bry. Does any of this make sense? God, what will I tell Mum and Dad? 'Sorry folks, the wedding's off. My girlfriend has discovered she's gay and is off making hay with a paraplegic old lady.'"

Bryony decided enough was enough.

"I don't think we'll achieve anything by carrying on talking like this. Here, this is my share for the lunch. I'm sorry it hasn't been what you wanted to hear, but it is what it is. I don't expect you to understand now, but hope you might eventually."

She put a ten pound note down on the table, and stood up. "I am sure we are best apart for the rest of the summer. I'll see you around next term, and I really, really hope you find someone who will be the right one for you, whom you can take home to your parents, who doesn't need to be such a faker as I have had to be."

Aiden said nothing, just scowled out across the river. He was obviously very upset, and part of her wanted to hug him, and tell him it would all be all right. But she wasn't the person to do that right now. Maybe they'd never speak again.

She picked up her bag and pushed her chair under the table and then walked quickly out of the bar area and away down the river frontage in the direction of Westminster. It was only once she had had turned the corner and had put five hundred yards between them, that she leaned over the railings and allowed the tears to come. It wasn't just the wreckage of her two year companionship and her friendship with Aiden which was sailing away on the muddy tide; it was her whole understanding of who she was, and what she needed from a lover.

For someone with no parental support, no siblings or even any wider family connections, Bryony realized breaking up with Aiden made her quite, quite alone. Alone, that was, except for Isabel, whom she had only just met, who was fragile both physically and emotionally, and who remained an enigmatic and powerful mystery. The way Aiden had put it, her whole change of direction seemed fraught with danger, and maybe she had behaved really stupidly.

She sat on a bench near the London Eye, and cried miserably for at least ten minutes. In the end, an elderly man walking his dog stopped by her and solemnly passed her a clean cotton handkerchief, the sort only his age-group kept in their pocket these days.

"Don't cry over him, dear," he said, very courteously. "He's probably not worth it."

Bryony managed a teary smile and took the handkerchief with a nod of thanks. She wondered if he, or anyone, could sympathize with her actual reasons for weeping. The old man and the dog walked away, while she blew her nose and tried to dry her tears.

The meeting with Aiden had been as painful as she had imagined it would be, but it was done now, and she could move on. Her mind turned back to Isabel, and she pulled out her phone. She could send her a text to say what had happened. It gave her just enough hope to stop crying. She could just imagine what Isabel would say If she could see her. She'd think she was a complete wimp.

"Stop crying, girl. I can't do with sniveling."

But sometimes, sniveling was exactly the right thing to do.

Isabel's Healing

Chapter 20

Isabel's response to Bryony's short text message was not as harsh as she imagined. She read between the two lines, and immediately called her.

"Hello, sweetie, don't cry. Don't cry Bryony girl, it will all be all right."

"I...I just didn't want to upset him, or myself. But it wasn't so good. I had to tell him straight."

"Yes, you did. Sometimes men need to know. You're not on this planet to make them always feel good, especially when they are so insensitive they never notice how you feel. We do have to hurt the people we love sometimes. It's inevitable. But it saves time if we're honest."

"Did you ever have to hurt people, tell them you didn't love them enough to carry on?"

"Oh, I am a master of it. Jane will tell you I'm a heartbreaker. She as good as told me I'm a cold bitch. But I'm learning not to take love for granted. Look here; do you want to come home tonight? I'll pay for you to change your train ticket if you need to?"

Bryony liked the way Isabel called their little cottage 'home', but turned down the offer.

"No, I will stay on tonight in your lovely flat, and work on my dissertation. I'm bringing the laundry back to Wales with me to do. I'll also water all your pots outside if you like. They look very thirsty. It's super-hot down here in London."

"Do you like the flat? So much of the stuff there belongs to Carrie, and I haven't had the heart to sort anything else since she died."

"I think it's a beautiful flat." Bryony almost wanted to offer to help Isabel sort out Carrie's many possessions, even the many clothes she had seen, which she could tell belonged to her, as they were for a taller woman than Isabel, but she didn't dare. She might only be in Isabel's life for the summer. She had no rights over her beyond that, and didn't want to jinx their current relationship.

"Where are you now?"

"Walking across Westminster Bridge. I've done a lot of walking. What have you and Jane done today, anything nice?"

"We have come to lunch on the coast at Barmouth. She's a restless soul and doesn't like just sitting in the cottage. She's now finishing a large portion of haddock and chips, while I'm outside, sitting on a bench in the sunshine."

"And you? I hope you had some fish and chips. The fattening up of Isabel project continues, you know, as soon as I return."

Isabel laughed. "Don't worry. All of our projects can resume when you return. Don't forget we have another trip to the hospital on Monday."

"Of course not."

"Good, and you've stopped crying now?"

"Yes, Isabel. How did you know I was?"

"Your text had tear-stains on it. Figuratively speaking. So, see you Sunday afternoon?"

"Yes,"

Bye for now, darling."

"Bye, Isabel."

Bryony smiled as she put away her phone. Isabel was a woman in a thousand, and for now at least, she belonged to her. She had called her 'Darling.' That was twice now.

On the way home to Isabel's flat Bryony bought a bag of fresh peaches, and when she let herself back in through the door, she immediately went outside into the beautiful little garden and turned on the water pump. The sound of the trickling fountain immediately refreshed her battered heart, and she sat on the bench to enjoy one or two peaches which she'd washed quickly under the kitchen tap.

The sunlight shone through the leaves of the old Plum tree by the back wall, and the garden was full of the scent of nicotiana and phlox flowers. It was a real oasis in the city and Bryony breathed in its perfumes and the other assaults on her senses. She watered all the pots, and then the borders, and almost sensed how grateful the flowers were.

But work drew her back inside, and she curled up on Isabel's sofa with her laptop on her knee. She began to plot out her dissertation with all the focus of a real scientist. It didn't matter that she was crazy about the subject of her study; she could still do a professional job.

***

At five o clock the following afternoon. Bryony was driving up their hill in Wales, having retrieved the Berlingo from an unofficial long-stay car-park near the station in Machynlleth. As she drove through the cottage gateway, she saw Jane's Rav4 had disappeared, so she and Isabel would be alone once more. She felt undisguised happiness, but was worried that Isabel had been alone for a while and might need help.

She found her sitting on the sofa, with her feet up, and a copy of the Economist in her hand.

"Hi, I heard the car."

She went forward and took Isabel's outstretched hand.

"Are you very tired from all the train travel?"

"Yes, a little. But it's so good to see you. How long ago did Jane leave?"

"After lunch. It's been wonderful, just being alone for a few hours."

"I'm sorry to spoil that."

"Do not be foolish. It's different with you. I have been waiting for you to come back to me."

"I brought you your post. I'll fetch you a letter

opener, and you can go through it all while I fix us some tea if you like."

Isabel took the thick pile of letters and placed them beside herself, but then grasped Bryony's hand and pulled her down until she was forced to kneel on the floor beside her. She put her arms round Isabel's shoulders, and leaned in for the offered embrace. Isabel took her face in one hand and cupped her cheek, then kissed her passionately on the mouth.

"You have been much missed," Isabel said quietly. "I am so happy to have you back here in one piece. Would you like to shower away all the dust and dirt from the journey, and then let's just go to bed? I don't really feel hungry for anything else. Besides, I've eaten like a pig all weekend. I could do with working some of it off."

Bryony's eyes widened, and she nodded. It sounded a wonderful idea.

"I'll shower now. I'll be quick." She began to pull off her shirt as she went into the bathroom, and as she was under the shower, she could hear the tap of Isabel's crutches moving into the bedroom. By the time she emerged, wrapped in a bath-sheet, Isabel was laying back on the pillows, her top half already naked and her slacks unbuttoned.

She looked so beautiful, Bryony's breath caught in her throat, and she almost jumped up onto the bed next to her. Isabel chuckled and lifted her breasts, deliberately teasing Bryony with the hardness of her pink nipples.

Bryony met the challenge by gently kissing each one in turn, and then she ran her fingers down between them as far as Isabel's waist.

"Here, let me help," she whispered, and moving down, efficiently removed Isabel's trousers. "This could be the last day we have to worry about this pot," she said, as she had to negotiate the trousers round the plaster cast still on her right leg.

"Can you lift your butt? Good, thanks," and she had stripped off Isabel's underwear as well. The panties were flung across the room.

"We can call this a goodbye party to the plaster casts,"

Isabel murmured, "or a hello party after your terribly long absence."

"Was it too long?"

"Totally. You have three days care and attention to make up for now."

"So what would you like me to do for you?"

"Take your towel off for starters."

Bryony complied. Her hair was still a little damp where the shower had caught it, but her flesh was warm and rosy pink, and her eyes were almost glazed with arousal.

"Now lie here, next to me, and just let me love you."

"I can...just about...manage that," and Bryony melted under Isabel's kisses.

Much later, after the summer sun had finally set behind them over the hill, and she had slept in Isabel's arms for a good hour, recovering from yet another scarily powerful orgasm, she enjoyed the resulting cuddle, with Isabel's arms tightly round her, possessively pinning her down in the bed.

"Why is it so easy with you?" murmured the older woman. "You're so accommodating to what I need, such an unselfish lover."

"I don't really know how to do it differently. You give me everything I need as well, so I just love you back. I adore you. You are so beautiful, and scary and funny. I want this to never end."

"Well, turn over, and open your legs again, and it may not."

"Not finished yet, Isabel?"

Isabel growled. "Hardly started."

She put her hand down between Bryony's rounded buttocks and run her finger all down her slit from front to back. It was still so wet, her hand was almost slipping and she felt Bryony bucking under her.

"Tonight I am going to show you what the big girls do," she said and slid down the bed.

"Up on your hands and knees!"

Bryony complied and Isabel wriggled down underneath her, then she pulled her down over her mouth so that Bryony's whole sexual area was totally at her disposal. Bryony tried to take the weight on her knees, as Isabel sucked and almost ate her out, but all she remembered afterwards was hearing herself moan, then giggle, as some vicious tickling was involved, then start to scream.

Their sex games grew rougher as Isabel herself began to come and Bryony writhed and tried to twist herself away from the agony and the ecstasy of Isabel's wicked tongue. Somehow they were flipped over, so that Isabel was on top again, and she made the most of it. Bryony started to fuck her, with the heel of her hand on her clit, and two, maybe three fingers deep inside her. They were as deeply attached as they could be, and when Isabel exploded into a climax, Bryony thought she might die with excitement. Wow, if this was how gay women made love, she sorely regretted leaving it so long before she came out.

After Isabel recovered, her hand itched and she gave in to the urge to spank by walloping Bryony on her deliciously rounded ass, as she had the other evening.

"Ow! You sadist! You really like doing that, don't you?"

Isabel smiled. "Of course. I have to keep you under control. And you like it too, don't you? Tell me the truth."

Bryony was shy, and buried her head in the pillow. She nodded her head up and down.

"I'm ashamed to say I do. It's one of my fantasies, being spanked by you. It turns me on dreadfully."

"Then we're both going to be happy. Don't be ashamed. Sex is meant to be fun. Fantasies are all part of it, and you know I'll never hurt you, well not enough to make you cry seriously!"

"Tell me one of your fantasies then, with me."

Isabel nestled Bryony's head against her shoulder, and fondled her hair.

"Well, it might involve a little uniform of some sort, just a bit too tight, with no underwear, and a little bit of light discipline. You might need tying up, and blindfolding, and then you would have to convince me to release you, but you could only use your mouth."

"I can see you have given this some thought."

"Not really, darling. I have some way to go before it is properly polished up. You can contribute your own ideas if you like..."

"Isabel, Bel, I think I'm in love with you. I would do anything for you."

"Good, that's how we sadists like it."

"Is there anything you need before we go to sleep?"

Isabel sighed. "Yes, I need a pee. Help me to the bathroom, will you, darling?"

Bryony laughed and heaved herself out of bed. She held out her hand and pulled Isabel to her one good foot. Maybe this would be the last time she'd need to do it, but she sincerely hoped it wouldn't be the last time Isabel would let her share her bed. They fitted together like a pair of spoons.

Isabel's Healing

Chapter 21

Sleeping with Isabel was glorious, but one of its best attributes was how it allowed Bryony to lie and watch her face in sleep against the crisp cotton pillowcase with its faint scent of lavender. Isabel had beautiful bone structure and luxuriant eyelashes, almost like a small child's, even though she was over forty. Her hair waved round her head and flicked up in little curls in front of her ears, and she slept very tidily, hardly breathing and certainly not snoring.

Bryony observed her for a full five minutes without moving on Monday morning, and just enjoyed the view, until she felt Isabel's hand grip her wrist, and a voice growled, "Whadyalookingat?"

"How do you know I am looking? Your eyes are shut."

"Magic powers and I can feel your breath."

"Oh, well. You are right. I am just enjoying gazing upon your beautiful face, oh, my Queen. But now I am going to get up and start breakfast, which I insist you eat this time. We need to be away within the hour."

"Bossy boots."

The eyes on the pillow remained closed, but Isabel released her hand. Bryony rewarded her with a little kiss on her nose, and slipped out of the bed. She went through to her room and pulled on a dress, a sleeveless linen shift which was long enough to protect her thighs from the hot plastic of the car seats. It was going to be another scorcher, and they once again had a four hour round-trip ahead of them, especially if the traffic was bad.

She looked at the calendar hanging in the kitchen.

Today was a red-letter day in Isabel's recovery, and she just hoped and prayed all would go well and the final plaster cast could come off with no complications.

She made tea for them both, and then helped Isabel dress. There was a mark, definitely like a hickey on her collarbone, for which she realized she was responsible, so she encouraged her into a high-necked tunic, over the balloon pants again. Isabel was bouncing with energy and excitement.

"Just think, in a few weeks I'll be able to drive. I need to get my nerve back, after the accident, and you can help me. We can go up into the hills, on those quiet back lanes."

For now though, she willingly let Bryony take the wheel as always, and they made it to Chester in record time, especially now that Bryony knew the route so well, including a secret detour which cut off five miles round Oswestry.

This morning Claire had arranged to meet them briefly at the hospital, and was very pleased to see Isabel's happy face, rounded cheeks and bright eyes. If she didn't know better, she'd say she was a woman in love. Her sister-in-law and the young medical student did not speak much to each other, but they seemed still to be in tune, and Bryony was as efficient and helpful as always. While they waited for Isabel's name to be called, Claire explained the reason for her wanting to meet them at the hospital.

"I'm sorry I have to go out to lunch today so I won't be able to see you later, but I needed to float an idea with you. You're now into your third week in Wales, and I'm so happy that your recovery is well on track. But we need to plan ahead.

"Ted and I want you to know that we think you should come and stay with us at least for the months of September and October, maybe up to Christmas. Bryony will be gone back in college by then, of course, and we feel it would be better for you still to have some support. We don't think you can manage in London alone just yet."

Bryony and Isabel both stared at her in silence. Was it really only five or six weeks away, the end of their partnership? In Isabel's mind, the summer was stretching ahead into some endless misty shimmer of happy sex and book writing. She had not remembered it could be counted in just a few more weeks. Bryony, who well knew how insecure her role was in Isabel's life, was simply plunged into a premature sense of loss. Claire somehow had taken half the joy out of the day.

Isabel said, "Thanks Claire, but let's not worry about the autumn just yet. I'm living from day to day at the moment. There! I think they've called my name. Let's go, Bryony. Will you come in with me, please?"

"But you will think about it, won't you?" Claire seemed anxious to tie up her life as firmly as possible, which Isabel automatically rebelled against.

"Of course, I'll think about it. It's a kind offer. Bye for now."

Bryony passed over the crutches and followed Isabel through the inner clinic door to see her doctors. She nodded goodbye to Claire as she went, but couldn't bring herself to smile at the bearer of such bad news. She realized that from this day on, she and Isabel had somehow to define their relationship and work out what, if anything it meant.

Maybe it was simply part of the summer project. Maybe she and Isabel would part company and never see each other again? If that was to be the case, then she vowed not to waste a single second of their time together.

The doctor who saw them this time was a different, older consultant from Sri Lanka. He pronounced the need to get the cast off Isabel's leg, and then they would x-ray it again to see the status of the healing. When the little circular saw was grinding through the plaster, Isabel gripped Bryony's hand and looked away.

For some reason she felt more nervous about this procedure than she had about having both her arm casts cut off. Then she had been so desperate to be released that it had superseded everything else, but now she could only think what might happen if her shattered leg bones hadn't fused properly. Supposing she was left with a bad limp, or worse, might still have to have her foot amputated?

However, her leg, when it emerged, very pale and thin, did look remarkably like a normal leg, and seemed straight. The scar from the operation to repair and set the bones ran right down the outside of her knee into her calf, but the stitches had dissolved naturally and what had been an ugly gash was now just a fine red line. Modern medicine had obviously done a really good job on her behalf.

Bryony also observed the scar with a semi-professional eye.

"It looks good Isabel. It's healed well."

The nurses helped Isabel into a hospital wheelchair and Bryony pushed her down to the x-ray department, while Isabel held their bags and her referral paper. When the x-ray was complete it was sent by computer back up to the fracture clinic, and the women retraced the journey back up in the lift to hear the verdict.

"You're lucky, or maybe just a great natural healer," said the doctor, staring at the x-rays on his screen. "You will need to take things very gently, and not put your full weight on it for at least another week, but I think your leg will be fine and you'll make a full recovery. Your family, or is this your friend? – She'll have to keep a close watch on you, but I see you're in good hands. How have your arms been? I read you had the casts removed from them last week. Any serious pain?"

"No, not serious. I've been doing a little light exercise. And resting for much of the time."

"And the ribs?"

"They are fine, just a twinge or two when I cough or laugh."

"Yes, avoid the comedy hour for a while, and don't catch a summer cold. Some people break their ribs from a bad cough."

"I try to avoid crowds. Bryony here, she looks after me."

Isabel took Bryony's hand and held it. She didn't let go.

The doctor's eyes crinkled at the corners and he smiled at them both.

"I see. Well Dr Bridgford, I think I can sign you off. If you feel any serious pain, make an appointment. Otherwise, follow the exercise plan, and carry on with what you are doing. Whatever your regime has been, it obviously works."

They said goodbye to him and the other staff, and made their escape down the corridor. After a few yards Bryony pulled something from her bag and waved it at Isabel who was still hopping on her crutches like a pirate.

"What's that?"

"Your other sandal! Here let me put it on for you."

She knelt down and fastened the shoe round Isabel's slim foot, and because no-one was looking, lifted it up slightly and dropped a kiss on her toes.

"There you are, the kissing of feet, the ultimate demonstration of undying fealty."

"Come on silly girl. I want to show you how I can walk."

"Use the crutches to take most of your weight though."

"OK."

Isabel put both feet to the floor and using the crutches as an aid, walked steadily towards the exit.

"You did it! You are now officially back on your feet. This is all going in the log when we get home."

"Yes, sweetie, let's go home. It's been four days since we worked on the book! We have so much to do!"

***

Isabel stayed awake this time on the journey back up into the Welsh hills and was very animated. She told Bryony a few stories from her years with Carrie, and could actually mention her name on several occasions without her eyes filling with tears. She seemed to be slowly coming out of her grief, and she felt strong enough to share with Bryony something of the agony and the ecstasy of loving Carrie, and what a rollercoaster their life together had been.

"Despite all the rows, I truly thought we'd be partners for life, I mean a long life until we grew old together. I never expected she'd be taken so soon, and so suddenly. I suppose I've been in shock ever since, now I think about it."

"Who was there for you? Who did you have to share it with, all the grief?"

"No-one close enough to understand. Jane was supportive, but she had never really understood how Carrie and I worked as a couple. I was the crazy unstable one in Jane's life. She couldn't imagine I could live with someone who was even more unpredictable.

"Ted and Claire as well, they knew what she meant to me, but they had a kind of myopic view of gay relationships. They can't see that a gay marriage can be identical to a straight one, more intense sometimes, because of the social pressures against gay relationships lasting.

"The people at work were all shocked when it happened, and respectful. My colleagues carried me really, at least for the first six months when I was quite out of it, but no-one really understood. I think I've been just lonely all this time, until you popped up. I think you get me, and you are a good listener. I feel I could tell you anything."

"Isabel, that's a lovely thing to hear. I feel the same way about you, if I'm allowed to say it. So were you and Carrie planning to marry?"

"Yes, she'd proposed, up a mountain in Ethiopia actually. Her mother is Ethiopian and we were there making a film together. Anyway, I accepted, after a lot of heart-searching. We were planning a big bash, but work got in the way, and we never managed to fix the date before she died. So now I will just have to die an old maid!"

Bryony squashed a tiny fantasy which had been starting to throw out a bud or two in her heart, and laughed back at Isabel.

"Anyone less like an old maid I've yet to meet." She sought for something to change the mood and decided to pull into the filling station ahead of them.

"I need to fill up the car. Look, they have a café attached. Can we stop for lunch?"

"Only if you let me walk up the steps by myself. Here, use my card for the petrol. I'll go on in and order us some food."

Isabel obviously reveled in the fact that she could leave the car and walk in a balanced manner across the forecourt and up the three steps into the little Welsh tearoom. She used her crutches, but Bryony could see how they'd be thrown in the corner before the week was out. When she joined her Isabel had ordered salads for them both, tea and water.

They ate, and then she said, "Go over and choose yourself a cake for dessert. I'll share it with you."

Bryony came back with a large slice of chocolate cake and two forks, and they consumed it together.

"This is to celebrate," said Isabel.

"What?"

"Goodbye to the hospital! I never want to set foot in one again."

"Well, good for you, but I am looking forward to a working life spent inside one, so poor me."

"You will be a wonderful doctor, Bryony. I can see you in a year's time in your white coat, fully qualified. You have a fantastic career ahead of you. You'll go far. You have real talent, I can tell. Nothing should be allowed to hold you back."

Bryony had been about to mention Claire's plan for Bel to live in Chester for the autumn months, so far from London, so far from her. But she just didn't dare. She didn't want to hear the bad news that she could predict would come from Isabel's mouth.

"Well, let's ask for the bill and get away. As you say, we need to concentrate on the book and only the book from now on."

So they did, Isabel walked back to the car, carefully putting one foot in front of the other, and Bryony drove them home.

***

In so many ways, the next few weeks fulfilled Isabel's dreams about the summer. The weather held, and the book developed. They worked on it for four hours every morning, from eight to twelve. Then Bryony fixed lunch, while Isabel read over her typed drafts from the morning and they edited what they had done.

From then on, they took the rest of the day off. Isabel followed Bryony's exercise regime obediently some days, and under duress on others. At times Bryony had to chase her round the living room with the bean can weights, and bribe her with kisses to knuckle down and complete the physio program, but before long she was developing real muscle tone. She was also putting on weight, ounce by ounce until Bryony could no longer count her ribs or feel her hip bones jutting out.

Once a week they went shopping, usually on Wednesday when Machynlleth had a street market, but otherwise they were alone, which was exactly as they liked it. Meals without meat were a breeze, and Bryony bulked up Isabel's diet with as much full-fat milk and carbs as she dared.

The cottage was so isolated; no-one ever passed the door. Not even the postman called, but left any circulars or letters in a box at the corner of the lane below. So because of this, after a couple of weeks they started to sunbathe naked in the garden in the warm afternoons, lying together on a blanket on the small stretch of lawn which had grown tall in the month they had been together.

Isabel had suggested the nude frolicking outside, and Bryony had not had any will to refuse. Now she was outside, lying naked on the rug and letting the sun warm her whole body, she realized just how liberating a sensation it was.

"You know, there is something about you, which has done something profound to me this summer, Isabel," she said, one afternoon as they lay together under the sky. "You've brought me up, somehow, made me mature. You've educated me about life, about possibilities. My background was so restricted, so provincial. I thought I was being very daring, going to university, training to be a doctor, but my teachers and lecturers really just pushed me through, because I have a good memory for facts and figures. It hasn't stretched me like you have. You've opened up the world to me, and you've opened me up as well. I'll never be able to thank you enough."

"You have a way with words, darling. Thank you. I'm supposed to be the writer, but I can never, ever express what I owe to you in bringing me back to health. You are a complete joy."

Bryony leaned on one elbow and picked a daisy to push behind Isabel's ear.

"Isn't there a passage in Lady Chatterley's lover about them playing around with daisies?" she asked as she picked another flower head and positioned it over Isabel's tummy button, and then another three to rest over her neat little patch of pubic hair.

Isabel smiled and flung her arms wide. "Lawrence understood about sexual desire. His lesbian descriptions in The Rainbow was the first description of gay women's sex I ever read as a girl," she said, "But I think we could teach him or anyone a thing or two about desire."

Bryony placed two more daisies on Isabel's breasts, and another in each of her open arm pits. "Now you are dressed as a votive offering to the gods. My queen."

"Am I to be sacrificed out here, in broad daylight?"

"Only the birds can see us and maybe the people in the International Space Station if it happened to pass by overhead. It goes round the world every hour and a half."

"But perhaps not over North Wales. Bryony..."

"Yes?"

"Please make love to me."

"Yes, Isabel."

Isabel's Healing

Chapter 22

Much later, when they were decently dressed and curled up together on the sofa after supper, Bryony talked about her decision not to return to Aberystwyth. They had missed two Fridays already, because she could see how much Isabel needed her with her to finish the book, and she really didn't want to put herself in danger from Miss Melanie from Mississippi or wherever. Besides, every day was precious while Isabel and she were together.

"I can finish the dissertation from personal observation. I have more than enough material, no need to disappear on Fridays."

"But I worry about you overworking. We should both take Fridays off in that case. There is somewhere I've been reading about, somewhere I want us to see while we're in this part of the country."

"Hmm?"

"The shrine of Saint Melangell. It's a very ancient druidic site with a circle of yew trees in a churchyard. The trees are more than two thousand years old, so they pre-date the time of Christ, let alone when Christianity came to Wales. The church there now is a place of pilgrimage, but I think it sounds magical. It's all about re-birth, as the yew trees constantly regenerate themselves. I want us to go."

"How far?"

"Oh, less than an hour away. Will you drive us there, on Friday this week?"

"Sure. Of course."

***

The trip to the shrine was on a shimmering, hot day. The month had now slipped over to August, and the trees above their heads were in full leaf with a canopy above the car as they drove down lanes, dappled in sun and shadows. The Church was remote, and the lane to it wound back and forth through a long valley. They seemed to be travelling back in time as well as through contemporary Wales.

"Tell me about the legend of St Melangell," said Bryony as she navigated the single track road. Isabel read from her little guide book.

"She was meant to be an early Celtic virgin princess who shielded a hare from the hunter who was about to kill it."

"Easy way to be made a Saint, especially for a woman. I read somewhere there are ten times as many male saints as female? There seems a little bias going on there. Do you suppose it'll be all men as well in heaven?"

"I can't see us wanting to go to the traditional idea of heaven, can you, in that case, or in any way? Actually there is a strong argument that the Christian version is a transplant from the much older Druidic tradition of the Moon Goddess, who had a hare as her symbol. It's amazing all the different layers which make up our history as a human race. Everything is a synthesis. That's what makes history so fascinating, real history I mean, not just the political shouting match which makes the headlines."

"The hidden histories of the hunted, as opposed to the propaganda written up by the hunters?"

"Precisely."

When they arrived at the shrine however, their chat about history and syncretism faded away as they were drawn into the deep 'thickness' of the place, hidden away in the green valley. For hundreds, thousands of years, people had been coming here on pilgrimage, to worship, to touch an Immanence, and to feel the wonder of the ancient trees.

"These are meant to be some of the oldest trees in the British Isles." Isabel stepped inside one of the massive yew trees and placed her hands against the hollowed out trunk. She could somehow feel its life communicating to her through the gnarled wood.

"Come, and join me. Feel it too."

Bryony stood beside her. The tree could comfortably house them both, and they touched the wood.

"I can't believe this place is so quiet, so unprotected."

"Maybe its own spirits protect it."

The red berries from the yew trees fell all around. There were so many trees, and all looked to be thriving. The size of their trunks and their huge overhanging branches confirmed their age.

Isabel and Bryony entered the church and read the copious displays on the walls. It was the oldest Romanesque church in the whole of the United Kingdom, maybe in all of northern Europe, and like the church yard it too had a spirit of peace and regeneration. But the feeling was more powerful outside than in. They spent an hour there and left an offering. Then they looked round the churchyard. Some of the tombs had oak leaves on them. Were druidic beliefs still prevalent in the area?

Isabel thought of Carrie, and her rebellious spirit against both the Catholic faith of her Italian father, and the Coptic tradition of her Ethiopian mother. Where was Carrie now? Was she causing positive trouble somewhere else in the universe, or did she just live on in Isabel's memory?

If the evidence was true, then this little church and the grove of yew-trees went back just as far as both those traditions, and for the trees, way beyond. The very length of the time-line somehow comforted her, and reinforced her determination to fight against climate change deniers with all the strength in her.

Maybe, as well as what they owed to future children, her generation owed it to those people in the past as well, who had planted trees, and built churches, had grown crops and raised children in the hope of a better future, not a worse one. It made her very thoughtful.

Bryony took her arm and walked with her back to the car.

"Are you OK?"

"Yes, just thinking."

"It's a wonderful place. I'm so pleased we found it. Thanks for suggesting it."

"It strengthens one, doesn't it, thinking it's not just our little story we need to tell, but the much wider one, of all the life here on earth, all the history. It's so strong and yet so fragile."

"Like the hare hidden under St Melangell's cloak?"

"Yes. That's a powerful symbol, whoever first thought it up. They say you can see a hare or a rabbit on the moon, that's probably where the connections started."

"I like hares. There used to be lots in Derbyshire where I grew up."

"Derbyshire? There's so much about you I have yet to learn."

"Hmm. And you, for me too."

Bryony's final comment was almost under her breath, as she opened the door and helped Isabel back into her seat. Acting as her career was second nature, even though she was getting stronger every day. She still felt she had only explored the top inch of Isabel's depths, and their time together was already flying by.

Bryony wondered how it would end, whether she would ever have the courage to ask Isabel for more, more time, more commitment, and more wonderful sex. But she simply lacked the courage. She couldn't bear to think of the probable answer. It would all be so painful; she would postpone raising it as long as she could, right up to the very last moment.

Chapter 23

The day visiting St Melangell's shrine marked the centre point of their summer together, and the following weeks just saw Isabel blossom even more and regain all her healthy muscles, and flexibility. She began to practice yoga as she'd done it for years, and showed Bryony how to move from one pose to another. She was pleased to have something she could offer back to the girl who had cared for her so well and given her so much therapy.

The only reason Isabel wasn't as gloomy about their personal future as Bryony was that she simply refused to think beyond the immediate. It had taken her so many months of regret, and a lake full of shed tears to stop living in the past, and her academic writing and current book's subject took so much of her mental energy about the future of the planet, that she had no mental resources left to dwell on anything. All she knew was how good the present felt with Bryony, on her arm, or in her bed.

She assumed she'd be a total disaster for Bryony long term, that the girl was far too young and too talented to be tied down to someone eighteen years her senior, and pushing a wheelbarrow of experiences and failed relationships. She was simply grateful that someone so beautiful, so kind, so clever, and so sane should choose to like her enough to have sex with her.

Oh and also do all their housekeeping, act as her nurse and physiotherapist and even type up her book! She didn't dare ask for any more.

One thing she did want to do for Bryony was to celebrate her birthday which must be coming along soon. She waited until the girl was in the shower one evening, and then quickly opened her wallet to search for her driving license. It showed Bryony's date of birth, August 16th, and she popped it back and closed the wallet, before Bryony emerged from the shower. It was the Friday of the following week. They must definitely do something special.

Bryony walked across the room, a towel round her body and another round her hair, looking as gorgeous as ever.

"Here, why don't you let me dry it for you? Holding the dryer will be good for my arm muscles."

Bryony smiled in agreement and went to fetch the hair dryer, then she sat at Isabel's feet in front of the sofa, and let the older woman rub her head and put the dryer onto full power, holding it in one hand, while she let the blonde hair spill out and tumble down through the fingers of her other hand. It was so wonderful to have the ability to do it again.

"I'm thinking of cutting my hair off, to make it a bit butchier, what do you think?"

Isabel reverted to her original stance of ice-queen.

"Don't you dare! It's lovely hair. I would be seriously displeased if you cut off even an inch. In fact I think I might measure it to make sure you don't sneak any of it off."

"Or what about a tattoo? Wouldn't that be a good thing to show I've come out?"

"Now you're being ridiculous. If you want to suffer needless pain, I can provide that for you without ruining your skin for life."

She gave Bryony's hair a sharp little tug to show she meant business.

"Ow! Oh very well. If you put it like that."

Isabel continued for a few more seconds and then declared Bryony's hair was dry. But having her sit at her feet, her naked shoulders within reach of her mouth was more than she could resist.

She put down the hair dryer, and then with both hands flipped away Bryony's bath towel and grabbed both her breasts from behind. When Bryony's head flew up and back in surprised response, Isabel bent over her and took her mouth in her own, twisting the girl's body round. Her intention had been to pull Bryony up onto her lap, but instead she found herself brought down to the floor, so they were both lying on the hearth-rug, laughing.

"It's a bit grubby down here. I haven't vacuumed for a day or two. Let's go to bed", said Bryony.

"All right. I wouldn't want to get your nice clean hair all dusty again. But as for your stupid ideas on tattooing, I think some serious punishment is needed. Come on!"

She literally pushed Bryony through the bedroom door, and slammed it shut. Bryony was naked now, and vulnerable. Her eyes shone and she trembled slightly.

"You can start by doing your handmaid thing, and undress me. I need full freedom of movement for what I plan for you."

"Yes, Isabel."

She went over to Isabel and slowly undid the buttons running up her shirt-waist dress. Then she lifted it up, as she had done so many times before, and pulled it away from Isabel's shoulders. But this wasn't a caregiver's move. Bryony's eyes were as bright and predatorily as Isabel's ever were.

She stared into her eyes and stood very close, then leaned behind her and unclipped the light sports bra she had started to wear.

Isabel's breasts gleamed in the evening light. The nipples were beautiful tight rosebuds as they tightened automatically whenever Bryony gazed on them. She ran a finger down each breast, meditatively gazing at them as they quivered.

"Stop that! You don't do anything unless I tell you. You're in real trouble tonight, Bryony. Tattoos indeed!"

There was a moment's silence, while they enjoyed the tension. Then Isabel pointed to the floor.

"Kneel! You can take off the rest of my clothes from there."

Bryony obeyed and knelt directly in front of Isabel, who could now stand as straight and as strong as anyone.

She was only wearing a light waist slip and silk panties, so Bryony's task was not exactly arduous. She tugged down the slip until it fell to the floor, and then delicately lifted each of Isabel's feet in turn to step her out of it.

Then she put her hands up behind Isabel and pulled her panties off over her backside, just until they rolled under the buttocks. She then put her head against the front of the panties and took the front in her teeth. When they dropped forward an inch, she cheekily nipped Isabel's mound of Venus and then slipped her finger just inside, rubbing her erect clitoris and forcing her hand past it, further inside the folds. If she was going to get spanked, she might as well make it worth Isabel's while. Isabel was soaking wet.

Isabel groaned, but refused to submit. She pulled Bryony's hand away, and held it against her underwear. "Just take them off!"

Bryony pulled down the panties completely and was delighted to see how drenched they were. She could tell that Isabel was more than ready. But Isabel had regained the upper hand now and was determined to use her power.

"Now lean over the bed and put your butt in the air. Higher! I'm going to have to teach you a little lesson about bad ideas. Where did you say you thought you'd like a tattoo?"

"I didn't, but how about on the left cheek?"

"Oh, let me see, How about here?"

Isabel's first stinging slap was light enough, but Bryony still jumped in the air, and could feel the mark of her fingers across her bottom.

"It would take a lot more pain than that if you got tattooed. What a silly girl you are."

And the hand came again, harder this time, and the pain spread a little further. Bryony felt the arousal go straight through her. This was incredible.

"Maybe the right side would be a better choice," she whispered.

"You want to find out?"

Isabel actually came forward now and took a

proprietorial grasp of Bryony's long hair which she wound round one hand. Holding her tightly she pulled her other one back and then gave an almighty slap, dead centre on Bryony's right buttock.

Bryony squealed, which earned her another hard slap, followed by three more.

"This is hurting me more than it's hurting you." Isabel felt she wasn't lying, as she shook out her tingling hand. She looked at the red flush across Bryony's buttocks, and thought she had administered enough pain for now. Bryony was still pinned down by her hair and bent over the bed.

"Now repeat after me, "Darling Isabel, I promise I will never get tattooed.""

"Darling Isabel, I promise I will..."

There was a pregnant pause and so Isabel just gently stroked a finger right across her bottom, warning of more punishment.

Bryony felt herself almost flood with so much juice that she didn't dare make things any more intense. "I promise I will never get tattooed."

"Good. Now get into the bed and wait for me. I'll go and lock up tonight."

Isabel walked swiftly out of the room and Bryony heard the key turning in the main door. Not that they needed to lock the door, but it had become a little ritual. She went to lie on the double bed, face down because her bottom really felt on fire, but she was as sexually aroused as she could stand, and she knew Isabel felt the same.

As soon as Isabel returned to the bed, Bryony grabbed her lover by the waist and pulled her towards her like a wild thing. But she felt Isabel flip her over and then dive straight south towards the end of the bed.

"Open for me!" Isabel was still in dominant mode, kissing her inner thighs and pulling her knees apart. She bucked her hips up so that the feathery touch of Isabel's lips could connect with her vagina and remove the ache which ran there from top to bottom. Isabel now lay upside down on top of her, her beautiful ass right in front of her eyes, so she followed suit and pulled Isabel's legs apart and buried her head underneath her, licking her out. They were near enough the same height to make it work beautifully.

So Bryony learned something else which gay women could enjoy in bed and without the need for any toys at all. She didn't need to dream of orgasms any more. Her employer provided them as a benefit in kind, and the number 69 would never just stand for the local bus route anymore.

***

After their first successful 'games night', Bryony kept teasing Isabel to 'punish' her again, but she seemed unwilling for some reason, and pushed them back onto the book schedule and the need to concentrate on work whenever Bryony plagued her or tried to lure her into the bedroom.

The book was going well, they were well ahead of Isabel's schedule, and she knew Isabel was due to have a period again, so maybe that was the reason, but Isabel's sexual fire had definitely cooled down. It bugged Bryony and she tried to figure out what she could do. Then she remembered Isabel's little fantasy, the one she had said she was still 'polishing up'.

On a trip to town for grocery shopping, she saw a sign in the local clothes shop, reminding customers of the need to stock up with school uniforms for their children before the end of August. Discounts were available on all the uniforms for primary and local secondary schools.

A feeling of pure wickedness went through Bryony, and while Isabel was perusing a selection of political weeklies in the newsagent's shop next door, she sauntered inside the outfitters' and bought a white shirt in a size smaller than her own, a little pleated grey skirt, and a school tie. She had no idea which school uniform she was pillaging for her proposed little drama, but it didn't matter. She paid cash for the clothes, and exited with them hidden in a paper bag.

"What have you bought?" asked Isabel, a copy of both the Spectator and the New Statesman under her arm.

"Oh, nothing, just some underwear." It was the first time she had lied to Isabel, but she felt it was justified for the fun she could provide later.

When they reached home, she hid the bag in her room, under the bed cover, and busied herself with lunch. They took it outside, sitting in the shade under the tree.

"It's your birthday next week," said Isabel, out of nowhere.

"How do you know?"

"We witches have all knowledge at our disposal. What would you like to do?"

Bryony rolled her eyes naughtily.

"Apart from that! I'm serious. This will be my treat. What would you like to do? Where would you like to go?"

Bryony thought back to all the unhappy and disappointing birthdays she had lived through with her Granny, who had thought a game of Pass the Parcel and fish-paste sandwiches constituted an adequate party. Her eighth birthday had been the worst, when her mother was on her deathbed, and a promised trip to the sea-side at Skegness had come to nothing.

"I think I'd like to go to the seaside, to a proper beach, with sand, and somewhere we can swim."

Isabel's eyes sparkled and she looked happy.

"Then I think I know just the place. Have you ever been to Abersoch?"

"No."

"Then that's where we'll go. I saw a picnic basket in the pantry. Let's take a really old fashioned British picnic, complete with ginger beer, and spend the day there. Does that sound a good idea for you?"

"Yes Isabel!"

Bryony went inside to pack away the rest of the shopping, and the remains of their lunch, and Isabel thoughtfully surveyed the view.

She knew Bryony was a little puzzled by her sudden reticence to indulge in their rather gentle and domestic version of S&M sex, but the girl hadn't heard the very definite upbraiding Jane had given her on the phone a few days ago, while Bryony was occupied typing up notes, and editing her current chapter. Jane had obviously been thinking about them since she had returned home to Bristol, and had built up quite a head of steam.

She had given Isabel the fruits of all her reflections, and they weren't pretty. She claimed Isabel was selfish, over-sexed even, and was only interested in her own sexual gratification. She was also unstable, and completely oblivious to the long term misery she would inflict on this perfectly innocent girl who had no idea what sort of relationship she had fallen into.

If Isabel cared for her at all, she needed to step back and let her down gently. She should show her that their sexual attraction was a fleeting, temporary thing, and that she should view it as just a summer fling.

Jane had no idea just what Isabel and Bryony had really been up to in the cottage, but she was convinced it wasn't healthy.

She had then put another spoke in the wheel, urging her not to go to live with Ted and Claire for the autumn, but to join her in Bristol. She lived alone, her house was quite big enough for Isabel to have her own room, and they could be house-mates for as long as Isabel needed. It would be like old times! Wouldn't it be more fun?

This phone-call had really shaken Isabel, and set her back on her heels. She was still vulnerable and fragile enough to half believe what Jane said, and the last thing on earth she wanted to do was to hurt Bryony.

She had not dared to make plans for the future. Probably Bryony would want to tank back to university and submerge herself in her final year's training, anyway.

So what Jane said made sense. She probably was bad news for the girl, she didn't deserve her. Her only comfort was that at least Bryony now knew she was gay, and could embrace her sexuality with someone her own age. But parting from Bryony without the promise of seeing her again very soon, would be much worse than ripping off a sticking plaster from her heart. How could she ever be strong enough to let her go?

Isabel struggled for days, and nights, as Bryony wrapped herself around her and tried to entice her into all the naughty things they both loved to do. By the day they went down the hill to do the shopping, she had definitely decided to be a good woman for once, and just concentrate on helping Bryony have a lovely birthday. Then she would manage a gentle transition away from their more extreme games into just gentle cuddling, and saying goodbye to each other at the end of August. That was the theory, anyway.

Isabel's Healing

Chapter 24

Towards the middle of August the weather broke and there were more showers than before, but the day of Bryony's twenty-fourth birthday gave them a clear sky, with full sunshine and a warm breeze. It was going to be a perfect day for visiting the seaside. Isabel was determined to spoil her, and for once insisted she stayed in bed while she went to make tea and bring her a cup.

Bryony smiled at her when she accepted the drink and looked at her mistress, wrapped in her blue dressing-gown with her hair standing on end above those beautiful clear blue eyes.

"I am so happy today. This is going to be my best birthday ever!"

"I hope so; at least I hope it will live up to those you had as a child."

"Isabel, you have no idea!" Bryony could feel a tightening up of her stomach muscles even at the mention of her early years. She was still burying so much away, and had realized that the feelings around her mother's death were threatening to escape from their tomb more and more frequently.

She couldn't understand it. Isabel was filling her life with love and excitement and yet those childhood memories she hadn't recalled for years were now seeping up to the surface, totally on their own. The last thing she wanted was for them to spoil today's pleasures. She bounced out of bed as soon as she had drunk her tea, and bagged the shower first.

Isabel let her. She took the time to go into the kitchen and make their sandwiches, and then assembled the picnic. It was worthy of an Enid Blyton adventure story, with cheese and tomato sandwiches, hard-boiled eggs, cakes and apples, and two old fashioned little bottles of ginger beer. Then she fetched the wrapped present she had bought for Bryony and put it inside the picnic basket and fastened the straps.

As Bryony emerged, all the work was done, everything on the table had now been cleared away, and Isabel was ready to take her own shower. When they left, Bryony simply picked up the picnic basket and put it in the back of the car without opening it. She fed the word Abersoch into her phone, and set it on the dashboard.

Isabel sat beside her. She wore navy slacks with a red belt and a striped blue and white top. She looked adorable to Bryony, who wondered how she would be able keep her hands to herself all day. Then, just as they were about to leave, she gave a little yelp, and turned off the car key.

"What?"

"Swimsuits and towels! We forgot. I'll run back in and get them."

Isabel nodded, and remembered she did indeed have an old black swimsuit tucked in the corner of her suitcase. Claire had thought to get her one in case hydrotherapy ever became an option, but it was still unused.

Bryony returned with a pair of rolled up towels and tossed them on the back seat.

"I brought one too. That was lucky. Let's go!"

It was a golden day, one of those days you remember for years. Their drive over the mountains and round the coast of the Llyn peninsula was a joy and they were early enough to secure parking as close to Abersoch main beach as possible, even though the little resort was packed with tourists making the most of the sun, and all the sailboat enthusiasts were crowding out the marina.

Isabel looked a different woman from the miserable bundle of humanity she had been six weeks before. Her whole way of being was transformed. Her default expression was one of happy pleasure, and her frown lines seem to have vanished. She looked ten years younger, and she was now walking without her crutches.

She kept her arm linked in Bryony's for much of the time as they walked around, but Bryony hoped it was as she assumed, that Isabel simply liked being close to her, rather than using her as a human walking stick. Isabel had also put on the much needed ten pounds, and no longer resembled a bag of bones.

"We used to come here when I was a child, from Chester," she said. "It has always been a popular seaside resort with the English."

"It still looks very traditional. I want to make a sandcastle and buy some of those little paper flags to put on it."

"If that's what you want to do, darling, it's your birthday! But I've booked us in for a spa treatment at 2 pm as a treat, so let's go down on the sands now, and get on with playing at construction workers."

Bryony chose a little plastic bucket and spade and a packet of flags from the nearest booth, and they made camp on the beach. With her legendary ability to focus, she concentrated on recreating a sand castle, which looked set to rival Caernarvon.

Isabel sat in a deck chair and looked at her very fondly. Then she noticed a very alarming thing. Bryony was sitting by her finished sandcastle with tears streaming down her face, and her shoulders shaking.

"My love, what's the matter?" Isabel managed to heave up out of the deck chair and sat beside her on the sand. She wrapped her arms around her, and rocked her, while Bryony very painfully, between sobs, told her about the aborted seaside trip on her eighth birthday, and how instead she had had the horrible experience of watching her mother being carried from her bedroom away by ambulance out of their little terraced house, never to be seen again.

"I'm sorry. I don't do crying. I'm not sure why it has just come flooding out. I'm ashamed. But no-one, no-one talked to me about it when I was a child and we never went to the sea-side again."

Isabel just rocked her, and passed her a tissue. "You've been so brave. You're so much more stoical than I am. It's good it's come up of its own accord. It needed to. You must miss your mother very much."

Bryony nodded and blew her nose. "I do, but I only have a few photographs, and her face is so hazy in my memory now. I worry it will fade completely."

"No it won't. You may forget the exact way she looked, but her love for you, and yours for her, you'll remember forever."

"Can we go for a swim now? Will you come in with me?"

Isabel smiled. Bryony's quick change of mood was almost like Carrie's, though their characters were so different. She looked around and saw a very comfortable family camped on the beach a little way away, and decided to ask them to guard their keys and possessions while they swam.

Having wriggled into their swimsuits under cover of towels and clothes, like a postcard cartoon from the 1950s, they then walked down to the water and bravely marched straight into the waves. Isabel's breath caught with the shock. It was a hot day, but still August in Wales and the Irish Sea was not the Mediterranean. She had swum in many of the world's oceans but usually only south of the Tropic of Capricorn.

Bryony grabbed her hand and took her lovely mistress forward with her, so her shoulders were soon under the water. It was just what she needed too, to jolt her out of the embarrassing fit of weeping.

She didn't really understand what had happened, but it made her somehow feel much better than she had before, healed somehow. It had maybe taken sixteen years, but Isabel had organized it so she could now have her birthday at the seaside and she was determined to enjoy it.

They were both strong swimmers, and Isabel could feel her arm and leg muscles working as they should. It felt wonderful.

Afterwards they lay on their towels, drying off and enjoying the sunshine on their faces.

"I should get out the sun-cream," said Bryony.

"Oh, pooh. Just relax nursie. Think of all this lovely Vitamin D we're getting."

Bryony reached over and pulled Isabel's sun hat across her face.

"I love you too much to get your face burned."

"Hmm." Isabel tried to not think about the word 'love' too much. For four letters it was a huge word, and she doubted Bryony had yet had a chance fully to explore what it meant. It was so easy to say when you were twenty-four, much harder when you were forty-two. If Isabel was to use it back to her, and truly prove she meant it, it would be like jumping off one of those enormous cliffs in New Zealand at the end of a bungee jump rope.

Oh, she knew she did love Bryony, more than was rational, and certainly much more than Jane Walkley had imagined, but where could it go? She would just have to steer them both in another direction, and live with the consequences. Her poor battered heart could just suffer the emotion alone.

"Picnic time!" she shouted, when these thoughts became too intense, and then pulled across the basket. Bryony remembered the Wind in the Willows story, and felt like Mole excitedly unpacking the picnic he and Ratty had prepared. She pulled out two plastic plates and several small boxes, and then noticed a cardboard box in the middle, tied up with a little length of string.

"What's this?"

"Happy birthday, darling."

Isabel handed her the box and watched as she untied the string and tore open the seal. It was the latest model of an Apple I-Phone, as powerful as a large computer, and as sleek and wonderful as she could imagine. What a luxury!

Her own phone was so old, she'd had it since her eighteenth birthday when she had treated herself to one, and then it had been reconditioned and sold in the second hand IT store. Isabel had somehow managed to charge this new one up as well, so it was ready to go, and also with a beautiful blue cover.

"Thank you Isabel! Thank you, thank you, thank you! It's wonderful!"

"Oh, the youth of today! How easily they are beguiled by gadgets!"

"Absolutely!" Bryony reached across and kissed Isabel on the mouth.

"Don't you want one? This is more powerful than yours."

"No, sweetie. I don't need to play candy crush or watch films all the time. You just enjoy it, and don't lose it!"

"Let's eat."

They enjoyed their picnic, and then Isabel directed Bryony to the local Spa where she had booked two sessions online. They enjoyed a wonderful two hours, and Bryony for once, could for once experience a massage herself, instead of always being the one to give them.

As the sun was moving west over the country hills behind Abersoch, they turned the old car for home, and drove together in perfect harmony, back towards the cottage.

The sea air had predictably given them a very pleasant feeling of exhaustion and relaxation. Bryony had intended to end her birthday with a spectacular display of dramatic creativity, involving the little uniform and school tie, but when the evening turned to night, she was actually too tired to do anything other than roll into bed next to Isabel and let herself be held and gently cuddled as she fell asleep. Life didn't always have to be sexual fireworks after all. Her appreciation of Isabel's curves was just as genuine when they were motionless, spooned against her, and warming her from hip to shoulder.

Chapter 25

The day out in Abersoch did somehow mark the beginning of the end of their idyllic summer at Ty Bach. The book, the all-important book, took Isabel's whole attention for up to six hours a day from then on, and Bryony faithfully tagged along behind her, furiously typing to her dictation on the student lap-top which had served her right through university. When they finally came to the end of the main chapters, she felt as though she'd run a marathon in flip-flops.

"I think it's a miracle we've managed this. I really could have done with a large screen editing desktop computer. I'll copy everything onto a data stick for you and then you can take it back to London to do the proper editing."

Isabel looked at her wearily rubbing her eyes, and felt very guilty.

"You're right. No-one else would have coped with what I've put you through. I've been so stupid. I wouldn't have let my staff at work ruin their eyes writing a whole book on a lap-top."

"No harm done. I have strong eyesight. It's been fantastic, actually. I've learned so much, just from typing up what you've said. I've travelled the world, places I never thought I'd see, like where we are now in this end chapter, Fiji!"

"Yes, it's ironic. I've been a gypsy and my own carbon footprint must be enormous, the amount of flights I've had to take."

Bryony counted the days they had left together, they were frighteningly few. She decided they had to have a conversation about the future if she was to have any peace. She dreaded what Isabel would say, dreaded even more that she wouldn't say anything.

"Izzy,"

"Oh, dear, what does that mean?"

"I just like it. I don't see why your friend Jane should commandeer it. Anyway, we need to talk, so I know what to expect. What are your plans for the autumn? Will you return to London? Is there any chance I can see you there?"

Her lovely green eyes were troubled and Isabel could tell she was very nervous. The poor kid was braver than she was, as she hadn't been even up to starting the conversation.

"I...I do know what you mean. Bryony dear, what can I say? These weeks, they've given me back my life. More than that, they have restored my hope of a future. I can never repay you for everything you've done for me. But what that future is, well it's too early to say. Ted and Claire want me to go back to Chester with them; Jane thinks I should live with her in Bristol."

"I think you're already fit enough to look after yourself," Bryony broke in. "I thought we might go for a drive tomorrow, so you can get behind the wheel and get your confidence back, and then you'll be good to go. Will you buy another car?"

"I'm not sure. But, the point is, darling, that whatever I do, you've already done enough. You have your own life to lead, and a really busy year ahead. You don't want me weighing you down."

"Weighing me down? Is that what you think? Isabel I worship you. You inspire me and excite me. You could never weigh me down!"

Bryony was beginning to lose it. She was perilously close to tears and they had only just started this conversation.

Isabel tried to channel Jane's thoughts and judgments of her through her own words.

"Darling, I'm not this wonder-woman you've idealized in your mind. Remember how cranky I was when we first met? I can be an absolute bitch, and I used to be notoriously unfaithful. You deserve someone much, much better. You need to have fun as well, take your beautiful self and play the field."

"Is that your best advice? Is that what you really want? So you want to say Cheerio and wave me off to sleep with any girl in London, as though none of this matters, as though it hasn't been important?"

Isabel looked away from her so she wouldn't see those exasperating tears which were threatening to come into her own eyes. She was determined to push on with her argument, even though it was actually the direct opposite of what she felt in her heart.

"Yes, that's what I'm saying. It's for the best, for you. I'm your first gay relationship, but I shouldn't and won't be your last. I've decided what will be best when our time here finishes. I don't want to go to stay with Ted and Claire, but I can cope with Jane for a few weeks, just while I finish the editing. If you take me to the train in Machynlleth, she can meet me in Bristol. Meanwhile I'll pay you extra to drive the Berlingo, with all the medical paraphernalia and the wheelchair etc. back to Chester to Ted and Claire's house. I'll arrange with them to take you to the London train. So everything will end in an orderly fashion."

She had her employer's voice on, as though by using it she could shut Bryony's objections down and brook no more argument. Bryony panicked for a moment and then realized that there was a lot more going on inside Isabel's beautiful head than she was letting on. One lost battle didn't mean she needed to give up the campaign. She was used to hiding her emotions, and wouldn't cry like a baby in front of her. Instead she took a deep breath and replied in a similarly objective vein.

"Well, I see you've thought it all through. Maybe you are right. I don't think you are of course. But I respect your decision. We can end everything in an orderly fashion, as you say."

Isabel winced as she heard her own banalities quoted back to her. Bryony stood up.

"I'm going to go and take a bath, if you don't mind now. My shoulders ache and I would like a soak."

"Fine, of course, dear."

Bryony left her, and disappeared into the bathroom. Isabel heard the taps running into the bathtub, and the radio turned onto a cheerful pop channel.

"Oh, hell," she thought. "She's gone in there to cry, but she doesn't want me to hear her."

Which was exactly what Bryony did, for at least the next half hour.

Lying in the bath-tub until her fingers grew wrinkly gave Bryony time to get over her initial panic, stop the emotional overflow of her deepest feelings and regain her legendary ability to internalize misery and look on the bright side. She and Isabel had five more days together. A lot could happen, and even if Isabel didn't change her mind and still wanted to finish whatever they had between them, those five days could be joyous or horrible. It was down to Bryony to make sure they were the former.

When she came out of the bathroom, wrapped up in Isabel's dressing gown and heading for her own room to find some pajamas, she looked red-eyed from crying, but not furious and not seeming as though she was about to launch them into a blazing row. This was so different from the way Carrie would have reacted that it almost knocked Isabel sideways.

She had been sitting on the sofa, trying but not succeeding to read a magazine, and she was more nervous than she could admit. Bryony only stayed in her room for a few moments and when she emerged she had put on her pajamas and was drying off her hair. Isabel stood up and stopped her from crossing the kitchen. She drew her into her arms, and Bryony sank into the hug.

"Don't cry, sweetie. Don't cry. I don't want to make you sad. You're so precious to me."

Bryony caressed her cheek.

"I know Isabel. I understand. Let's not spoil our last few days together then. I'm thinking we should instead just make them as wonderful as if they will last forever."

"Come to bed."

Bryony seemed to hesitate, and Isabel wondered if she had burned her bridges already and their lovely times together were already a thing of the past. But then Bryony smiled and almost drove her through into the bedroom.

"Those are the nicest words you ever say to me," she said. "I adore you everywhere Isabel, but I love you in bed more than any other place."

"Let's go then."

Isabel also knew the feeling was mutual. Now she adored Bryony, all pink and damp from the bath. She picked up the Aloe Vera gel as she passed the chest, and closed the bedroom door behind them.

"Let me give you a massage this evening. I think you deserve one, and it will be good for my arm muscles."

Bryony lay down on her stomach on the bed and gave herself up to Isabel's hands. As work went, this posting really wasn't that bad was it? And when they fell asleep together it was as two united women, after all.

Isabel's Healing

Chapter 26

The penultimate day of August had come. Isabel had stuck to her guns, and kept insisting that Bryony's future would be far better without her in it as her lover. She phoned Edward and Claire, working very hard to keep the tremor out of her voice, and arranged for them to take Bryony to the train at Chester station and send her safely back to London. She also gave them some additional instructions, which eased her troubled conscience just a little, and then turned to make another phone call to start negotiations with Jane.

Her jock friend had been absorbed with the various female sporting events throughout the school holidays, so had not been back on her case too much, but she certainly leapt in when Isabel voiced the thought that she might join her for a few weeks in Bristol. "Great, just like old times! Thank God you've come to your senses! I'm glad you're not still playing about with that girl."

"I've never been playing, though she is very good at games."

"Well, make sure you finish it with her properly. I'm not having you stay with me if we have loads of loose ends hanging around."

Isabel flinched. Bryony was anything but a loose end. Cutting the tie with her would be like severing an artery, but she was still convinced it was for Bryony's best, if not hers.

"Look Jane, cool it, OK? I will come to you just until the end of September. I think I need to be out of London for some weeks yet, and while you're in school I can edit my book and be back in touch with the publishers in peace. Once people hear I'm back in circulation, there'll be no letting up. I probably also need to buy a car."

"Are you back behind the wheel?"

"No, I've not driven yet. Bryony is taking me out today."

"Well, make her let you drive. You've been too dependent on her."

"Oh and by the way, I'm now firmly vegetarian, and heading towards veganism."

"No way, Jose! Well I'm not changing my eating habits."

"No, you don't need to change your whole life for me."

"I suppose that was your girlfriend's stupid idea?"

"No, it's not a stupid idea. Bryony didn't make me, of course not, but she has had no trouble at all in..."

Here Jane broke in again and complained.

"Are you going to talk about nothing else but the sainted Bryony?"

"No, I'm not going to keep talking about her!"

The conversation was getting out of hand. Honestly, Jane was as bad as Carrie had been, in arguing all the time. Isabel closed her phone, and took a deep breath.

Bryony came through the room, waving the car keys.

"Come on, Madam, let's get your sea legs going again. Do you want to drive from here, or shall I take us up on the hills somewhere first, and then we can swap and you can drive us home?"

"You drive first. I know this is ridiculous. I've driven since I was seventeen. But I keep getting flashbacks of the collision, and I seem to have lost my nerve. "

Bryony came over and kissed her on the cheek. "Let's go. It will only be a little outing, but it will break the spell. I think you'll be fine, but if you feel wobbly, then I'll be there for you."

She drove Isabel a few miles even further up into the hills so they could look north across to the mass of Snowdonia, and then parked beside the road, and jumped out. Isabel cautiously took her place in the driver's seat and adjusted the mirrors.

Bryony said, "Why don't you drive us back to that little café we passed? Then we can stop for coffee and buns."

Isabel put the car into gear, reversed up onto the grass verge and then started to drive them back down the single track road. She was breathing heavily, and could feel her heart thumping, but within five minutes the threat of panicking had passed and she was driving as smoothly as she always had.

A farm tractor pulling a trailer full of sheep came into view, but he pulled over for her, and she passed him without incident. By the time they had reached the café, she was ready to hand back to Bryony, but she'd conquered her nerves once, and could do it again. They went inside and Isabel ordered a flat white coffee and two welsh cakes. Bryony's order of the same drink, alongside a toasted tea-cake provided a very pleasant pit-stop for them.

"What will you do when you get back into London?" asked Isabel.

"Book back into the student accommodation, in a shared flat probably. And then finish this dissertation I've been working on. I have a few weeks before my next placement starts and I want to get it finished."

Isabel nodded. "Did I answer all your questions OK? Do you have enough material?"

Bryony had given her sheets of questions to fill in, and had also done a series of mini videos on her phone, charting her progress week by week. Coupled with all the tables of weight gain, sleep patterns and flexibility tests, she knew she had enough data to make it a competent submission.

"Would you still like to read the final version, before I submit it?"

"Of course. Please send it to me. Bryony..."

"Yes, Isabel?"

"I hope, after a while, after what I think has to be a necessary separation, I do hope we can stay friends. I will take a keen interest in your progress."

Bryony tried to think through what Isabel was asking. Did she really imagine it would work, to turn what was the love of her life, so far, into just a friendship? She tried to compare what she felt for Isabel with her affection for Aiden.

It was in another universe.

Aiden had not contacted her since their explosive lunch meeting, and she had not missed him at all. But Isabel? She really didn't see how she could live if there was even a faint chance that Isabel might call her anytime for a chatty Cathy catch-up. The true depths of her attachment only now really came home to her.

"I'm...I'm not sure. I don't know how I am going to adjust. Can we leave it, at least for a month or more? You are breaking up with me, Isabel. Have pity on my poor heart."

"I will miss you more than..."

"Don't say it, please. This is your choice, your decision, which I respect. I don't even want to think about next week now, so let's concentrate on the here and now."

They went back to the car. She offered the keys to Isabel, who shook her head. "No, enough is enough. You drive." For some reason she wanted Bryony to carry on looking after her. The girl's reticence about keeping in touch as friends made her realize what a huge hole she was digging for herself in her life, and it made her very sad.

Bryony said, as they set off, "When we get home, I have a heap of cleaning and packing to do, but then I thought we might have a little party tonight. I have a little surprise for you, to remember me by."

Isabel raised her eyebrows.

"Oh? I wonder what that can be about."

"Wait and find out!"

Chapter 27

The cottage was scrubbed clean, the windows washed, and the carpets hoovered within an inch of their lives. Isabel marveled at how efficient Bryony was in all things domestic. She even polished all the glasses with a linen cloth she found, and had washed and ironed the sheets and the pillow cases from her own bed.

The only bed still to strip and make up again, was the double bed, which had been their location for so many happy hours of fun.

"I'll sort that tomorrow."

"Do you like housework? You are certainly wonderfully efficient."

"Strong working class stock. My granny would have chalked her doorstep if her knees had let her. I don't know, I have always been like it, cleaning and clearing out my environment helps steady what goes on inside my head."

"I'm sorry, darling. I don't think I have helped with any of this. And I'm sure I have messed up your life, with all my sexual advances, and my silly fantasies. Will you forgive me?"

"Forgive you? You have transformed me! Isabel, please don't imagine for a moment I haven't had a ball this summer. I've actually grown up. If I was a kid before, I now feel a woman. I can cope with pain and passion. I even know what an orgasm feels like! Let's have one last beautiful night together, without any regrets or guilt. OK?"

"OK."

The nights were drawing in now, compared to the mid-summer long evenings of eight weeks before, and

Isabel drew the curtains across the cottage windows. The lamp-light was low, and she moved through to the bedroom to finish her own packing, very heavy at heart, but trying to copy Bryony's apparently positive attitude to their imminent parting, one for which she was solely responsible.

"Isabel..."

"Yes?"

She turned at the sound of her name, and caught her breath at the sight of Bryony in the doorway. She was dressed in very little, a school girl shirt which was held together at the front with just one button, and a grey mini skirt which showed the length of her slim, tanned legs.

Round her neck she wore a loosely fastened school tie, and she carried an open bottle of champagne in one hand and two narrow glasses in the other. She waved the bottle cheerfully, and then placed it beside the bed. Her hair was loose, and she already looked a little tipsy.

"I thought it would be fun to have a little role play, as a piece of end of term fun."

"Oh, yes? St. Trinian's?"

"Not quite. How would you like to play my old Math teacher? The one who gave me private coaching to get me through additional math early?"

"Ah, did she achieve it?"

"Yes, in the end, but it was touch and go for a while. I was dangerously close to not succeeding. I was so unmotivated. I needed convincing I should work harder."

"You mean, you respond well to discipline?"

"You could say that. Would you like a drink? I've been hiding this bottle out in the woodshed."

Bryony's eyes were huge, and the lamplight reflected gold flecks in them. She poured out two glasses and passed one to Isabel. Isabel came forward and slipped effortlessly into her role. She looked caustically at her attempt at a uniform.

"How dare you come to a private lesson like that? Is this your idea of proper attire? Your tie is not even done up properly."

She swallowed most of the glass of champagne and then went forward, tightening Bryony's tie so it lay tightly round her neck, well above her collar. She took one end of it and gave it a little tug.

"Now, let's examine this shirt. I think you have bought the wrong size here. Take it off at once and show me the label."

Bryony caught her breath and then slipped her finger behind the little white button on her breastbone. When it opened, her naked breasts tumbled out, and the size ten shirt jumped back. She let it fall and then held it up for Isabel's attention.

"Hmm, as I thought. It's a nice little shirt but far too small for you. I suspect your skirt is equally inadequate. Let me look at that."

She couldn't keep her hands off Bryony any longer. The tie was left for now, and Isabel slowly rolled up the little grey skirt, until it bunched round Bryony's waist. Then, she unzipped it and let it fall to the ground.

Bryony was now naked apart from the tie. Isabel grasped it and pulled Bryony onto the bed. She lay on top of her and adjusted the tie so one end was much longer than the other, and then fastened the long end round the bed head. Bryony could keep her head on the pillow, but not move much beyond it.

"A little light discipline might improve your adherence to a dress code, I think. But first I need to give you something to numb any pain."

She took another drink, this time from Bryony's glass, and then holding the champagne in her mouth, slipped it down Bryony's throat as she enveloped her in a kiss. Bryony was caught under her and forced to swallow. The champagne made her nose feel fizzy as the bubbles invaded her throat. This was repeated at least four times, until the champagne bottle was seriously depleted.

Isabel was now really getting into character. She was still fully dressed, but now stripped down to the waist to give her arms freedom of movement.

Bryony began to pant as she watched her throw off her shirt and bra, and Isabel decided she needed further restraints. She pushed her over until she was lying on her front on the bed and then fastened her arms above her head with the twisted shirt acting as a set of soft handcuffs.

"Up!"

Bryony lifted her bottom up in response to a light slap, and Isabel placed a large pillow under her pelvis so that her buttocks were fully tilted skywards.

"Now, then, you say this is a math lesson? How about a little mental arithmetic?"

"Hmm?"

"If you get the answers right, you'll have nothing to fear. Do you understand?"

"Yes, Isabel."

"Right. We'll start with something easy. 17 x 9? "

"170 less 17. 153."

"Good. That's 153 in your prize fund. 42+ 138?"

"Um, 180."

"Good, but not quickly enough. 189+584?"

Bryony felt her brain turning to mush and her insides beginning to catch on fire. This was her game, but she wondered if she'd been wise to invoke the spirit of her math teacher.

"Er, I'm sorry, I can't think..."

Isabel's hand came suddenly crashing down on her buttocks.

"Concentrate, Bryony, or I'll keep smacking you."

"Ow, oh, wait please, 684, and..."

Another slap, this time just on the left hand side.

"684 and 100 less 11."

The smack came from the right this time. It really hurt.

"773!"

Isabel heaved an exaggerated sigh of relief.

"At last! I couldn't have carried on much longer without getting something else to hit you with. My poor hand is throbbing."

"Poor you. Maybe you need to rub it up against something smooth and soft."

Isabel released Bryony's arms and turned her over. She saw her staring as she removed the rest of her clothes and then poured lotion over her stinging hand.

Bryony's sore backside was pushed back firmly against the sheets, and her legs roughly parted. Isabel then invaded her with her hands and mouth and wiped the lotion from her belly, right down under her sexual organs and through until she reached her behind. She could feel the heat still in the delicious mounds of flesh, and it enflamed her. Bryony, now that she could use her hands, tore away the tie holding her neck against the pillow and brought Isabel's breasts into her mouth. They were entwined together like Venus and Adonis. Their bodies blended into one. And the sex was very, very good.

**

It was late when they woke up in the morning, as Bryony had turned into some wild animal in the night and had woken Isabel, demanding another lesson and bonus orgasms. She was a different girl in the dark, completely raunchy and outrageous, and hugely disrespectful of Isabel's seniority and status.

It worked really well. There was no way she was passing into Isabel's memory as a casual lay. She had decided she would make Isabel really, really miss her, and judging by the sobbing, the cries for help and the screams at multiple orgasms coming from her lover, she had achieved her ambition.

However, morning did come, and it was raining heavily, and the clouds were dark, and Isabel finally achieved the cosmic sympathy for her emotional state that she had asked for on the day they had first met. Bryony was calm, and tight-lipped, and totally into healthcare assistant mode. She drove her down to the station, and helped her on to the train with her suitcases.

"I've registered online for you to have assistance at Birmingham, when you change onto the Bristol train. It's all sorted."

"Bryony, thank you. For everything. How about a hug?"

But Bryony shook her head. "Not a good idea. Sorry, but I need to stay focused. I need to be able to see the road, and I'll turn into a blubbering wreck if we touch again."

"Bye, then, darling. I am so sorry..."

"Bye, Isabel."

So their summer ended, as it had begun, with two journeys, but this time, in opposite directions.

Chapter 28

The train left the station and Bryony drove back to the cottage, finished loading the car, left the key as instructed under the third pot from the left, and drove north to Chester. Her face was set in steel, and her lip almost bled from the way she forced herself to bite back the tears.

When she handed over the car, and all the medical equipment borrowed from the hospital, Edward and Claire thought what a sensible and placid girl she must have been, to have coped so calmly with their crazy sister all this time. They saw her off, as arranged at Chester station, with her little suitcase, and rucksack and Edward handed her a brown envelope as he said goodbye.

"Isabel wanted you to have this. She said it's a small present, towards your student debt bill. Don't worry that it's my signature on it. But it comes from her part of our family trust fund."

As the train pulled out, Isabel opened the envelope. Her salary had been paid into her bank account already, but this "small present" was something else. It was a check for £10,000. She honestly didn't know what to say or think, and when the train reached London, she still didn't.

Of course, nothing ended, neither for Isabel nor Bryony. Isabel felt she could have written the script herself, about how horrible she felt as the train moved south towards Birmingham. A great wave of longing engulfed her for Bryony, for that last forbidden hug, for the sweet perfume of her, for the touch of her almost magically healing hands.

It was all quite ridiculous. They had only known each other for eight weeks, and yet they had somehow fitted together, more perfectly, and, yes, she could now admit it, even better than Carrie and she had.

Where Carrie had thrown everything in the air when she was upset, tossed every toy out of the pram, caused a huge emotional showdown, what had Bryony done? She had internalized everything, had stoically absorbed the pain Isabel caused her, accepted it, and had not made any fuss, carried on loving and helping her to the very end.

It was hard to read Bryony, but it wasn't that hard. Isabel knew she was hurting, knew how much the girl truly loved her, so why had she done this to them both? Why had she made them both so miserable?

Isabel had arrived in Bristol, being met off the train by the ever competent Jane, and shuttled off towards her house, before she had begun to solve that question. Jane seemed oblivious to anything Isabel could identify as mixed feelings about the wisdom of her decision. She seemed to be more interested in what they were going to do together in the coming weeks, the sports matches they could watch together, meeting up with the girls, even introductions Jane had lined up for Isabel.

"Now that you've obviously worked Carrie out of your system, you can start dating again, move forwards."

Isabel looked at her in horror. There was nothing less she wanted in the whole world, and she tried to say so.

"No, it's too soon, much too soon."

"It's been nearly two years, for heaven's sake!"

"Not after Carrie, I mean Bryony. I'm just not interested. Sorry."

"Oh, pooh, that was just a little summer fling. She'll have forgotten you by the weekend, and you should do the same."

Isabel wondered if anyone could be quite as insensitive as Jane. She might have been granted more understanding by Ted and Claire even, and regretted her decision to come to Bristol if she was going to have to endure all this bullying positivity.

But Jane ploughed on regardless. She had cleared the exercise bike, and all the weights out of her spare room, and Isabel could see a month stretching ahead for her having to fit all her global passions, and her squandered love for Bryony, into a narrow bedroom, looking at the terraced houses from her dormer window. Bryony had always given her space, had let her have agency, even when she'd been at her most vulnerable. This made her feel claustrophobic.

The final straw came when Jane suggested they go out to eat at the local steak house. "You weren't seriously about all that vegetarian nonsense, were you? What difference will that make to the future of the world?"

***

Isabel decided to treat her time with Jane as some masochistic lesbian boot-camp experience. Jane did like running early every morning, so Isabel joined her, panting at first behind her at a slow and painful jog, but then eventually managing to keep up more or less for the first half-mile or so, when she dropped out and walked home while Jane ran off at speed, and completed her full 5k circuit.

When the tireless woman had left for school, Isabel used the peace and quiet in the empty house to work hard on the book, and was methodically ploughing through all the footnotes. It was fine.

Well that was a lie. It wasn't fine at all. But the footnotes connected her to the text and the text kept her in touch with the echo of Bryony's fingers clicking over the keys for all those hours. She had somehow brought her words to life, and she remembered every question she had asked, and each comment she'd made.

It was usually around 2 pm each day before Isabel started embarrassingly to cry from missing Bryony, and she had usually dried up her tears before Jane came waltzing in at 5 pm. As a misery coping mechanism, it worked like a dream, except at night, when she did dream. Then Bryony's face, her hands, her lips, her tongue invaded her every fiber, and she would wake up trembling in a cold sweat. She felt she was moving backwards, even losing some of the weight Bryony had helped her gain.

She knew Bryony wouldn't write or call. Hadn't she told her not to? Why had she been such a total bloody fool? Why hadn't she trusted her heart, or even more sensibly, trusted Bryony when she had quietly challenged this ludicrous idea of separating?

Then Isabel's mood slumped even further. Bryony enjoyed following her orders. Supposing she had already obeyed Isabel and had embarked on an exciting new fling with a woman unknown? God, the girl was sexy, full of libido and loveliness. There was no way she'd stay celibate, faced with all the opportunities open to her in London. The sharp dagger of jealousy stabbed her heart. This was unbearable.

Isabel need not have worried about Bryony playing the field, however. September in London was proving as difficult for her young caregiver as it was for her down in Bristol. Bryony certainly had no interest in sex with anyone, female, male, or even with herself. She just ached for Isabel, day and night, and only her Grade A self-control stopped her jumping on a train and pounding the streets of Bristol city until she found her.

She concentrated on completing the 'Isabel dissertation', as she called it. It kept her in touch with the lovely woman, and when it was finally finished and she was ready to submit it, she held it back, remembering her promise to let Isabel see it first.

So they continued in mutual isolation until Isabel decided after three and a half weeks that one more day of Jane's company would lead her to commit buddycide or whatever killing your best friend was called, and told her she was preparing to return to London.

Jane looked up from the sports science papers she was marking, and actually said something which surprised Isabel.

"Yes, I knew you would. I've seen it coming. You can't

stay away from her any longer, can you?"

"What?"

"Bryony, your young lover. Don't tell me she hasn't been on your mind all this time! I've seen how many boxes of Kleenex you've gone through. And I'm sorry."

"For what?"

"For not realizing just how much she means to you. For thinking you are still twenty eight, not forty two. For not taking you seriously and maybe for giving you really bad advice."

Isabel stared at her. "You think?"

"Yes, I think I was wrong. If it's right, then you need to test it out. You can't feel worse than you do now. And maybe, you won't break her heart after all."

"I may have broken it already."

"Well, go and find out."

Isabel was in a fluster, excited as a young thing suddenly. She realized she'd been idiotically leaning on Jane to give her the right leadership, when Jane didn't have any clue how Bryony and she worked together. She bundled all her things together within the hour, and booked a mini-cab to take her to the station.

She was too nervous to call Bryony's new phone. It was so important not to say the wrong thing. She decided to wait until she was home in Highbury. She just needed the door key to get in.

It was then Isabel realized she had never taken it back after Bryony's trip to London back in July. She had a spare, obviously, but it was locked away in a drawer, inside the flat. Did Bryony even have the key still, and how could she get it from her?

She would have to call, but then Bryony would think it was just because she wanted the key. She needed to do something serious to prove she was for real, that she was coming after Bryony, and that she was totally committed to a future with her, that she would stay faithful.

Isabel left her suitcases and briefcase in the lost

luggage office at Temple Meads railway station, and took another taxi into Bristol city centre. The driver was bemused by her request, but together they found the answer, and her expedition ended three hours later with the desired result. Isabel then caught the late afternoon train to Paddington. It was very crowded and she needed to stand for most of the hundred mile trip, which wasn't a bad idea as it happened.

When the train stopped at Reading, Isabel texted Bryony. She didn't want to disturb her work.

"Hi, I am coming back to London tonight. Do you by any chance have my flat key? I have missed you very much."

It took a few rewrites before it sounded with just the right amount of urgency and longing, but not too needy. She sent it from the train, so hoped it made it through the airwaves.

When she reached Paddington she looked for an answer to her message but nothing had popped up, to her great disappointment. She swallowed her pride and tried to call, but Bryony's phone went to voicemail, and it wasn't even her own voice but a recorded message.

Isabel stuttered something incoherent into the phone, and then gave up halfway through. She would just have to go home, and maybe break a window if her neighbor could help. She went off to find another black cab.

The taxi wound its way up the main roads from North Islington to Highbury Corner and then north past the playground and tennis courts. It was already dusk, so Highbury Fields park was quiet, apart from a group of boys playing basketball on a floodlit court, and a few evening dog walkers. Her own road flanked by its tall plain trees showed the lights of people's kitchens and living rooms, as they recovered from an exhausting day at work, and prepared their evening meals. She gave the taxi-driver the number of her house, and indicated which lamp-post he should aim for. She was in for a very tricky struggle to break into her own flat, without the alarms all going off, and the sound of glass breaking.

But like an angel out of the shadows, as Isabel emerged

from the taxi, a tall, slim, beautiful vision of her Bryony girl stepped forward from where she had been sitting, out on the front steps. She even waved the door key.

"I tried to call you back but my phone died. I thought I should come at once, as this is my fault. I have had your key in my wallet all this time. I'm so sorry."

Isabel paid the driver, and the cab disappeared into the night. Bryony walked forward, as helpful as ever, to help her carry in her luggage. She turned the key in the lock and they went in together. Isabel went to turn off the alarm, but Bryony had already done it.

"Sorry, I have just been inside to pick up your post again, and to check that everything is OK."

You've cut off your hair! All your lovely hair!"

"Well, not all of it, obviously. I thought I should follow your advice, and come out a bit more. I thought this cut would be just about the right amount of butchiness. I know you didn't want me to, but I thought I'd never see you again. It was kind of to remember you by."

"Oh, sweetheart, as if! Bryony, I've been the biggest fool, but I hope you can forgive me. These past three weeks have been..."

"Pretty hellish. I know. For me too. I was so delighted when I received your text, and then the phone went dead. I just want you to know, Isabel; I will take any small morsel of your time, any crumb of your company. I know you don't want us to be lovers, but I will take any level of friendship over what these weeks have been."

Isabel ran forward, reached across and gripped her short blonde locks. She pulled her mouth forwards and stopped what she was saying with a desperate kiss. Bryony wrapped herself around Isabel and they stayed like that, pushed back against the hall table, for what seemed like months, but was possibly about thirty seconds. Isabel wasn't counting.

"Not want to be lovers...it is all I want! I have been

such a fool. You have filled my mind every moment of my life since I left you."

"Oh, well, you mean then, we're good?"

"Of course we're good, silly girl. If you forgive me."

"I have brought you my dissertation to read."

"You have? We'll look at it afterwards."

"After what?"

"Come with me. I have a little bit of writing of my own I want to show you."

Isabel pulled Bryony into the bedroom, still kissing and hugging her, and then Bryony took control of their situation, as the realization of what Isabel meant for their future sank into her brain. When they were in a bedroom together, it seemed inevitable that they should end up in bed.

She began to undress Isabel almost reverently, and then let her do the same to her. It took quite some time, as they were both shivering with nerves and arousal, but then they were standing in the room together, pretty well naked. Bryony reached up and gently smoothed back Isabel's waves. She still had those adorable flicks at the ends of her hair. Bryony thought she was the most beautiful woman in the world.

"Come under the covers. It's chilly."

Isabel turned on the light and drew Bryony down beside her in her bed. The mutual warmth of their bodies gave immense comfort and they melded together in a head to toe embrace.

"So what was the writing you wanted to show me?"

Isabel chuckled.

"It's something I think you might like. Remember the promise I made you make? Well that was for your gorgeous body, not mine. I had something done this afternoon, to show you how much I love you. It's still sore, but they said it will settle soon. What do you think?"

Isabel turned over onto her front, and tugged the sheet down behind her. Isabel's gaze went down her back and then she gasped as she focused on Isabel's perfect ass. On the left buttock was tattooed, in a very elegant script and discreetly small letters, the word *Bryony*, and on the right, the words, *My Love Forever*. Then, to finish, there was a perfect little rose in red and green.

Bryony was speechless. Her eyes shone, but she couldn't say a word, until she said, "You do understand this is for life? You'll be stuck with it until you die."

"As long as I'm also stuck with you, I don't see any problem. I just needed you to know it really wasn't just a summer fling, that you have transformed my life, that you are my perfect rose. I love you so much, Bryony."

Bryony reached round her and held her closely against her body.

"Then I will get one done as well!"

"No, you can't. Remember I made you promise not to."

"But that was under duress. I don't think it should count."

"Yes it does, nothing should mark your exquisite skin."

"It must have hurt you, a lot. I thought you never wanted to feel pain again."

Isabel looked into her eyes, and ran a finger very gently down Bryony's arm.

"You're right, and it did hurt more than I expected, but nothing like the pain I've felt after leaving you in Wales and that was self-inflicted as well, and much worse, it hurt you as well. I needed to punish myself somehow, but also to make amends, and imprint your name on my backside, just as surely as it is imprinted in my heart."

"Then I will have to do something just as permanent to tell the world you're mine."

"Hmm?"

Bryony decided to dive from the highest springboard.

"Will you marry me, Isabel Bridgford?"

Isabel jumped in the air.

"Are you serious? A battered bag of old bones like

me?"

"Well, yes, though I would hardly agree to your description, oh, glorious goddess."

Isabel was so flustered; she decided to change the subject.

"Why haven't you banked my check? You've not paid it in yet."

Bryony hesitated. "I was unsure. It is so much money. I just didn't want to think it was some sort of payment for services rendered."

"Oh, darling, it isn't payment. It's tax-free I assure you. It's simply a present from me to you, because I love you, I will always love you. You have given me back my life,"

Bryony walked her fingers up Isabel's spine until she shivered.

"Then please take my proposal seriously. Please say yes, so then I can live with you in this super convenient flat, and use all your lovely cooking utensils, and lie in your grade A bed...and..."

"Yes!"

What?"

"Yes, my darling, I'd be delighted to marry you, of course I would."

There was a delighted sigh from Bryony, and she buried Isabel's mouth under her own. It took several more minutes before Isabel could speak, but then she whispered, "Only first, could you find me some nice Aloe Vera gel to put on these tattoos? They do sting rather."

"Roll over darling. I have a better idea of how to take your mind off the pain."

And Isabel smiled, and then closed her eyes in pure contentment. "Yes, Bryony," she said.

Chapter 29

Everyone they consulted told them a Christmas wedding was a bad idea. The weather would be awful; no-one would be able to come, because of work or family commitments and traffic hold-ups. All the venues would be booked, and anyway wasn't it rather too soon?

Isabel and Bryony sensibly ignored all this advice and went ahead. They booked their marriage ceremony for December 18th, just after Bryony's term finished, and once the chaos caused by the early general election would have died down.

Isabel had spent most of October engaged in the Extinction Rebellion protests, and had been interviewed on several TV and Radio current affairs programs. She even had a ten minute interview on Channel 4 News about the themes of her book, which was being rushed through the presses to be launched in January. It was also going to be serialized in a Sunday newspaper.

Bryony had hardly seen daylight during this time, pursuing her surgery elective, and perfecting her suturing skills with typical focus. She already performed a range of small tissue and skin repairs, under supervision and knew she wanted to focus on orthopedic surgery.

Giving people back the ability to move their limbs, and restore strength to shattered bones still seemed as worthy a vocation as it ever had. Someone else could find a cure for cancer, and other specialties. She knew the only person she wanted to give complete and holistic care to from now on, was Isabel.

From the moment they reconnected, there was no hesitation. Bryony's possessions had been so few, that there was no need for the legendary U-Haul hiring cliché, but they spent several weeks together, gently making space for her within the Highbury flat. Bryony played it really gently, but helped whenever Isabel needed her, to sort through all of Carrie's collections of artifacts and musical instruments, her clothes, files, books and DVDs, and even her make-up still stored in at least half the bedroom drawers.

"I just couldn't face any of this before, but I can now. I know she's gone. I will always have the memories."

"I think we should keep her portrait somewhere central, maybe not over the mantelpiece but where you can see it. I feel she has given me permission to take her place, and I would like her to be around."

"Thank you, sweet Bryony. Let's put her up in the dining alcove, and see how we feel later, after a few months."

After many of Carrie's things had been sold or disposed of, the flat seemed to double in size, and Bryony realized that Isabel did actually like things simple and cleared away. The one thing they definitely kept was Carrie's water feature in the garden, though as the nights drew in they turned it off for the winter, and wrapped the pipework in insulation to stop it freezing.

Isabel took Bryony round to her agency headquarters near Old Street station, and introduced her to all her colleagues. Their offices were a jumble of small rooms in a block for NGOs, and Isabel's friends all seemed delighted to see her alive and well and to welcome Bryony into their circle. Isabel planned to return to her post in January, after the wedding, and after a short honeymoon.

Then it was Bryony's turn to shyly present Isabel to her colleagues on the medical course. Aiden stayed well away, but she was pleased and not surprised to learn he had certainly taken on a new partner, a pretty Chinese student who was in the year below them. None of Bryony's girlfriends seemed at all fazed by her coming out, nor by her choice of partner. Ted and Claire were relieved it was Bryony who would now take care of Isabel, though they still found it hard to comprehend that Bryony was as gay as she was. Jane simply sent a funny email when she heard the news, offering to give Isabel away.

People seemed to assume they would fly off to somewhere warm for a honeymoon, but Isabel's new found conscience about accruing yet more air-miles slid exactly alongside Bryony's own idea of where she wanted them to go.

"Are you thinking the same thing?"

"Yes, of course. It will be cold and dark though, this time of year."

"But we can take lots of warm clothes, and light the fire. Besides, if it's too cold we can just stay in bed."

"Shall I see if it is free over Christmas?"

So Isabel made the enquiry and came back waving the print out of her booking receipt. They were going back to Ty Bach.

"We can travel first class if you want a bit of luxury, and hire an electric car when we get there."

"When we get there I simply want to wrap you up in silk sheets and kiss every inch of your beautiful skin."

"Well first we have to arrange the wedding, and work out what we wear."

In the end it was all so simple. Bryony wore a dress, looking like a cat-walk model in an ivory satin shift which scooped round her shoulders and emphasized her breasts. Isabel felt more comfortable in a tailored pant suit which hid all the faint but still present scars on her arms and legs.

The civil ceremony was short, sweet and completely in tune with their desire for a no fuss event. The reception for fifty of Isabel's friends and Bryony's fellow students was in a restaurant where the owners knew Isabel from old days, and really provided them with a wonderful vegetarian banquet, and by the next morning they were away on the train heading north-west.

In Aberystwyth the hire car was waiting, and Isabel took the wheel, all her old confidence regained. Bryony sat beside her and enjoyed the view of her lovely profile. When they climbed the last hill up to the cottage, she surveyed the little house with complete happiness. It was winter, and the deciduous trees had all lost their leaves, but the great pine and larch plantations around them were still in full leaf. A clear sky above was already studded with stars, even though it was barely tea-time, and a frost made the ground crunch under their feet.

Isabel found the key in its usual place and turned the lock. Then they stepped into a lovely warm room. The owners, or their agent, had lit the big fire and the Aga was already sending warmth through the entire cottage. A Christmas hamper had been set up on the kitchen table, full of lovely vegan food. And there was a seasonal scent of cinnamon, ginger and pine cones from a large wreath hanging on the wall.

Isabel gathered Bryony to her and hugged her as tightly as she could. The younger woman could feel a surprising shaking of her shoulders, and lifted up her face to see tears on her eyelashes.

"Hey, what's up sweetheart?"

"Nothing, nothing at all. I just can't cope with how happy I am right now, compared to last time, when I came here on the first of July."

"I love you Isabel. I will always love you."

"Me too."

"Now let's eat some of this lovely food we've been left. I'm starving."

And so they did. The winter woods embraced the little cottage like a green blanket. The owls ruffled their feathers against the cold, and the deer in the forests sniffed the frost in the night sky.

But later, after the feast was consumed, some warm mulled wine drunk, no-one within a hundred miles, neither human nor animal, bird or beetle, slept as well or as contentedly as Isabel and Bryony, wrapped up together in each other's arms. They were in love, partners for life, and Isabel was completely and utterly healed.

THE END

About the Author

This is Maggie McIntyre's first novel in her own name. She has been happily writing for most of her life, and especially enjoys writing about women in love with women. Dividing her time between the USA, the UK, and Spain, and between mainstream writing and fanfiction, she invites you to travel with her and enjoy the ride. She believes a good story can inspire, entertain and also console in times of trouble. It also has the power to break down barriers of hatred and fear between people, and help people live their lives to the full.

You can find Maggie on her Facebook page, Maggie McIntyre Author, and at her website: www.maggiemcintyreauthor.com.

COMING SOON BY MAGGIE MCINTYRE

website: www.maggiemcintyreauthor.com
email: maggie@maggiemcintyreauthor.com

Trafficked

If you enjoyed this book, why not meet Isabel's colleague, Steph, who has romantic challenges of her own...a mystery to solve and a huge decision to make. Set in London in the winter of 2019, the novel takes us through the swinging doors of a radical women-led international aid agency. It also explores the dilemma all working women face when caught between glass ceilings and the calls of parenthood. But many women have it so much worse, as Steph and her lover Celia discover to their cost when they try to answer a call for help. A lesbian love story in the real, often scary, world of trafficked girls and hidden networks of power.

- Contemporary Romance
- Tentative release, 2H-2020

TRAFFICKED

BY

MAGGIE MCINTYRE

CHAPTER 1

"Kittens."

"Kittens?"

"Kittens. The most sought after images on Facebook apparently."

"You don't say. Well I know not to find any kittens on your pages anyway. You're allergic to cats."

"And too cute. Don't forget, cute. You know how that sends me up the wall."

"Hmm. Definitely allergic to cute."

As she spoke, Steph Miller flung her I-Pad across the sofa and stretched out her arms and legs in a move which did make her resemble a cat languidly pulling itself from sleep. She looked and felt exhausted, having just returned from three grueling months in the DRC. Her clothes were creased and covered in dust.

Her travel bag was dumped by the sofa, and her rucksack had fallen by the door as she'd come in. She had merely collapsed for a few minutes, giving in to the urge to check the internet for any urgent messages, and spend a few minutes on trivia, before picking up the pieces of a very hectic life, and emailing her perpetually anxious mother.

Celia Forrester, the opposite to whom she was seriously attracted, had just walked through the door of their South London flat, but in her case, after only a short train ride from an accountancy firm in the City of London. The enforced separation had been a long twelve weeks this time, and she had grown used to her own immaculately tidy ways.

Their laconic exchange about kittens was typical of the way they often slid cautiously back into their relationship after months apart. Neither of them seemed good at spontaneously showing their emotions without an ice-breaker.

Celia was overjoyed to see Steph had returned from Kinshasa in one piece, but couldn't deny she was slightly irritated by the way her beloved spread herself and her luggage across their main room in total ownership. Stephanie was a woman whose whole lifestyle never seemed to know its rightful boundaries.

She liked to live rough even when the way promised to be smooth. She travelled constantly, and she invaded Celia's heart, dreams, bed and wardrobe with casual disregard for the mess she left behind whenever she departed again. As she did all the time.

Celia swallowed her pain. Now wasn't the time for nagging. She put out her arms and Steph stood up and went quickly over to her. She helped her pull off her coat, and then gave her a big bear hug.

"I have missed you so much. God, I think I'm getting too old for these trips. And the Internet connection was terrible. Sorry I couldn't Skype you more often. If we weren't having a power cut, it was the water which stopped running in the taps, and we were carrying buckets round the compound. The nights were hotter than hell."

"I know. I understand." Celia kissed her warmly, half on the mouth, half on the cheek. They had been together three years. They were almost family. "Go and jump in the shower, and I'll fix a meal. You'll feel better once you've eaten."

"Yes, that stale croissant in Brussels airport seems a long time ago."

Then she remembered, "Oh, and something really weird happened on the flight home. I want to run it past you and see what you think."

"OK. Over supper. I'll put some pasta on."

"Great, anything but rice." And she dragged her smelly, weary bones into the bathroom, and turned on the shower. Ah, the bliss of hot water!

They sat together an hour later on the small terrace behind the flat, enjoying a glass of Tesco's best red together despite the cold night air. Steph who loved to sit out and listen to the night sounds of London had grabbed the duvet off the bed and wrapped them both up in it against the December frost. A scented candle made by a Ukrainian women's collective gave them a little pool of reflected light.

"So what was the problem on the airplane from Kinshasa?"

"Not so much a problem for me, but something troubling. At the gate, as we went through to board, there was a large, Nigerian family in front of me, with several children, and a young Congolese woman in tow, who seemed to be their nanny or maid."

"And you knew this, how?"

"By the general way they treated her, with the haughty disdain with which wealthy treat their minions. She was carrying most of their hand luggage, and seemed to have responsibility for the younger children. I know she wasn't Nigerian like the others, because, when she stepped backwards and accidentally fell over me, she apologized in Liguana. I answered in French, and we knew we were at least on the same wavelength, language wise."

"So? Sadly that's a scenario you see everywhere, especially in airports."

"Yes, but when we were flying and I stood up to use the toilet, this young woman suddenly arrived behind me in the queue, and thrust a small scrap of paper into my hand with a phone number. She whispered in French, "Please, phone my sister. Tell her you met me on a flight to Brussels. Tell her…""

"Then we were thrown apart by the toilet door opening, and I was pushed inside before I could reply. When I emerged, I saw that she had returned to her seat in the centre of a row of five, towards the back of the plane. Her employers were all in business class, naturally. I walked back and looked at her with raised eyebrows. I mouthed, "Are you all right?""

"She looked very scared, and I saw the man next to her, maybe another employee of the family, was scowling at her. She just gave a tiny shake of the head and looked away from me, so I took the hint and retreated.

"When we landed in Brussels, there was no sign of her. She may have gone forward to be with the family when they left abruptly from business class. Perhaps they had a quick connection, but I couldn't see them anywhere as we went through to the transit area. So now I really don't know what to do."

Celia was surprised. "Call the number, obviously."

"Well, obviously, duh. But there's no country code. Is it the UK, the Congo, somewhere on the continent? I tried the basic number at once, but they said, "This number does not exist. Please check and dial again.""

"Give it to me. Let me look at it."

Steph pulled it out of her I-Phone wallet and passed it across. It was on the squared paper, universally used in francophone countries, in ballpoint pen, and had nine numbers.

"It's a puzzle, and it worries me. I can't get her face out of my mind. She looked both exhausted and terrified, and I am sure she was much younger than I had first thought."

"Have you tried Googling it?"

"Yes. It's not a postcode. It's just a seemingly random set of numbers. But it may mean a lifeline to this girl. "

"Let me ask at work tomorrow. Some of the tech team might crack this. I expect it's quite simple. We should try the DRC first anyway, don't you think? Oh, and why don't you ask your boss tomorrow? Isabel will know. She knows everything. "

"Isabel won't even be back at work yet. She's still on her honeymoon until after Christmas, I expect."

"Perhaps, but maybe you could text her. You know what a workaholic she is. I went to her wedding on your behalf by the way. Everyone was there, and they all asked why you weren't and where you were. I told them you had to stay on in DRC to wind everything up."

"Yes, I was so sorry to miss the wedding. I adore Isabel, and want to get to know Bryony. We should have them round for a meal in the New Year."

Celia nodded. It would be a positive new start if

Stephanie could stay in the UK long enough to issue invitations and still be there to honor them.

"Anyway, this mystery phone number, I'll help you sort it out, don't worry."

Steph was grateful Celia was taking it seriously, but the hour was late, and she was exhausted. They retreated back into the warmth, left the paper on the kitchen table, turned their wine glasses upside down in the sink, next to the unwashed supper dishes, and fell into bed.

Celia curled around Steph like a spoon behind her back, slowly rubbing her shoulder with one hand and cupping her left breast with the other, but Steph was just too tired to respond in any sexual way. She mumbled an apologetic, 'love you, Night...' and promptly fell asleep.

"Story of my life," muttered Celia. "In bed with a sleeping beauty," and turned over, hugged her pillow and followed her into la-la land.

There was so much she needed to talk to Steph about, serious stuff, but it would just have to wait now until the following evening. Stephanie Miller, West African Project Officer for the "Righteous Anger" charity, was never good in the morning, and Celia needed her full attention and most positive mood if she was to respond well to what she had to say. It was perhaps the most important decision they needed to take in their lives, and she desperately wanted Steph to say "Yes."

Celia was going through inner turmoil here, and what really scared her, was that she suspected Steph hadn't even noticed.

New Releases from Fellow Authors

Sliding Doors

Author: Karen Klyne
ISBN: 978-1-9164443-8-6
Release date: 15 June 2020
https://bit.ly/S_Doors

Gemma Tennant's life is in a downward spiral, and she doesn't know where to turn. She longs for something different, something new. When she finds a strange flyer suggesting she could start over, all she has to do is find the courage to go through a sliding door to switch lives with a woman on the other side…

Alex Gambol is content but a little lonely. She runs her own business, looks after her ill mother, and goes for long walks with her dog. She's got no time for love, and that's okay. But when a strange woman on the beach shoves a bag at her and insists it's hers, she has no idea how drastically her life is about to change.

Gemma knows the risks she's taken and embraces her new life with enthusiasm and delight. But Alex is bemused, thrown into a life completely alien to her, and she has to learn to live with a wife and kids she never knew she wanted…until now.

About the Author:

KAREN KLYNE lives in England and is a passionate globetrotter. When she's not travelling, she likes walking, cycling, and chasing a little white ball around lush green fairways.

New Releases from Fellow Authors

Call To Me

Author: Helena Harte
ISBN: 978-1-8380668-0-2
Release date: 1 August 2020 (via Amazon)

Ash Smith has plans. Sort of, anyway. Still a kid at heart, she loves working with young people, especially the ones who need a bit of extra attention. She's determined to make something of herself but knows enough about love to know it's not what she wants right now. Life is too full, too wild, to get tied down. That is, until she finds Java, a beautiful, abandoned dog who steals her heart.

Evie Jackson is all about stability. She and her son live a calm, happy life, and although Evie misses companionship, a recent relationship taught her not to trust her instincts when it comes to women. Passing dalliances are all she'll allow so she keeps her heart, and her son, safe.

When Ash and Evie meet at the Hound Hotel, sparks fly. Ash is a free spirit, something that calls to Evie despite her knowing better, and Ash can't get enough of Evie's strong, sexy fire. But will they hear love's call, or will they let it pass them by?

About the Author:

HELENA HARTE is an incurable romantic with a marshmallow heart, whose favorite pastime is finding love and romance in the strangest of places. Call to Me is her debut romance novel.

Printed in Great Britain
by Amazon